continued . . .

"A story that you cannot just help falling in love with. Ms. Hayworth is fast becoming my go-to person to read, with heartfelt stories that steal your heart. . . . If you enjoy a heartfelt romance that has laughs, sighs, and more, then you need to race to get *Winter at Mustang Ridge* immediately. You won't be disappointed!"

—Love Romances & More

"With lyrical storytelling and genuine characters, Hayworth has created a love story that will wrap itself around any reader's heart." —*RT Book Reviews* (4½ stars)

SUMMER AT MUSTANG RIDGE

"A superb read: a gorgeous setting and a beautiful love story."

—*New York Times* bestselling author
Catherine Anderson

"Warm, witty, and with a great deal of heart, *Summer at Mustang Ridge* is an instant classic."
—*New York Times* bestselling author Kristan Higgins

"The Wyoming backdrop is beautiful, watching a foal being born is miraculous, ranch life sounds like a lot of fun, and Foster and Shelby are sweet and tender with each other."
—*Publishers Weekly*

"Hayworth paints the setting so beautifully, you won't want to leave. The romance is slow and subtle but with enough encouragement to keep you reading all night. I can't think of a better recommendation for a sweet romance: horses, scenery, and working cowboys."
—*Kirkus Reviews*

Also by Jesse Hayworth

COMING HOME *to* MUSTANG RIDGE

JESSE HAYWORTH

A SIGNET ECLIPSE BOOK

SIGNET ECLIPSE
Published by New American Library,
an imprint of Penguin Random House LLC
375 Hudson Street, New York, New York 10014

This book is an original publication of New American Library.

First Printing, August 2015

For more information about Penguin Random House, visit penguinrandom-
house.com.

ISBN 978-0-451-47082-9

Printed in the United States of America
10 9 8 7 6 5 4 3 2 1

Penguin
Random
House

To Wallaby. You were so worth the wait.

Author's Note

Greetings, Reader-Friends!

I don't always know which comes first for me—the chicken or the egg—but my life often imitates my story-art and vice versa. When going through a long-overdue breakup, I wrote about a relationship that was on life support and a husband and wife trying to decide whether or not to pull the plug. Sure, there were Mayan demons and an apocalypse in the mix, but the central question was universal: Do I stay or do I go? *They stayed together. I split. Then, newly single, I wrote about a cop struggling to find herself in the aftermath of a shooting. And later, freshly in love and ready to write happier, more hopeful stories, I turned to a new pen name and a new series, and Mustang Ridge was born.*

Five books and two novellas later, I'd like to invite you to turn the page and share Ashley and Ty's story with me. It's about how love can bloom when and where you least expect it—even between an artsy dreamer who's out to prove herself, and a solid, practical cow-

boy who'd rather be alone than risk trusting his heart again. But more, this book is about fresh starts like the one I've been blessed with. And it's about new beginnings . . . like the son I conceived while writing it, and whom I'm holding right now.

Thank you for being on this journey with me, dear Reader-Friend. Welcome back to Mustang Ridge, and I truly hope you enjoy Ashley and Ty as much as I do . . . and that maybe you see a little of your own story in theirs.

Love,
Jesse

1

"Sign here and here, and initial wherever you see a yellow sticky arrow." A thick stack of oversize papers came sliding across the glass countertop toward Ashley Webb, obscuring the costume jewelry that glittered in the showcase. When she hesitated, Penny Trueheart, lawyer extraordinaire, said, "Do you need a pen? I brought one with me."

Fighting an image of her flinging the paperwork in the air and bolting for the shop's back room—*down, brain*—Ashley nodded, then shook her head. "Yes, I'll sign. No, I've got my own pen."

There it was in her hand, bright blue and embossed with: ANOTHER FYNE THING ~ *the best in vintage couture and thrift shop treasures, Three Ridges, Wyoming*. And it was shaking, ever so slightly. *Don't freak*. This was what she wanted more than anything else, ever, in her life.

It was also a buttload of money. Especially for someone like her.

"This is so exciting! I can't believe you're buying the shop!" Henrietta squeezed her arm, then danced away in a swirl of fabric.

Today, Ashley's sole employee had paired a floaty green sundress with a pair of purple capris and yellow sandals that had big plastic happy faces on them. But, hey, it worked on a woman who wore her long blond hair in dozens of braids and claimed to have been conceived at Woodstock while Jimi Hendrix played "The Star Spangled Banner."

Penny, on the other hand, wore a blue pantsuit with a starched white shirt, which made her pretty much the anti-Hen. Still, the savvy lawyer had been the perfect go-to for the paperwork when the shop's founder, Della Fyne, had agreed to split the down payment into two installments that Ashley could sort of, but not really, afford.

If business stayed very, very good.

And she didn't eat or use any electricity.

Oh, God. What was she *thinking*?

"Ashley? Are you okay?" Hen's face came into view, eyes worried beneath a striped headband that might have started life as a sock. "Penny, I don't think she's breathing."

Whooshing air into her lungs—what do you know; Hen was right—Ashley said, "I'm fine." To prove it, she signed her name on the first line, making herself focus on each letter and not get distracted by the part of her that was going, *This is nuts. It's too much, too soon, too everything. What makes you think you can stick it out this time?*

Hen beamed. "Hey, you're a lefty. Me, too. Did you know we can see better underwater, and we tend to hit puberty faster than righties?" She frowned. " 'Course, we also die younger. Oh, and there's that link to insanity."

"Exhibit A," Ashley muttered, and signed next to a yellow arrow sticky.

> *I, Ashley Webb, do solemnly swear that, having just wiped out my savings for this first payment, I will make the second one in forty-five days. Despite dropping out of college and having never held a job for more than six months before this one—which is on month seven, yay me—I promise that I will be smart and responsible. I will keep up with the regular monthly payments to the bank, insure everything I can think of, do all the paperwork on time, file my taxes, turn over the inventory as fast as possible, make regular buying trips, update the Web site—*

Gack.

Turning the page, she initialed next to a sticky. Then another. Her head spun. She was really doing it. She was buying Another Fyne Thing from Della—the whole shoot and shebang, everything from the Armani sunglasses to the thirties-era Zelinka-Matlicks, plus the thousand-square-foot retail space, the warehouse out back, and the five-room apartment upstairs.

"Are you ready for me?" Henrietta buzzed back in, bumping Ashley's elbow and turning her initials into a scribble.

"Almost." Ashley dealt with the last few stickies, then handed over the papers. "Okay, witness. Do your thing."

"Yippee!" Hen went to work with her pen, signing her name with a flourish in vivid purple ink.

Watching the lines appear on page after page, Ashley pressed a hand to her belly and regretted the cinnamon bun she had bought to go along with her coffee, even knowing she shouldn't spend the money. She could do this. She could. The numbers worked, more or less, and she had been running the shop solo ever since Della moved down to the city to be with Max. Really, all she was doing was taking Della's name off all the official forms and replacing it with her own. Nothing else was going to change.

Which was a total lie, but at least it kept her breakfast where it belonged. And as Hen finished witnessing the last few pages, Ashley managed to resist the urge to swat the pen cup off the counter and shout, "Wait! Stop! I changed my mind!"

"Okay, Ashley." Penny made two neat piles with the contracts. "Moment of truth."

"The checks." They lay on the countertop, looking up at her with their fat round zeros, like little eyes. Lots of them.

She didn't know which was scarier, the one from the bank with all the digits, thanks to the thirty-year commercial loan she had gotten by the skin of her teeth, and then only because it was a local bank . . . or the one she had written off her own account at the same bank, wiping out her meager savings plus the overdraft, and including a cash advance from her credit card.

You're nuts. You know that, right? Utterly mental. The most expensive thing she'd ever bought prior to this was—what—A drum set for Kenny? New tires, maybe? She was still driving Bugsy, the pimped-out VW Beetle her mom and Jack had given her as a high school graduation present, all smiles because she was headed off to art school, the future bright.

Just do it. You can make it work this time. Pressing her fingers onto the checks, she trapped them against the cool glass of the display case. Then she slid them across to Penny. "Here you go."

And, just like that, she was the new owner of a vintage shop smack in the middle of downtown Three Ridges, Wyoming.

"You did *WHAT*?" Wyatt loomed over Ashley, seeming to momentarily forget that he was holding his eleven-month-old daughter in the crook of his arm. "Are you out of your *MIND*?"

Little Abby let out a startled *"Awoooo!"* that reverberated off the rough-hewn log walls and overstuffed couches of the sitting-room-slash-reception-area in the main house at Mustang Ridge—aka the gorgeous dude ranch Ashley's brother had married into last fall, and where Ashley had lasted six weeks as an employee before deciding that working there wasn't nearly as fun as being a guest.

Thank God there had been a HELP WANTED sign in the window of Another Fyne Thing. Though Wyatt probably didn't see it that way now.

He gave the baby a bounce, rearranged his face to a fatuous smile, and sweetened his tone to say, "Sorry, sweetie. Auntie Ashley started it." With his hat off and his dark, russet-streaked hair standing up in agitated spikes, he looked like an irate porcupine.

A very large irate porcupine.

Ashley just folded her arms. "You're the one doing the yelling." Though she was pretty sure she was the only one capable of hitting her big brother's bellow button.

"What did you expect?" he demanded, halfway losing hold of his baby-soothing voice, so he sounded like an irritated cartoon character. "Of all the harebrained, irresponsible—"

"Annd, that's my cue." Krista stepped in and scooped Abby out of Wyatt's arms. "Come on, kiddo. We're going to go find somewhere else to be." Propping the baby on her hip, the pretty, fresh-faced blonde kissed Wyatt's cheek, shot Ashley an encouraging finger wiggle, and whisked down the hallway leading to the kitchen.

"But—" Wyatt took a half step after them, then stopped himself with a muttered curse and took a couple of deep breaths. By the time he'd turned back to Ashley, he looked less like a furious porcupine, and more like a concerned patriarch of a porcupine.

Which was worse, really. She could deal with his bluster, but his disappointment always got to her. There was too much history there.

"I can do this," she insisted. "It's a fantastic opportunity. And aren't you the one who was always telling me I needed to find something I love, something I'm good at? Well, this is it." From the first moment she had stepped through the shop door into the bright, chaotic interior and heard the jingle of the little bell overhead, she had been in love.

"I was talking about you going back to school and getting a degree," he grated. "You know, giving yourself a shot at a real future? Sound familiar?"

As usual, he didn't even try to understand where she was coming from. "Seems to me you went right back to cowboying after college." Sure, he was famous now—in a few high-dollar art circles, anyway—for the Wild West–themed sculptures he made from recycled farm equipment. But those successes hadn't come out of any classroom.

"We're talking about you, not me. And I've gotten plenty of use out of my degree. You would, too, if you'd just give it a try."

"Too late. I've already signed on the dotted lines. All of 'em."

Besides, she was allergic to school. Her brain was too quick, too flighty. Too ready to get distracted when things stopped being fun and started feeling like work. That was why Another Fyne Thing was perfect for her—the stock was always changing and the customers were a fascinating blend of locals and tourists. And as of today she could mix things up even more—the advertising, the sales, the window displays, all of it. Nothing at Another Fyne Thing would ever be boring again, now that she owned it.

Ohmigosh. She owned it.

Even though she and Hen had thrown an impromptu celebration after they finished the paperwork, inviting everyone up and down Main Street to stop by

for cookies, coffee, and ten percent off, there was still a
frisson of shock at the thought.

She. Owned. The. Store.

It was impossible. Incredible. Wonderful. Terrifying.

"Are you even listening to me?"

She blinked at Wyatt. "What?"

"You can't afford this," he said between gritted
teeth. "What if you miss one of the payments? You'll
lose what you've already put into it, and destroy what
little credit you've managed to scrape together since
you left the Douchebag Drummer."

Her chin went up. "I'll make the payments." She
didn't want to talk about Kenny. She could only say
You were right and I was wrong so many times.

Yes, her ex had been a douchebag, and, yes, she had
followed the family tradition—the female half, anyway—
by staying way too long in a relationship that was going
nowhere but downhill. That was over and done with,
though, and just because she had made a whopper of a
mistake in her choice of men didn't mean buying the store
was a terrible idea, too.

That was her story, and she was sticking to it.

Scrub went Wyatt's hand through his hair. "You're
getting in way over your head. You don't have the first
clue how to run a business."

"Della is going to help me. Not to mention Krista,
Jenny, and the others." The friends she had fallen
into—married into, really—when she'd crossed the line
into Wyoming with zero to her name but Bugsy, some
clothes, and her boxes of art supplies.

He scowled. "What happened to starting small? I

thought you were going to stay at the shop until Della sold it, then come back to work here while you got an online storefront up and running."

That had been his plan, not hers. "I changed my mind."

"Change it back."

"No." It was a single word, a complete sentence. But it was one of the hardest things she had ever said to him. Unable to leave it like that, she added, "Please, Wyatt. Try to understand where I'm coming from. I can do this without your support—I will if I have to. But it won't be the same. I know I've let you down before, but this time it's going to be different. You'll see."

"Ashley." He sighed as some of the fight drained out of him. "Be—"

"Happy for myself?" she interrupted before he could say *reasonable* or *logical* or any of those other words he was so fond of. "I am. And I hope you will be, too, eventually. In the meantime, what would you say to making me a few mannequins? It'd be killer to have some F. Wyatt Webb originals in my window."

"I'd say you're pushing it." But his scowl lacked the punch it had carried before. "Have you told Mom what you're up to?"

"I'll call her in a day or so. I wanted to tell you first." And when it came to talking to their mother on the phone, she needed a dark, quiet room. Wine and chocolate would be good, too. She stepped in, gave him a hug, and said, "Love you, bro. Even when you treat me like I'm still ten years old."

"Back then, I could take away your allowance."

"Now the bank can do it for you."

He winced. "Don't say that. Don't even think it." A pause. "On second thought, do think it. Maybe knowing that you're just a couple of missed payments away from having it all yanked away will help keep you on track."

"I'll keep myself on track, thank you very much." And, yeah, the whole bank think gave her a definite twinge. Hiding that behind a saucy smile—flirting was one thing that had always come naturally, even with Wyatt—she patted his cheek, near where she had kissed. "I'm leaving before you decide to scare more babies."

"Going back to the store?"

"That's the idea." It was closed to customers, but there was plenty to do. And it was all hers! Well, hers and the bank's.

"Change of plans," Krista announced, appearing in the doorway, carrying Abby, who was armed with a fat chocolate chip cookie and back to her usual smiling self. Popping the baby in Wyatt's arms, she said, "You're on kidlet duty, because Ashley and I are going out. I already called the others, and they're going to meet us at the Rope Burn."

He cradled the baby, looking offended. "Hang on there. Abby and I aren't invited?"

"Nope." Krista hooked an arm through Ashley's and urged her toward the door. "Sorry, cowboy. Girls only. We're going to celebrate Ashley's big news!"

2

The kitschy cowboy bar outside of town was best known for having cheap beer, dartboards in the back, and food with silly breakup names like the Let's Just Be Friends Spinach Dip and the I'll Call You Burger. To Tyler Reed, though, it was the buzz of the Thursday night crowd that mattered, and the stage and speakers that were half visible through the cracked-open office door.

"Checking out the local talent?" The question came from the other side of the room, where Chase was sprawled on a thrift store reject of a couch, flipping through song notes. Wearing tight jeans, glossy black boots, and a silver-plated belt buckle the size of a paperback, the younger man looked like your typical lead singer at a small-town dive bar—the kind who would unbutton his shirt halfway through the set and let it hang open through the encore if there were enough women on the dance floor making eye contact. Supposedly the kid could hold a tune, though, and Ty figured that was good enough. Wasn't like he had anything to prove. He just wanted to play for a crowd.

Looking beyond the stage to where the bodies stacked at the bar were a pretty good mix of blue collar and tight skirts, Ty said, "Go figure. I thought *we* were the talent."

"Not the tunes, man. The babes." Tossing his notes, Chase sprang up and came across the room to prop a shoulder on the doorframe, scanning the room like the two of them were at a stock auction. "Three Ridges might not be more than a pimple on the map, but it's got some mighty fine fillies."

Fillies? Ty was tempted to ask if he had ever swung a leg over anything four-legged other than a barstool. They were just playing together for the night, though; there was no point in knocking the kid down. "I'm not really in the market."

"You married?"

"Nope. Just not looking to start something serious."

"Who said anything about serious?" Chase shot out a bony elbow that completely missed Ty. "I'm sure you've had your share of road hookups, being out on tour with a band like Higgs & Hicks." The kid was trying so hard to be cool about Ty backing him up, like it was no biggie that the owner of the 'Burn had found a real road musician to fill in when Chase's usual guitarist decided to splurge on some gas station sushi and wound up splurging from both ends.

Ty snagged the old, mellow-noted Martin guitar he had propped nearby, and strummed a chord before saying, "Last I checked, this wasn't the road."

And thank Christ for that. His first year or so with the mega-successful country band had given him exactly what he had needed at the time—a break from small-town gossip and room to clear his head. By year three, though, the cracks in the band's foundation had started wearing on him. Or, rather, the fact that A.J. Higgs had the impulse control of a flea, Brower Hicks was a drunk on a downward spiral, and their rat-faced manager, Weasley, didn't give a crap what was going on backstage as long as they were making money. And when Ty tried to make him care, tried to go about setting things right, he got shown the door.

Which was for the best, really. It had been past time for a change.

Chase gave a restless shrug. "Sure, Three Ridges isn't the same as being on the road, but if things get too complicated, it's no big deal to bail. There's always another little cow town looking for someone to sling hay and fix tractors, and there's always another bar with pretty girls ready to throw their panties up onstage."

Ty figured he had been that young once. Now, though, he settled back in his chair and picked out the opening to "Home on the Range." "What do you say we go through the set list again? I want to make sure we're on the same page."

And he'd far rather talk music than women.

"I'll have a Let's Get This Party Started Cosmo," Ashley said as she and the other four members of the Girl Zone settled around their usual high-top bar table.

"Sure thing." The waitress poised a pen that had a miniature cowboy boot dangling off the end. "Do you want it in a light-up glass?"

"Absolutely." Why not? They were celebrating.

"White wine for me," Shelby said, then shot Ashley a wink. "A regular glass is fine." With a slick manicure and a soft summer sweater, both in a deep, rich crimson that brought out the highlights in her dark hair, the big-city advertising-exec-turned-cowboy's-wife didn't need a glass that blinked red, white, and blue to make a statement.

Danny wrinkled her nose at them. "You two are such girls. I'll have a Corona."

"That's not exactly a manly-man's beer," Shelby pointed out.

"Better than a cosmo. In a blinky glass, no less."

"Tomboy," Ashley said.

"Priss," Danny fired back, and they grinned at each other.

The two were a study in opposites. Where Ashley flirted, Danny was no-nonsense. Where Ashley flitted, Danny kept her hiking boots firmly planted. And where Ashley rushed headlong, Danny planned everything out to the last detail. But despite their differences, they totally clicked.

"Can I get you guys something to eat?" the waitress asked. "The It's Not You It's Me Loaded Potato Skins are fun to share."

"Sounds good," Krista said from the other side of the table. "Plus a basket of fries."

"The You Frenched My Sister You Bastard Fries?"

Jenny snorted. "With a name like that? Sold." Although she was Krista's identical twin, the professional photographer—and local vet's wife—had short, dark hair and an edgier style, in tight black.

"Okay. I'll put that order right in."

As the waitress bopped away with a jingle of the fake roweled spurs attached to her Smurf-blue boots, Ashley said, "Is it just me, or do the names of things change like every week around here?"

"It's not you," Danny confirmed. "I think they do it to keep us on our toes."

"That, and it's good branding." Shelby tapped the drink menu. "You're having relationship problems? Head down to the Rope Burn and order whatever fits your mood. The Kick Him To The Curb Wings, maybe. Not having problems with your relationship? You can feel all superior when you put in your order, because you and your sweetie would *never* say something like, 'Let's just be friends' or 'I love you, but I'm not *in* love with you.' Single? Order a Come And Get Me Wrap and stick the flagged toothpick behind your ear, and everyone knows you're looking for love. It's brilliant, really." And Shelby knew a few things about branding and market presence.

"Besides," Krista added. "Since we just spent an extra minute or two talking about the menu, I'd say it's mission accomplished."

"Here are your drinks!" their waitress announced, arriving with a spur-jingle that somehow carried over the crowd noise. She offloaded the wine and beer, and then set Ashley's tall glass in front of her and pushed the button on the bottom to activate the LED embedded in the stem, making red, white, and blue stripes move up and down.

As the waitress said something about being back in a minute with their food and jingle-jangled off, Shelby raised her wine, which looked classy and grown-up in its traditional housing. "To Ashley. Congratulations on being the new owner of Another Fyne Thing!"

Danny held up her beer. "To being your own boss!"

Jenny added her glass to the group salute. "To loving what you do."

Krista raised hers. "To taking a leap of faith!"

"Hear, hear!" The four of them clinked, then looked expectantly at Ashley.

Who sat there, holding her blinky glass as she fought back a sudden wave of emotion. "I . . . You guys . . . Wow. I can't breathe."

Sometimes when she was out with her friends, it was hard not to feel like the little sister, even when Wyatt was miles away. The others were so educated, so accomplished, each of them a business owner in her own right. Now, suddenly, they were looking at her like she had done something important. Something they understood, even admired.

"So don't breathe," Jenny advised. "Drink." That got another round of "Hear, hear!" and the five of them clinked and drank.

The first slug of cosmo tingled going down; the second spread a warm glow that eased the pressure in Ashley's lungs and let the air back in. With it came some of the positive vibes she had been practicing.

Della believes in you. The customers love you. The window displays rock. You can totally do this.

And she could. She would. Starting now.

"Speaking of the store," she said, setting down her blinky glass, "I could use some brainstorming help." Considering how many times she had helped the others spitball ideas for their businesses—everything from new theme weeks for Krista's dude ranch or Danny's adventure trekking business, to slogans and photo shoot locations for Shelby and Jenny—she got a buzz out of it being her turn.

Eyes lighting, Shelby beckoned. "Bring it on."

"The second payment is due in forty-five days, and it's going to be tight." She had already filled them in on the financing. "The window display contest that Mayor Tepitt is running during the Midsummer Parade has a big cash prize, but it's right before the money is due, and there's no guarantee I'll win."

"I'd bet on it," Danny said, lifting her beer. "Your windows rock. The way you linked the Easter egg one to a whole-town scavenger hunt? Genius."

Jenny nodded. "I think my favorite was the one you did for the equinox, with the mannequins acting out how the sun, moon, and earth are aligned, with winter colors on one side and spring on the other."

"That *would* be your favorite." Krista rolled her eyes. "Geek."

"Says the rodeo princess."

"Anyway," Ashley put in, raising her voice a little to interrupt before the twins got going, "Bakery Betty could give me a run for my money, especially if she does free samples again. I mean, really. Who doesn't vote for brownie bites?"

"Bakery Betty?" Shelby asked, amused. "Do you call her that to her face?"

"Sometimes, especially when Fish and Chips Betty is there." Ashley took a look around—you never knew who might be sitting a couple of tables down—and lowered her voice to confide, "When she took over the restaurant, I guess the Main Streeters agreed that Fish and Chips was better than calling her Clam Strips Betty."

"Much better," Jenny agreed. "Do you have a nickname?"

"Nope. I'm the only Ashley, and Feed Store Billy says I'm still too new. I'm working on them, though. One of these days, I'll be Fyne Ashley, maybe, or Vintage Ashley, and you can say you knew me when."

Krista's laugh bubbled up. "Until you started at the shop, I had no idea that downtown Three Ridges was its own little world, with everybody up in each other's business. And to think, you got claustrophobic at the dude ranch, with so many people coming and going all the time. Seems to me this is just another version of the fishbowl."

"Maybe, but it's my version. And at the end of the day, I can lock my customers out. You have to live with yours."

Jenny lifted her glass. "To finding what's right for ourselves, rather than letting other people tell us how it's going to be."

"Amen," Ashley said, and clinked. "So, here's the deal. I want to run a couple of special events at the store as a way to get customers through the door, and hopefully put product in their hands while they're there. Which is where I could use some help. I was thinking of holding a sale and letting people spin a roulette wheel right at checkout to 'win' an extra discount. Or maybe having a fashion show. Or what about a handyman auction? Highest bidder gets stuff fixed around their house. I figure there aren't enough eligible bachelors in Three Ridges for a sexier sort of auction, though that would tie in better with vintage clothing."

Shelby whipped out her phone. "Hang on. Let me jot down a few notes."

"What about a costume contest?" Krista suggested. "You know, sixties and seventies, that sort of thing. You could charge twenty bucks per entry, less if they buy everything from the store."

But Shelby shook her head. "You don't want the store to become a Halloween go-to, especially after Della did all that work for the Drama Club and helped out with the haunted house. Branding-wise, you need to focus on how you can make hip, trendy combinations with vintage clothes. That's the message you're trying to get out to your customers, right?"

"That's exactly what I'm going for!" Ashley grinned, feeling suddenly like she was surrounded by a warm glow of friendship. Or was that that the cosmo? Probably a little of both.

"So no costumes." Shelby hummed, tapping her lower lip. "But a contest isn't a bad idea. Or the fashion show. You'll want to make sure it stays really down-to-earth, though. None of that Fashion Week stuff of sending a model down the runway in a couple of Band-Aids and a skirt made out of twist ties."

"Dang it, there went my signature piece."

They bounced ideas back and forth for the next twenty minutes, through another round of drinks, and pretty soon Ashley decided she should totally claim the night as a business expense, because they were getting more planning done over drinks than she had in the past three weeks of sitting up late at night, moving numbers around on her laptop, and seesawing between *I can totally do this* and *Eeek!*

"Food!" Their server announced cheerfully, plopping down a couple of plates. "The It's Not You Skins and the French My Sister Fries. Don't they smell great?"

"Food." Shelby snapped her fingers. "You could link one of these events to a can drive for the Three Ridges Food Bank."

"Enough!" Jenny made a time-out with her hands. "Let's eat. We should let some of these ideas percolate, anyway." She raised an eyebrow in Ashley's direction. "That cool with you, Miss I-Just-Bought-A-Big-Ass-Storefront-Downtown?"

Ashley stared at her—at all of them—with her throat tightening, and not in a bad way. Growing up, she hadn't had that many friends—she had lived on the wrong side of town, wore the wrong clothes, grew too tall, said the wrong things, and always felt like she should be doing something to make up for her mom and Wyatt scrimping for everything . . . And even once she outgrew that awkwardness, her pool of friends had stayed small, limited to Kenny and his bandmates, who had been loud and self-involved, and hadn't had much interest in her until it came time to pay the delivery guy for their pizza.

It was crazy, really, how much things had changed in the past year and a half.

"Yeah." Her lips curved. "Thanks, guys. I mean it. Thanks for the ideas, for coming out tonight, for being happy for me, even though some people—*cough-cough*, Wyatt, *cough-cough*—think I'm completely nuts for jumping in like this . . . for all of it."

"Well, we kind of think you're nuts, too, but that's why we love you." Danny lifted her glass. "To Ashley!"

"To Ashley!" the others chorused, then clinked and drank, with Shelby giving Ashley's glass an extra tap and adding, "We're here for you, girlfriend."

Forcing back a surge of emotion that the others might not understand—they had been friends for years, after all, and Krista and Jenny had spent their whole lives having each other's backs—Ashley surveyed the heaping plates. "Did we really get potatoes and grease to go with an order of greasy potatoes?"

"See?" Shelby said. "Branding. They totally got you."

"They got *us*," Ashley corrected, sectioning off one of the loaded potato skins. "And I'm not sorry in the slightest. I'm celebrating." She bit in with a moan. "God, are these good."

"Was that a sex noise?"

"With a potato? Sounds uncomfortable."

"Well, you did just say that pickings are slim in Three Ridges."

"It's not the pickings, slim or otherwise. This is the post-Kenny era, which means I'm focusing on myself, and now the store. Heck, I haven't even kissed a guy since I crossed the Wyoming border." Except for that one incident, but she wasn't about to bring *that* up. "I don't have time for kissing."

Danny narrowed her eyes speculatively. "Hmm . . . Methinks the lady doth protest too much. And if you ask me, a girl can always find time for kissing, if it's with the right guy." To Krista, she said, "How about your new head wrangler? I heard he—"

"Stop!" Ashley ordered, holding up both hands. "Don't even."

"What? You don't like cowboys?"

"I like cowboys just fine." Almost as much as she liked musicians. "But I'm not dating the new head wrangler. I'm not dating anybody, thank you very much. I've got a store to run, events to plan, and a big, scary payment to make." Besides which, she was pretty sour on the whole crappily-ever-after thing right now, and had zero faith in her own judgment when it came to men.

She was too much like her mother. And wasn't *that* a terrifying thought?

"Hello?" The hail came from the stage, where Jolly Roger—the bar owner's name was actually Roger Jolly, but he lived up to the nickname with his long, dark hair, grizzled beard, and the patch-and-peg-leg routine he pulled out for special occasions—stood at the mic and did a *tap-tap*. "Is this thing on? Testing, testing. Are we ready for some live music?"

The crowd buzz dimmed for a second, then burst out in applause.

"Awesome." Ashley turned in her chair. "I could dance." It would be a good way to burn off the potato skins, and grooving to the beat should quiet the jitters that came from having had a Very Big Day.

"I'd like to introduce tonight's performers, who are guaranteed"—Jolly drew it out like the three-syllable word had become a dozen—"to get your boots tapping and your booties shaking. Let's put them together, folks—your hands, I mean, not your booties—for Chasen Tail!"

The door behind him opened up and a guy came out, giving a big wave to the crowd. "Howdy, folks!" In his mid-twenties, with handsome features and sandy hair that brushed the collar of his shirt, he looked like someone had taken one of the cowboys from the crowd and turned the volume up a couple of notches.

"Oh!" Danny said. "I've seen him before. I like him."

"Meh." Shelby shrugged. "If a guy's going to pop the buttons on his shirt halfway through the show, his abs should be required to be seriously ripped. And his stage name sucks. I mean, really? Chasen Tail? Ew."

"I like his music," Danny clarified. "I agree that the name is dumb. And the shirt thing doesn't do much for a girl who's got a better set of muscles waiting for her back home."

"Now that's just mean." Ashley turned her back on the stage to complain across the table: "Some of us are living vicariously, you know."

"I can already see this is going to be a killer crowd," Chasen said behind her. "How about we give a round of applause to my boys?"

As the crowd whooped and hollered, Krista's eyes went beyond Ashley, and lit. "That's no boy. And speak of the devil. There's my new head wrangler in his very fine flesh!" She waved. "Yoo-hoo, Tyler! Hey, Ty. Over here!"

Ashley froze, the name going through her like a bolt of hot lightning—searing and paralytic.

Wait.

What?

No. It couldn't be.

Setting down the blinky glass with calm precision, she turned in her seat. Looked up at the stage. And stopped breathing while her brain sproinged back and forth between *Oh, hell* and *Oh, my*, with a bit of *Wow* thrown in.

Then back to: *Oh, hell.*

A drummer and a guitarist had set up behind the lead singer. The drummer was a cutie—young, flushed and nervous-looking, as if playing at the Rope Burn was the high point of his life to date. The guitarist was his exact opposite—thirtysomething, solid, and totally chilled out as he bent his head and strummed a couple of chords that should have gotten lost in the crowd noise, but thanks to some acoustic quirk of the room carried straight to Ashley.

She didn't need to see the face beneath the shag of sun-streaked brown hair—she knew him by the mellow undertones and upper twang of the old Martin. And by the way his hands moved on the strings—slow and steady, but with an underlying strength that said here was a man who always hit the note he was going for.

Tyler Reed.

His head came up and his eyes locked on hers, as if she had said his name out loud. His gaze pierced her, brown eyes so dark they were almost black, putting a hot-cold-hot shiver in her belly.

Behind her, the others were talking about how he had come back to Mustang Ridge after spending the past few years touring with a country band, their voices sounding normal, as if the world hadn't just shifted on its axis. As if it didn't shift again when she got a good look at his face, with its high Viking cheekbones and the strong slash of a nose, bumped across the bridge where it had been broken by what he had called "a short dive off a long bucking bull."

Last fall, at Krista and Wyatt's wedding. Where they had totally hooked up.

3

Ty stilled, staring at the woman sitting not thirty feet away at a high-top with his boss and three of her besties. And, just like that first moment he'd laid eyes on her eighteen or so months ago, the others might as well not have been there.

Close to his height in heels, with a model's bone structure and a great laugh, the violet-eyed knockout had captured him, captivated him. Now the honey-blond hair that had been swept up at the wedding was down around her shoulders, and the pale green dress had been replaced by a pair of long, trim jeans and a soft blue shirt, but she was no less a knockout . . . even with her mouth hanging open and her eyes channeling a whole lot of *What the hell?*

Well, that made two of them, as his fingers stumbled on the strings and the air heated up a few degrees. Because, damn.

Ashley. Her name was right there, even though he had tried to forget it once he was back out on the road. Hadn't worked, though, and when he decided to come back to Mustang Ridge and take the promotion Krista had offered, maybe he had figured his boss's pretty bridesmaid friend from LA might visit one day. Had even thought it'd be nice to see her again.

He hadn't figured on that happening on week one of his being back in town, though. And he damn sure hadn't figured on it feeling like he'd just come out of the gate on a world-class bull that had taken two jumps out into the arena, then dropped a shoulder and started to spin.

"What do you say, folks?" Chase hollered, and got a roar from the crowd in return. Flicking a quick glance back at Ty and the baby-faced drummer, he led them in with "And a one, two, a one-two-three-four!"

Ty was half a second late jumping in on the first song and might've missed a few notes in the intro if his fingers hadn't done him a solid and taken over for his brain. Knowing that wouldn't work for long, he tore his eyes off hers—shocked violet framed by milky white skin and golden hair—and focused on making the old guitar sing, weaving point and counterpoint, and shoring up Chase's lower register when it wanted to flatten out.

Wasn't easy, though. Not when he was fighting for balance on a barstool that felt like it was thinking about reversing the spin and throwing in a couple of back-cracking bucks for good measure. Not when *she* was sitting halfway across the room.

As the music kicked into high gear—a country song that Ashley didn't recognize, with breakup lyrics that sounded like the singer was going down the bar's menu—she reminded herself to breathe. Keep breathing.

And not stare. Much.

She didn't want the others to notice, didn't want them to ask things she couldn't answer when she was having a hard time believing her eyes. She had thought he was just a hired guitar, maybe a friend of a friend who had been flown in for the wedding. How could he be Krista's new head wrangler?

The others were talking about a midseason special Danny wanted to advertise, two-for-one on a hike up into the mountains, living off the land. Ashley, though, couldn't focus on anything except the man up on the stage.

Should she say something to her friends? If so, what? It wouldn't be easy to rock the whole *I'm turning over a new leaf* thing if she let on that she had sneaked out of her brother's reception to hook up with the guy who'd played the wedding march. A hot flush flooded her cheeks at the memory. At the time, it had felt exactly right, like she was striking a blow for her own independence—*See, Kenny? I'm totally over you.* Now, though, she found herself wishing she had kept her hands—and lips—to herself.

Okay, that was a lie. Because whoever he was, he was a hell of a kisser.

When the conversation behind her lulled, she said, "I hadn't realized you guys hired a new head wrangler."

Shelby's husband, Foster, had held the position at Mustang Ridge for going on a decade, but he'd been building up his own training business at his family's ranch, and had given Krista and Wyatt the heads-up last year that they needed to find a replacement.

"Ty isn't really new," Krista said. "He was Foster's second-in-command for years until Jenny posted a video of him leading a campfire sing-along, and it got some attention online. The next thing we knew, he got an offer to play with a country band. Have you heard of Higgs & Hicks?"

Ashley nodded, though she had only looked them up because her wedding hookup had mentioned the name. Country wasn't really her thing. "They're good. Popular." Though with a shaky reputation offstage. "Why did he leave?"

"He hasn't said, and I haven't pushed it. I'm just grateful that's he's back. So is Gran. He was always a particular favorite of hers."

"So that's how he ended up playing at the wedding. Friend of the family, and all that." She played it cool. *Nothing to see here.* Not even remotely freaking out.

"That's right. Did you meet him?"

"I recognized the guitar." The long line of his body. The width of his shoulders. The way his hair fell forward as he played. The air of concentration, like nothing else existed except the song—until those dark, dark eyes met hers and that focus shifted, locked on.

Heated agitation pooled in her belly, making her feel like she had swallowed the whole blinky glass, not just its contents.

Onstage, the band finished the first set—had it been that long already?—and the singer leaned in to say,

"We're going to take a quick break. Be back in ten." He gave the front row a slow smile and toyed with the bottom button of his shirt. "Stick around, ladies. The show's just getting started."

The whoops and hollers coming from the dance floor mostly drowned out Shelby's shout of "Keep it on. Keep it all on!"

"Shh!" Danny swatted at her, laughing.

Ashley watched out of the corner of her eye as Ty put down his guitar and headed for a door that led off behind the stage.

Heart drumming, she set her half-finished drink—her second, she thought, or possibly her third—on the table and slipped off her chair. "I'm going to hit the ladies' room, maybe talk to Jolly about renting his sound system for one of these store events we've been talking about."

As the stage crowd split like the Red Sea, one half heading for the bar, the other for the restrooms, she ducked through the door Ty had taken, hoping to catch him alone.

The rear hallway was empty save for two sun-starved potted pines and a trio of framed rodeo posters, but a back exit was cracked like a smoker had just gone through. Or a guy who had a feeling someone might follow him. Ashley hesitated for a beat, wishing that she was wearing something snazzier than the basic jeans, boots, and shirt routine that she had hoped would make Wyatt think she was taking things seriously, but now just made her feel bland and colorless.

Oh, well. There was no hope for it now, and she

needed to talk to him before he said anything to the others. To Wyatt. Taking a deep breath, she pushed open the door and stepped out.

The sun had set, darkening the mountains and purpling the sky, but she saw Ty instantly. He stood silhouetted at the edge of the parking lot, next to the post of a light that hadn't yet come on—tall, broad-shouldered, and staring out across the craggy Wyoming horizon.

He turned as the door creaked closed behind her, and a shiver of awareness said he was looking at her from the dark shadows beneath the tipped-down brim of his hat.

She had intended to walk across to him and do a "Hey, cowboy." Instead, her boots planted themselves on the last step leading down and her mouth went dry as the scene burned itself on her retinas, made her wish for a palate and brush, or grease pencils in vivid purples and dark, brooding black. She could capture him there, a lone cowboy at the edge of civilization.

If she did, though, nobody would believe the scene was real. She barely believed it herself. Because, damn, he was something to look at.

Then he moved.

Boots crunching on gravel, he came toward her slow and steady, like he was afraid she might bolt. Or maybe because, like her, he felt the sudden electric tension in the air. She couldn't tell, couldn't see his face or read his expression—not even when he got up close and personal, the two of them eye-to-eye even though she was a step above him on the short flight of wooden stairs.

His height was one of the things she had liked most about him that night. That, and the guitar. And the fact that he was just passing through.

Or so she had thought.

"Ashley," he said in a raspy baritone that sent tingles along the backs of her hands, making her want to reach out and touch. Except that he might have remembered her name, but he didn't know who she really was.

Forcing her voice level, she said, "Hey there." *Play it cool, play it cool, play it cool.* "Fancy seeing you here." Ugh, really? Who even said stuff like "fancy that" anymore? So much for the cool factor.

"It's a surprise—that's for sure." His voice warmed a notch, though his face remained in the shadows. "You visiting Krista?"

"Actually, that's sort of a thing. At least it could be. You see, I wasn't entirely honest when I told you that I was a friend of hers." She had wanted to be anonymous, unimportant. Free to do whatever she wanted, if only for the day. Except she wasn't, really. "I'm Wyatt's sister. I live here in Three Ridges . . . and now, apparently, so do you." She tried for a smile, felt it wobble around the edges. "So, um, howdy, neighbor! Welcome back to town."

Oh, hell, no. Ty's body might have held his ground, but the rest of him took a big step back. Because, damn. There was a big difference between hooking up with a random bridesmaid and locking lips with the groom's sister. And when you added in the whole part about Wyatt being damn near his boss now, there was a whole extra layer of awkward. As she said, a *thing*.

Unlocking his molars, he leveled his voice. "I take it Krista told you who I am."

"Seems we both held a few things back."

"I didn't lie." He wouldn't have, and didn't have much time for people who did.

"I'm very sorry," she said, and to her credit, her high cheekbones wore a flush of shame. "I didn't think that it would . . . Well, that's not your problem. In fact, this doesn't need to *be* a problem. I was thinking . . ."—her apologetic expression went hopeful—"that maybe we could just keep what happened to ourselves? It was just a few kisses."

He stiffened. "I'm no liar." Just kisses? Well, if that was how she saw it, so be it.

"I'm not asking you to lie," she said. Was that a flare of temper in her eyes? Please. "But if nobody asks—and they won't—what's the point in bringing it up? It's not like it's going to happen again."

"That's for damn sure."

"So you'll do it?"

"Fine," he said, biting off the word. "But if anyone asks, I'm not going to pretend it didn't happen." Though he almost wanted to now, as a near perfect memory went sour. Damn it. There had been days out on tour—gritty, grimy, angry days—that he had let himself replay the hour or so they had spent down by the lake together, needing something fresh and pure to keep him anchored. Maybe it had even been part of what had drawn him back to Wyoming. Not her, but the memory of how something could be simple, effort-less.

And, apparently, just another game.

Relief smoothed her face—heart-shaped, bow-lipped, and flawless in the half-light. "Thank you. I mean it, Ty. Thanks. I don't want my brother thinking . . . Well, that's not your problem, either. So I'll just say thank you and leave it at that. And, um, I guess I'll see you around."

"Sure thing," he said, pretty sure his tone conveyed a whole lot of *Not if I see you first*. Which might not be all the way fair—he hadn't told her that he knew his way around the ranch or that he'd helped build the dock they had been walking along when he'd kissed her for the first time. But that was different from pretending to be someone else.

She beat a retreat, boots knocking on the stairs. A moment later, the door swung shut behind her, giving a final-sounding *thunk* that reverbed for a two count before fading beneath the quiet noisiness of a summer night on the edge of the high country—the B-flat buzz-whine of bugs; the *ker-scree* of a nighthawk looking for some action; the rustle of the scrub moving in a low-lying breeze.

A minute ago, Ty had been content to let those noises seep into his bones, pushing out the bar noise. Now, though, he was more aware of sounds coming from inside the Rope Burn—the *badda-thud* bass line of whatever was playing on the old-timey jukebox and the rumble of patrons' voices as they no doubt returned to the dance floor or their tables with fresh beers, waiting for the stage to fill back up and get loud.

And among them, Ashley.

Knowing she'd still be there shouldn't have made him want to head for his truck rather than back inside for the second set. This didn't change anything. *She* didn't change anything—he had come back to Three Ridges for a job and a base of operations. Not because of the girl he had kissed down by the lake, and who had turned out to be more than she had said, and so much less than he had let himself imagine.

Maybe—probably—she was right about walking away, about it not mattering in the grand scheme of things. Hell, by dawn tomorrow, she would be a mental footnote. Wasn't like he didn't have better things to worry about.

Like the voice mail he'd gotten earlier in the day, terse and to the point. *Call me after ten. I might have something for you.*

Maybe Mac had something; maybe he didn't. Ty had heard it before. Still, when a check of his phone said it was five past, he scrolled down to the number and made the call.

One ring. *Don't get your hopes up.* Two rings. *It's probably another dead end.* Three—

"This is Macaulay." The private investigator's hoarse voice went with his pack-a-day habit, even though he smoked ecigs now.

"Mac, it's Tyler Reed. I got your message." Ty took a deep breath. "Did you find her?"

"No. But I might have a lead."

4

The next day, Ashley woke early with her heart banging away in her chest and her head filled with the remnants of a crazy dream about a herd of empty clothes chasing her along a roller-coaster track paved with dollar bills. "Whoa," she said, blinking. "That was . . ." Well, she didn't need a dream expert to interpret *that* particular gem.

Hello, store stress. At least there hadn't been any guest appearance by a certain guitar-playing cowboy.

Who she totally wasn't thinking about. At all.

Starting now.

The cracked-open window let a breeze through the screen, stirring the orange-and-teal-striped curtains against the white trim. Beyond, she could see across to the other side of Main Street, to the apartment over the feed and grain, where Feed Store Billy lived with his wife of thirty years, and the bedroom blinds went down every Sunday at three in the afternoon without fail, making her smile.

It was the same view Ashley had awakened to for the past five months, ever since Della had left and she'd moved in . . . except now it was *her* view. And how crazy was that?

Bouncing out of bed, she did a little dance. It was *her* bed now, along with the other things Della had left behind. Maybe the furnishings and decorations weren't all exactly to her taste—unlike the store's founder, she didn't always think that older was better—but Ashley was grateful for the squishy sofa, battered kitchen table, and the colorful mismatching Fiesta-type dishes racked on open shelves in the little galley kitchen.

Her dishes in *her* kitchen.

After going through her usual morning routine, she debated briefly between suede fringe and acid-washed denim, going with the denim because her budget no longer stretched to dry-cleaning. But then, because she was weak and Della's Mr. Coffee—now *her* Mr. Coffee, alas—was possessed by a bad-taste demon that alternated between toothpaste and motor oil, she headed to Butter My Biscuit two blocks down for a quick in-and-out and a small coffee. That was it. *Nada más.* She had pennies to save, and wasn't going to let herself get distracted by donuts and Danishes.

Half an hour later, carrying a large paper cup that wafted with the heavenly smell of a double shot of caramel and a paper bag that bulged with muffins, she came back up Main Street, humming "Sunny Days," because it was one and she was in a good mood. How could she not be, when there were a couple of cars parked in front of the store, one on each side of her beloved ladybug-painted VW, and Hen had flipped the sign in the window to OPEN ten minutes early?

Come on in, look around, and buy something. Mama's got bills to pay!

As Ashley passed her beloved car, she gave one of the spring-loaded antennae a flick. "Wish me luck, Bugs."

"Meow?"

"Excuse me?" Seeing a hint of movement in the shadows beneath Bugsy, she hunkered down. "Well, hello there."

A small, all-black cat huddled near the passenger-side tire with its yellow eyes narrowed to slits and its ears flat back.

"What are you doing under there? Are you new here?" It wasn't one of the shop cats she was used to seeing along Main Street. "Lost? Hungry? Would you like some muffin?" She reached in and broke off a piece. "Here you go. Blueberry, fresh out of the oven." She tossed the fragment.

"Sssss!" As if she'd lobbed a grenade rather than a baked good, the cat lashed out a forepaw that carried a whole lot of impressive claws, then bolted into the road.

Limping on three legs. Directly in front of an oncoming minivan.

Ashley shot to her feet. "Look out!"

The driver slammed on the brakes so hard that the vehicle shuddered and nosed down as the black cat gimped past. Ashley followed. "Wait!" she cried as the creature ducked under another parked car. "Come back! I'm not going to hurt you!"

But the cat had disappeared—*poof!*—into thin air.

The minivan's window buzzed down. "Did I hit her?"

"No, I— Oh, hi, Rose." Ashley finger-wiggled at Krista and Jenny's mom, belatedly recognizing the dark green vehicle with Mustang Ridge's logo on the door. "Nope. She—or he, who knows?"—though the female pronoun seemed right—"got away. Poor thing. There's something wrong with her leg."

"Let me park. I'll help you look."

There was no sign of the cat, though, and after doing a bunch of *Here, kitty, kitty* around the block and letting the other shopkeepers know to be on the lookout, they called it quits and headed back to Another Fyne Thing. The customers were gone, leaving Bugsy and the minivan alone out in front.

"Thanks for your help." Ashley hunkered down to look under the cars, just in case. "Sorry to interrupt your day." She straightened. "Where were you headed, anyway?"

Rose grinned. "Here, to see you."

"Oh?" Ashley gave the other woman an up-and-down, taking in the tailored gray pants, silk shirt, and upswept salt-and-pepper hair that made up a usual workday outfit for Rose, who orchestrated all the special events at Mustang Ridge. "Are you looking for something in particular? I've got a dark purple Chanel that's got your name all over it." The dress was sleek and sophisticated, but ruffled sleeves gave it a flirty twist that made it exactly right for Rose, whose brain could change directions in a snap, and who had so many great ideas she sometimes had trouble focusing on one or two.

Which was probably why she and Ashley got along so well. Like minds, and all that.

Sure enough, Rose's face brightened with immediate interest. "Ooh, I'd love to see the Chanel! First, though, I'm here on a mission . . . Rumor has it that we've got a fashion show to plan."

Right. Because last night, somewhere between the potato skins and the lake-sized brownie sundae they had ordered with five spoons, her "I need to do some special events to bring in revenue" had become "I'm going to do a fashion show next Friday." As in ten days from now. Which meant she needed a stage, a plan, permits, music, refreshments— *Oh, God.*

"Is that sudden panic I see?" Rose asked. "I recognize it from last summer, when Krista took an emergency wedding reservation, then realized she had double-booked it with a four-generation family reunion. If she and I made that work with three weeks' lead time, then you and I can absolutely pull this off."

Ashley didn't want it to be a *we.* It was her store, her gigantic payment due in forty-five—now forty-four—days, her chance to prove that she wasn't going to bail when the going got tough. But she also had to be reasonable. She wouldn't prove anything by falling on her face right out of the gate, and her friends were offering to help. "Okay, deep breath," she said, suiting action to the words. "I'm really doing this, aren't I? It still seems a little unreal." More than a little.

"Well, you know my motto: *One thing at a time.*"

"That's your motto? I thought it was *Look before you*

leap. Oh, wait. That's me. At least I'd like it to be, one of these days."

Rose hooked an arm through Ashley's. "First things first. What did you have in mind for a theme?"

"How about *Please buy something, I'm begging you*?"

That got a laugh. "I think we can do better than that."

"*Pretty please buy something*?"

"Come on, Ashley. I know you've been thinking about it."

Of course she had. Question was, which ideas were the good ones, and which were the creative black holes that would suck time and money while giving nothing back? She couldn't always tell. "I was thinking along the lines of *What's old is new again* or *Reinvention*, but neither feels exactly right."

"They fit with vintage, and would be easy enough to pull off in ten days."

"Still, they're . . . *meh*. And I don't want meh." She wanted vivid, vibrant, exciting.

"Hmm." Rose studied the display window, which was painted with the store name in foot-high gilt letters and was currently showcasing a volleyball game of mismatched mannequins, bright clothing, and purple sand that had been a special order Billy needed to dump. "So we need a theme that says reinvention without using the word."

"I want the audience to get something tangible out of the evening, too, more than just oohing and aahing over the clothes." Though the oohs and aahs would be important, too. "I was thinking I could show people how to take an old, tired piece out of their wardrobe and use it in a different way rather than getting rid of it. Maybe some of the models could even come out wearing things one way, then do a quick change and wear them another."

Rose's eyes lit. "Kind of like a butterfly coming out of its cocoon. I like it!"

Ta-da! Colored flashbulbs went off in Ashley's head. "That's it! You're brilliant. Butterflies. We could call it *Transformations* and have each model wear a butterfly somewhere—a pin, or a scarf, or whatever." She talked fast as the ideas tumbled one over the other, fluttering in her mind's eye. "We'll go heavy on the colors and patterns in the show itself, and line the walls with butterfly art. Maybe even put wings on the mannequins. Or how about the models?"

"Butterfly swag would be ideal as a giveaway."

"Yes yes yes! A butterfly-shaped gift bag with every ticket, full of promo stuff, coupons, a trinket or two. And after the show, we'll open the sales floor and offer suggestions on how certain pieces can be reinvented . . ."

Heads together, talking butterflies and percent discounts, they headed into the shop and were greeted by the perky jingle of the welcome bell. And for the first time since Ashley had started signing next to those sticky arrows, she was more excited than scared.

So what if she had another big payment to make? She wasn't just going to do this. She was going to rock it.

*   *   *

"I hear congratulations are in order."

Ty stiffened at the sound of Wyatt's voice coming up the barn aisle. He hadn't seen Krista's husband all day, hadn't heard him come through the rolling doors just now. Turning away from grooming Brutus to square off opposite the other man, who was a couple of inches shorter but built like a brick outhouse, Ty said, "'Scuse me?"

Wyatt propped a shoulder on a nearby stall door, letting the horse within—a spunky chestnut mare named Sassy—sniff his sleeve. "Junior says you slam-dunked it out on the trail today."

Okay, they were talking business. Ty could handle that. Krista had rehired him over the phone and handed over the keys to the posh above-barn apartment without batting an eye, but they went back nearly a decade and she knew he could do the job. Wyatt was relatively new to the operation and only knew Ty as the wedding singer. He had proven more reserved. Which probably made it a good thing that Ashley had wanted to keep her and Ty's little rendezvous between the two of them.

Ty didn't want to owe her, didn't want to think about her at all. But he had to admit, it made things easier not having to butt heads with her brother on that front.

Returning his attention to Brutus—he didn't like turning his back on the too-smart chestnut gelding for long—he said, "Thanks, but it was mostly par for the course. Singles Week, you know."

It was one of the dude ranch's most popular theme

weeks, complete with couples' roping games, horse-back speed dating, and musical saddles. It also tended to be their most dramatic, with sex—or the lack thereof—complicating the usual stew of nerves and bravado that came with mixing two dozen greenhorns with an equal number of mustangs.

So far, Ty had broken up a couple of almost-fights, consoled a heartbroken relationship columnist who had chucked all her own best advice on taking things slow and gotten burned for it, and dealt with a couple of attorneys who kept trying to kiss while trotting along on their highly annoyed mounts. All while keeping the line moving and making a bunch of city slickers feel like they could totally hack it on the pro rodeo circuit.

"Still," Wyatt said, "good work. You coming in for dinner?"

Swiping the last of the dust and sweat-salt off Brutus's hide with practiced flicks of a stiff-bristled brush, Ty shook his head. "No offense, but after today, a cold beer and a quiet sunset on my back deck sounds better than the dining hall."

"Don't blame you. There's chili, though. And cake."

Ty's stomach grumbled. "I'll keep it in mind."

"Do that. And when you're done with Brutus, you can call it a night. I'll finish up in here."

There wasn't much left to do, save for making sure the guest tack room was set up for the morning, topping off waters, and giving the aisle a last sweep, but Ty figured it wasn't about who did the chores. There were times a man just needed the barn to himself—

usually when things had gotten tense outside it. "Roger that. Thanks."

He picked out Brutus's hooves, dodged a too-hard nudge aimed at his shoulder, and led the gelding into his stall, which opened through a Dutch door on the far side to a small private paddock. When he came out, Wyatt was still leaned up nearby, letting Sassy nibble his sleeve.

Ty hesitated, then went ahead and asked, "Everything okay?"

The silence that followed sounded a whole lot like *I don't want to talk about it.*

"Right, then. I'll leave you—"

"It's my sister," Wyatt said unexpectedly. "Ashley."

Ty stiffened. "Oh?" *Uh-oh.*

"She's in trouble, in over her head. As usual."

That didn't sound like the lead-in to a round of *Keep your hands off her*, but it didn't sound like anything Ty wanted to get involved in, either.

"She bought a business downtown," Wyatt continued, "on a payment schedule that can't possibly work the way she thinks it will. Especially if she pulls her usual routine of starting off all gung-ho and then losing steam." He patted the mare's nose, then looked over at Ty. "What I can't figure out is where do I draw the line at bailing her out?"

"I don't think I'm the right person to answer that. Maybe Krista—"

"She thinks I'm overreacting. And, yeah, maybe I've pushed her over the years. Ashley, I mean. But she's got all these talents, these incredible opportunities, and she keeps bouncing around. It's always something new with her, something better. Now it's a big-ass store that she can't afford unless the stars align exactly right. Not to mention—" Wyatt broke off, scowling. "Sorry. Not your problem. You don't even know her."

Ty hesitated a beat. Now was the time to say something if he was going to. He didn't, though. What had happened between him and Ashley was over and done. History. "I've ridden out with a lot of family groups over the years," he said instead, "and it seems to me that the siblings that bust on each other the hardest are usually the ones who defend each other the fiercest when things start to go wrong. Maybe after a while of things going wrong and you needing to step in, that big reaction gets to be automatic."

"In other words, you think I'm overreacting, too."

"I think that she's lucky to have a big brother who has her back." Ty knocked some shavings off his boots. "I'll get along now, leave you to finish up in here."

"Yeah. I could use the quiet. Go on and get yourself some of that chili."

"I'll do that. Thanks." And a couple of beers to go with dinner, because getting too deep into the dynamics of other people's families always put an itch between his shoulder blades.

Seemed he was doomed, though, because a few minutes later, as he came through the side door into the ranch's main kitchen, with its hanging herbs, commercial ovens, and endless counters, he saw Gran, Rose, Shelby, and Krista sitting at the butcher block with their heads together, deep in conversation.

As he hesitated, trying to decide between greeting and retreating, Krista said, "Ashley said she's having trouble figuring out how to fit everything into the building along with enough people to make it worthwhile."

Pivoting, Ty headed for the door.

"Don't you dare sneak out," Gran said without looking at him. "Come over here and give an old lady a hug."

He turned back. "This sounds like girl talk. I'm allergic to girl talk." Especially when it involved Wyatt's flighty little sister, who seemed to be stalking him without even being there.

Blue eyes glinting, Gran beckoned him over. "Deal with it, big guy."

Unable to refuse her—he had zero resistance when it came to Krista's bird-tiny, white-haired grandmother, who cooked like a goddess and had a personality that filled every room she entered—he crossed the kitchen and leaned down to fold her in his arms, breathing in the scents of hot peppers and baked goods.

He was a guy who'd never had a gran of his own, so it was mighty nice of the Skyes to let him borrow theirs now and then. That didn't mean he wanted to get in the middle of their family stuff, though. He had it on good authority that he didn't have any talent in that department.

Okay, maybe his ex wasn't a good authority on much except cheating, but still.

Gran patted his cheek. "You're a good boy, Tyler." She slid off her barstool, which put the top of her head below his chin, and headed for the two big refrigerators. "You'll be wanting chili, sides, and seconds on dessert."

"Thanks. You're the best." To the others, he said, "Sorry for interrupting."

"No problem," Krista said. "We were just going over some details for the fashion show that Wyatt's sister, Ashley, is having next Friday."

"We've met." *Swapped spit. Lied about our identities. Agreed never to speak of it again.*

Shelby's eyes narrowed speculatively. "Hmmm."

He returned her stare. "Don't even think it." He liked Foster's wife just fine, but knew her too well to trust her when she was wearing that particular expression.

"Think what?"

"Whatever it is. The last time you looked at me like that, I wound up with my shirt off, starring as Mr. November in a gift calendar."

"You loved it."

"I didn't mind it." And along with that campfire video, it had gotten him the gig with Higgs & Hicks. But he wasn't taking any chances when flaky Ashley was the subject and Shelby was wearing that look. "That doesn't mean I'm doing it again, though. Or whatever else you've got in the works."

"You'll be perfect." She turned to the others. "He knows all about staging, acoustics, and making an entrance. What could be better?"

"Chili and a couple of beers, and watching the sunset from my back porch?"

Krista made a face. "Spoilsport."

"It'd just be an hour," Shelby put in. "Maybe two with the drive."

"Oh, leave the man be," Gran said as she finished packing his dinner in one of the wicker baskets she used for the guests' carryout meals. "Helping out our Ashley isn't part of his job description."

Which, darn it, really meant, *Be a good boy and help her out, will you? As a favor to me.*

Ty's gut took a quick ride on the down elevator, headed for his toes. *Oh, hell.* Because this was Gran, and it didn't feel right saying no to her. Especially when she was tapping the lid of the picnic basket with a look that might not be a threat, but was pretty darn close. They were talking about chili, sides, and dessert, darn it. And, yeah, if Ashley needed input on staging and a sound system, he could probably help. In fact, if it had been anybody else, he'd already be in his truck.

Taking a long look at the basket, he sighed. "Fine. I'll do it."

He didn't have to be happy about it, though.

5

"Here kitty, kitty, kitty." Ashley opened the can of Happy Moist Kitty—the cheapest brand Billy carried over at the feed store, and a truly questionable name—and wrinkled her nose. "Mmm . . . This smells"—*like low tide and week-old garbage*—"yummy."

Trying not to let any of the brown glop ooze onto her hand, she hunkered down on the sidewalk and stretched out an arm to set the can as far back into the live trap as she could reach. Made of wire mesh and about the size of two jumbo mailboxes put together end to end, the contraption had levers and pressure plates and had to be set up exactly right if she hoped to catch anything. And even at that, there was no guarantee it would be the scrawny black cat with the bad leg.

"You'd better appreciate this." She kept her voice sweet and lilting, figuring the tone counted for more than the actual words. "Nick said when I catch you he'll take a look at that leg, get you cleaned up, and find you a new home. Wouldn't that be nice?" Convenient that Jenny's husband was the local vet, and a softy when it came to strays.

There was no response, even though she had seen the skinny black shadow skulking around under Bugsy an hour ago. She did get curious glances from a couple of pedestrians, though.

"Stray cat," she said, not wanting to start a rumor about there being giant rats lurking on Main Street. After the foot traffic continued on, she fumbled to rig up the pressure plate the way Billy had showed her. But where he had made it look easy, she clearly needed another arm, maybe two. Like that Hindu goddess. What was her name? Katy? Cujo? *Focus. You don't have all day.* The to-do list loomed large. "Come on," she muttered under her breath as she fought to line up the little hook thingie with the corresponding hole in the pressure plate. "Behave, will you?"

Finally, everything slipped into place with a satisfying click.

"Thank you!" she exclaimed. "It's about time." *Kali.* That was the goddess's name. Score two for her.

"Talking to yourself?" a man's voice said from above her, amused. And suddenly there was a big shadow blocking the early-evening light.

Ashley stiffened, her mind blanking because she knew that voice, that shadow.

Ty.

Rocking back on her heels, she looked up at him—up, up, and up some more to where he stood over her, boots planted on the bricks and the brim of his straw Stetson casting that wide shadow. She couldn't read those dark, dark eyes or the set of his square, stubbled jaw, couldn't imagine why he was there. Didn't like the prickles that ran down her arms at the sight of him. Sure, he was hot, but she hadn't cared for the way he had looked at her last night, condemning, as if he'd never made a mistake in his life.

Not letting any of that leak into her voice, she said, "Ty, hey."

He nodded to the trap. "Skunk problem?"

"God, no." *Knock on wood.* "Stray cat." She rose, making a show of dusting off her jeans. "You headed over to the feed store?"

"Actually, I came to see you."

"You . . . really? Why?"

"Gran asked me to," he said. "Krista, too. Rose. Shelby." He added the names like he was piling on the evidence, just in case she got the crazy idea he had come to see her on purpose. "They said you're planning some big event for next Friday and could use some help with the stage design. So here I am."

"Here you are," she echoed, torn between her to-do list and a whole lot of *I can do it myself.* Especially if getting help meant it came from him. "I thought we were going to avoid each other."

"It's a small town." His gaze went a couple of blocks down, to where Main Street went from shops to practically nothing in one set of lights. "Might be better for us to figure out how we can cross paths without you turning a couple of shades of pink. That is, unless you think Krista and the others won't notice."

"I . . ." She pressed both hands to her warm cheeks, feeling them heat further. "Darn it."

"Besides, Gran is the closest thing I've got to family,

and I guess she's yours, too. Around here, folks help each other out, and I've got a free hour. Up to you whether you want to use it."

He was right, of course—about family, it being a small town, the two of them needing to get used to each other . . . and about her needing whatever help she could get, especially with the technical stuff. The deeper she got into planning the fashion show, the dumber she felt. There were so many moving parts—front and center being the stage, the lighting, and the sound. If he could help her get a handle on that, it would be major.

Suck it up, buttercup. Nobody said this was going to be easy. Granted, she hadn't figured on him being one of the challenges. He could be useful, though. Anyone who played like he did and had spent a few years on tour with a megagroup like Higgs & Hicks had probably picked up a few tricks along the way.

So, smoothing her expression to the one she used with her more frazzling customers—the ones who went on about how the size tags were wrong, the prices were crazy, and why didn't she have this particular one-of-a-kind gown in a different shade of champagne?—she said, "Then I'll use that hour and be grateful if you can help." It came out sounding more dubious than she'd meant it to, but whatever. Crossing the sidewalk, she pushed open the door. "Come on in. Welcome to Another Fyne Thing."

The scent hit Ty first, then the colors, in a one-two punch of *Hey, cowboy, you're not in the backcountry anymore.*

Sure, the air sometimes smelled like flowers out on the trail—first thing on a spring morning, maybe, or after a quick summer thunderstorm—but this took it to a whole new level, like all those flowers had gotten together in a hot tub and had a crazy party. *Crazy party* pretty much described the visuals, too. The big, high-ceilinged space was heavy on the primary colors and fabrics, none of which were put together how he would've expected. Not even after getting a load of the shiny red VW Beetle out front, with its big black polka dots, tennis ball antennae, and BUG-Z vanity plate, or the window display, where mismatched mannequins wearing bright dresses played beach volleyball with a set of stuffed Jockey shorts.

Nope. Not even close.

Disembodied and empty, wire-strung pants and shirts climbed the columns, skipped along the walls, and dangled from the overhead ducts that gave the place an industrial feel. Mismatched shoes hung from haphazard clotheslines, tied together by brightly colored laces, and mirrors made crooked zigzags everywhere he looked. There were racks of clothes everywhere, some topped with little scenes: a wire figure crouching down, petting a cat? dog? made of a stuffed-full turtleneck with an upturned hiking boot as a head; a couple of mannequins kissed as they danced.

There were signs, too. FUN AND FLIRTY, said one above a rack of dresses, while another hung above an empty hook announced, COOL THINGS I'M GOING TO TRY ON. They were hand-painted in bright colors and decorated with painted-on flowers. Those same flowers—along with starbursts and little caricatures of curvy women wearing pretty clothes—were also painted on a series of glossy white bookcases that held everything from jeans and shoes to handbags and little froufrou dustables.

He had to blink a couple of times to make it all settle into focus. Sort of.

Ashley sent him a sidelong look. "I know it's probably not really your speed." She hadn't seemed thrilled to see him, wasn't exactly gushing with gratitude, but what had he expected? They just needed to get through this and move on.

Still, he didn't need to be rude about it. "It's . . ." he began, but then petered out, because his gut reaction was that it was silly, spontaneous, and exactly the sort of thing he should've expected from someone whose car had tennis ball antennae and whose brother thought she was a disaster. It was also way too crowded to fit a sound system, never mind a stage and a bunch of people . . . But he didn't want to start off with a pointless argument—on either front—so he went with "Fun."

She blinked, surprised. Then she smiled.

And, damn, he wished she hadn't done that. The curve of her wide, full lips illuminated her face, punching right through him and lighting a fire in his gut. That was how she looked when he'd first seen her, when he'd first kissed her. When things had been simple, all about chemistry and nothing more.

Well, he didn't want anything more when it came to women right now—not in general, and certainly not with her. Shoving his hands in his pockets, he looked around again, studying the space and realizing that the place wasn't as small as he'd thought at first, just crowded. "I hear you bought it."

Her smile flattened. Which hadn't been his intention, but he would take it. Made it easier to think. "It's a big commitment," she said. "Like, scary big. How much did the others tell you?"

"Some. I heard that you've got six weeks or so to come up with the rest of your down payment, and you're looking to run a fashion show next Friday, hoping to get bodies through the door."

Her lips curved once more. "That about covers it."

Did she know what her smile did to a man? Probably, he decided. A woman who looked like her couldn't not know, and at the 'Burn he had seen her flirting up a storm with the grizzled old cowboy at the next table over. She wasn't turning it on now, though, with her shoulders stiff and her eyes mostly avoiding his. Was it because she didn't like needing help, or because she didn't like needing *his* help?

Doesn't matter. In and out, an hour of your life, and there's chili waiting for you at home. More, he'd rather have her at arm's length than up close and smiling. "What did you have in mind for staging?"

"I've got some sketches. Over here." She spun and headed deeper into the store, to where a glass display case was packed full of sparkly stuff and had a register at one end.

Feeling like he was walking into a box canyon crammed with flowers and parrots, Ty followed. His boots clomped on the wood floor like he was the bull in the danged china shop.

She had a bunch of papers fanned out beside a laptop, and a leaning tower of books wore library stickers on their spines and titles like *Event Planning Checklist* and *The Divas of Fashion Week*. Looked like she had been doing her homework.

"I talked to Della—she's the former owner of this place—and hit the mayor's office, so I think I've got a pretty good idea of what I need in terms of permits, parking, and code stuff. I'm going to need a runway that doesn't mess with the fire exits, a bar, enough floor space for a hundred people—that's the max I'm allowed, though I don't know if we'll sell that many tickets in a week and a bit—and a way to display plenty of product but keep it safe from spills." She nudged a sketch in his direction. "This is what I was thinking, but as you can see, my plans are bigger than my footprint. What do you think?"

He stared for a beat—at her, not the paper—and said, "Impressive." Between what Wyatt had said and the chorus of "Ashley needs our help" from the kitchen, he'd been expecting a half-assed mess. Granted, a bit of prep work didn't mean she wasn't exactly how her brother had described her—a flitter who bounced from obsession to obsession. He just happened to have landed in the middle of her latest fixation.

He knew the type. Though, in his mother's case, it had been men and drugs, not modeling and fashion.

Ashley's eyelids went down. "About the sketch, I mean."

"Right." When he leaned in, the smell of flowers brightened to a warmer, fresher scent that made him think of loping up into the foothills on a sunny spring day. Holding his breath, he focused on the job at hand and scanned the not-even-close-to-scale rendition of the store, with the racks pushed to the perimeter, rows of chairs, a wide catwalk winding around a central display, and spots for a sound system and a bar. He gave a low whistle. "This is—"

"Nuts?"

"I was going to say *ambitious*. Might be doable, though." If she had a month and a full crew. "What's your budget?"

"Think garage band doing their first paid gig. You know—lots of painted plywood and stuff scavenged from the basement."

He shot her a look. "You were in a band?" *How long did that phase last?*

"Me? Nope. I have zero rhythm and my pitch sucks, but I love music and dated a drummer for a while. Too long, if you ask my brother. Anyway." She tapped the sketch. "What do you think about the stage? I need a curtained-off space for the models to come through, here-ish." She pointed. "They'll strut their stuff around a central display—I'm thinking mannequins wearing high-end dresses, acting out a little scene—to the end here, strike a pose, and then head back around the other side, so everyone gets a good look."

"Kind of like a baggage carousel at the airport."

"Close enough. Will it work?"

He took another long look around the space, this

time seeing the solid bones and clean traffic lines beneath all the fluff. "It should," he said, stepping away from the scent of summer sun and back to flowers-in-the-hot-tub. "First things first. You're going to need to spread out your speakers more, and raise them up off the ground level. Got a pen?"

"Here." She fished one out of a pink coffee mug that sat next to the register and held it out.

Their fingers brushed when he took the pen, bringing a tingle, and her quick indrawn breath said she felt it, too. Ignoring it, Ty bent over the glass case full of froufrou and got to work.

An hour later, Ashley walked Ty to the door, not sure whether she wanted to throw her arms around him and profess her undying gratitude, or wrap her fingers around his neck and squeeze.

The wedding-singer-turned-cowboy-turned-potential-complication had proven to be darn near brilliant on top of everything else, at least when it came to set design. He thought like a concert planner, sketched like an engineer, and had turned her crazy-sounding ideas into something that might actually work. All while keeping a solid chunk of airspace between them and shutting down her attempts at being friendly.

Wasn't like she had been creepy-stalker prying, either—at least not at first. It was just her usual new-customer stuff, some basic getting-to-know-you-isms designed to find some common ground, create a rapport. But "It must've been cool, being out on the road with a big band like Higgs and Hicks" had gotten a terse "Less than you'd think," and "Is it nice being back at Mustang Ridge?" had yielded the gem, "Not bad." Even her go-to "I'm still learning my way around Three Ridges. What's your favorite place to grab a bite?" had been met with "Out of town."

Clearly, he thought she deserved the attitude. She, on the other hand, wanted to shake him until his perfect teeth rattled, and hit him with a one-two of *Get over yourself* and *It was just a couple of kisses.* Sheesh! *Let's try sticking with gratitude, shall we?* Thanks to him, she had a plan for the stage now, and it was a good one. Besides, it wasn't like she wanted to be his best friend, or even his friend. She owed him one for the help, and if the payback was putting up with his crap tonight and avoiding him from here on out, she could do that.

Except that his big, masculine presence had her on edge, as did the skim of heat that kept wanting to run along her skin every time he moved and his worn jeans and plain T-shirt stretched across impressive muscles. That, plus the monosyllables, had turned it into a challenge that flipped her flirt button to ON.

She had started with "I could hook you up with some threads, you know. Just because you're back working at Mustang Ridge doesn't mean you have to dress straight out of the Sheplers catalog," and when that got a grumble, she'd had a little fun with "You'd look just darling in Italian silk" and "Your coloring says autumn, but we could play with some spring colors, too. Lavender would be good."

By the time they'd finished up, the grunts had given way to glares, but she didn't think he was actually mad at her anymore. More like baffled, which she decided to consider an improvement.

Flipping the dead bolt, she pushed open the door. "Thanks again. And I'm serious. I don't usually handle menswear"—try *never*, but he didn't have to know that—"but I'd be willing to make an exception, seeing how you're helping me out. Lavender silk. Think about it, okay?"

He stopped outside the three-foot perimeter he'd been maintaining between them, planting his boots on the wide boards of the wooden floor. Even at that distance, she had to tip her head up a little to look him in the eyes. He hooked a thumb in one pocket, making her think that if he'd been a sheriff with a six-shooter, he would've had his hand on the butt of his gun. But all he said was, "Not gonna happen. And thank Shelby. Me being here was her idea."

Let him go. Enough is enough. She was on a roll, though, and perversely enjoying the game of wringing a response out of him. "The staging is going to be great."

He tipped his head in acknowledgment.

"I'm surprised you didn't design the emcee's stand in the middle with a trapdoor and some spikes below. Maybe alligators." She would be standing up there most of the night, after all.

"Rattlesnakes would be easier to get hold of." One corner of his mouth kicked up. "Besides, I was going to talk to Ed about those plans privately."

And then, darn it, he broke into a full-on grin.

The expression rearranged his face, turning the stern

lines into character, the heavy judgment into a different sort of intensity. Her head spun, her insides clutched, and she was suddenly taken back eighteen months, to the moment she'd come waltzing up the aisle in a floaty, flirty bridesmaid dress—her first purchase at Another Fyne Thing, in fact—feeling like a million bucks. Then twice that when she and the guitarist had locked eyes, and he'd smiled at her like he'd been waiting for her all his life.

In other words, it was the kind of grin that could make a smart girl do really dumb things. And when you weren't that smart to start with . . . Her palms went damp, her mouth dried out, and she did the only thing she could possibly do under the circumstances.

She stepped back and waved him out the door. "I'll see you around." Maybe. Probably not. She didn't get up to Mustang Ridge much, and it didn't sound like he was a fan of Three Ridges. And that was probably a good thing.

Settling his Stetson lower on his brow, he stepped through the door, breaching their unspoken perimeter and putting them up close and personal. His body heat touched the exposed skin of her face and throat, and his scent tingled in her nostrils, sharp and male. Then he was past her and out on the sidewalk, and she could breathe again.

She expected him to beeline for his truck. Instead, he paused and made a sour face, like he had just gotten a look at the purple Italian silk shirt she had been teasing him about. Except the expression wasn't aimed at her this time—it was being fired at her little town, like it was the smallest, crappiest place he'd ever been stuck.

Her cute, funky, *interesting* little downtown. The one populated by cute, funky, interesting people who had welcomed her, befriended her, made her feel like she wasn't an outsider anymore and like buying the shop wasn't the Stupidest Idea Ever, because, hey, they had shops, they weren't perfect, and they were doing okay.

The bristle was instinctive.

Let it go, she told herself. *Gratitude, remember?* "You should try the pizza place," she suggested instead. "I don't know what Gary's secret ingredient might be, but his sauce rocks."

He glanced back at her, expression unreadable. "I've been there. Been most places in town over the years, but I'm not interested in reconnecting. I'm just passing through."

"You never know. You might decide you like it here."

Again with the sour look up the block. "Doubtful."

"There are some new places in town, you know. Otter's Ice Cream is good, and the fish place."

"Like I said, I'd rather take a ride outside of town."

She told herself to let it go, but couldn't. "Why?" she asked, arching an eyebrow. "Afraid you'll run into someone you'd rather not see?"

He stiffened and turned back suddenly, warning her that she had pushed him too far. Two long strides carried him back to her, had him looming. The air between them went suddenly hot, and not in a good way.

She would have backed up, but the doorway kept her in place.

"Sweetheart," he growled, "you have no idea. Let's keep it that way." He glared down at her for a beat as if daring her to say something else. When she didn't, he jammed his hat even lower on his brow and gave her a terse nod that said they had just agreed to something, though she wasn't sure exactly what.

Then he turned on his heel and walked away, leaving her in the doorway with her heart thudding in her chest and the sense that she had just brushed up against something far bigger and more dangerous than she had expected. Like dipping a hand in a koi pond and cutting her finger on the edge of a shark's tooth.

Where had *that* come from? What had she missed just now?

Don't care, she told herself, which was a lie. Like it or not, there were still sparks between her and Ty, still heat buzzing in her bloodstream from their encounter. *It doesn't matter,* which was the truth—or it should be. Needed to be. Whatever was going on with him, it wasn't her business, wasn't hers to worry about. *He* wasn't hers to worry about, especially when she didn't want the others to know they had a past, however small.

Besides, she had vowed that when she got involved again—somewhere in the future, when she had everything else worked out—it wouldn't be with another project guy. She was through with trying to fix men. She had a business to run, a fashion show to plan, and a new, better life to build. One that was hers alone.

Taking a deep breath, she retreated into the shop and double-locked the door. Then, facing the sales floor, she zeroed in on the changing area, which needed to be rearranged for the staging to fit in as planned. "Okay. Time to get back to work."

That was what mattered, after all. Not a music-making cowboy who clearly wanted nothing to do with her.

6

The next morning, Hen rifled through Ty's sketches, her eyes bright and interested behind a pair of smoky-blue John Lennon glasses. "Hey, cool. Are these for the fashion show?"

"That's the theory," Ashley said from over by the dressing rooms, where Froggy Lemp was trying on dresses for a big anniversary weekend in the city, complete with theater tickets and a fancy dinner out. To the scuffling noises going on in the curtained-off cube, where Froggy's socks—one pink-toed, the other solid blue—were doing a little getting-into-a-dress dance, she called, "How's it going in there?" She far preferred to talk to her customer than tell Hen about last night.

Especially when, in the light of day, she knew it had been mostly her fault. Sure, Ty was the one who had copped an attitude and got in her face with it, but she had pushed and poked and backed him into that corner when all he was doing was helping her. Not cool. So much for being a newer and better version of her same old self. She was more like a project in progress.

A half-patterned dress with a couple of seams and lots of pencil marks.

"I know I picked this one out." Froggy's voice was beyond dubious. "It was so pretty on the hanger, but I wonder if it's not a little too . . . I don't know. Green?"

It's not easy being green . . . "Come on out and let's have a look in the mirror. Even if it's not the one, we can take a look at what doesn't work on you, and why." Not that Ashley would have picked the calf-length sequined mermaid for the short, perky, fortysomething rancher's wife, but she had learned that it wasn't always about what she thought looked right. More often than not, if a customer felt beautiful in an outfit, she became beautiful in it.

As Froggy swept aside the curtain and stepped out, though, she was looking more worried than beautiful. And very green.

The Alyce Designs dress, with its ruffles on the straps and sequins encrusting the entire fitted body, had probably been a knockout at a prom back in the nineties, on some curvy teen built like an old pinup. Apple-shaped Froggy, though, looked more like a bright green disco ball, especially when she stepped into the mirrored alcove and they saw the effect from three sides.

She heaved a sigh. "I don't just look like a drag queen. I look like I'm making *fun* of a drag queen."

"It's not the right shape for you," Ashley said bracingly. "You're leaner through the hips than the dress, and that's giving you the illusion of some junk that you most definitely don't carry in your trunk. And the straps are too long. If we shortened things up here"—

she pinched one strap, lifting the built-in bra an inch or so—"and took in a handful of material down here"—with her other hand, she eliminated the trunk-junk—"things would look a whole lot different."

Relief eased Froggy's reflected image. "Oh! You're right. Now I look more like a mermaid than a blinged-out watermelon."

"But it's still not the right dress for you," Ashley said before she could be asked to confirm or deny either resemblance. Letting go of her insta-alterations, she nudged the other woman back toward the dressing room. "Do me a favor? Try the blue Dolce next. I've got a feeling about that one."

While Froggy's mismatched socks did the getting-out-of-a-dress dance behind the curtain, Ashley made a circuit of the store, nudging jeans into a neater stack, tweaking a couple of sleeves, and winding up at the register, where her assistant was still studying Ty's sketches.

"Very nice." Hen tapped a diagram of the central display. "What are you thinking of for here?"

Not letting herself remember Ty's grin when he threatened rattlesnakes, Ashley said, "Some high-end pieces. Chanel, maybe, and a few of Della's designs." Not just because Della had founded Another Fyne Thing, but because her original designs rocked, and being her sole distributor had bumped the store's online and in-person sales. "Plus shoes and accessories. I want to make the central pieces feel exclusive, like a buyer would be darn lucky to wear one."

"Which she would, of course!" Hen traced the outline of the emcee stand, sans trapdoor. "Did Ed do the design work?"

It was a reasonable guess—Krista's father had been quick to volunteer his help. Then again, so had pretty much everybody in the extended family, from Krista making plans to bring her female guests to the fashion show, to Jenny's offering to do photos and videos.

From Wyatt, though . . . crickets.

Ashley shook her head. "Ed is going to help me build everything up to code, but these drawings came from another of their employees, who got press-ganged into helping." She hesitated, told herself not to ask, then asked anyway. "Maybe you know him? Tyler Reed?"

Hen's eyes brightened behind the John Lennons. "Of course I know Ty! He was here?"

"Ta-da!" Froggy whisked the curtain aside and made a grand entrance, looking like a million bucks in the blue tea-length dress. "What do you think?"

The interruption was probably a good thing.

"Now that's more like it." Ashley nodded her approval, making herself focus on their customer. Which wasn't a hardship, as Froggy had suddenly transformed.

The dress was mid-eighties, but instead of the decade's trademark shiny rayon, along with shoulder pads that would do a football player proud and puffed-up sleeves that needed big hair to balance them off, the fabric had a faint iridescent sheen and the cap sleeves were simple and unadorned. Better yet, the bodice had enough structure to give Froggy's ample bosom a little lift and then nip in at her waist, and after hugging her shapely—and decidedly junk-free—derriere, the skirt flared away to brush just below her knees.

"I feel pretty." Froggy did another skirt-flaring twirl. She let her head fall back and laughed as her dark, curly hair bobbed around her face, making her look every bit her age, but also youthful and energetic, and as if she wanted to grab onto life with both hands and take it dancing.

"You're beautiful," Ashley said. "Martin isn't going to be able to take his eyes off you." She grinned over at Hen, loving this moment.

After shooting her a double thumbs-up, Hen bustled down from the register, adding, "One of the nice things is that with this color blue, you can tweak the accessories to pull it from season to season. For summer, I'd go with an open-toed shoe in a jewel tone. Ruby, maybe, or green." She headed for the shoe wall. "You're, what, a seven? Seven and a half?"

Thirty minutes and almost five hundred dollars later, once they tallied up the dress, shoes, clutch, wrap, and two scoop-neck shirts that had found their way into the pile, Ashley helped a delighted Froggy load the bags into her car.

"You're the best!" The other woman turned back to give her a quick hug. "I'm so glad you took over the store when Della left. And I can't wait for next Friday!" She patted her purse, where she had tucked her ticket. "Front row, here I come!"

Ashley waved as Froggy reversed out of her parking spot; then she turned back to the store, where Hen stood in the doorway. "Well. That was a good sale!" Not just because it had put money in the till, but because Froggy would spread the word—and when it came to a town like Three Ridges, buzz trumped advertising. "I need to get busy on those tickets." She had hand-printed a version for Froggy, who had loved having hers custom-made with a #1 in the upper right corner, but if the word was going out, she needed to be prepared for a rush.

Fingers crossed.

"I'll do the tickets if you tell me about Ty. I'd heard he was back at Mustang Ridge, but I didn't figure on seeing him in town." Hen wrinkled her nose. "Bad memories, you know."

Ashley stilled. *Oh, really?* She told herself not to ask—*not my business, staying out of it, don't even like him that much.* "What kind of memories?"

"Oh, right, you weren't around for the drama, were you? He was engaged to a girl in town—a baker over at Betty's. They were head over heels, the cutest couple you ever saw. It was a whirlwind romance, the two of them always holding hands and sitting on the same side of the booth. Something happened, though, and the next thing we knew, the wedding was off and Brandi was gone." Hen snapped her fingers. "Just like that."

"He—" Ashley covered her mouth as her stomach headed for her toes. "Oh, God."

"He stuck around another month or so, but he wasn't the same guy at all. Then the dude season ended and he left, too. Really, I was surprised to hear he'd come back at all—I always figured he was gone for good. He didn't seem like the type to give second chances, whether you're talking about a place or a person." Hen shrugged. "I guess Krista must've made him an offer he couldn't refuse."

Ashley felt like crap. *You have no idea,* he'd said, and how right he had been. She had taken his look as a sneer against the town she loved, but he hadn't been staring at all of downtown. He had been fixed on the sign for Betty's bakery.

Suddenly realizing that she was standing where Ty had been last night, while Hen had taken her place in the doorway, Ashley crossed the sidewalk and perched on the end of Bugsy's hood. As her faithful little car settled under her weight and her stomach headed even lower, she dropped her face into her hands. "Ohmigod. Dumbass."

"Who, Ty?" Hen sounded surprised.

"No. Me. We . . . Well, anyway." Telling Hen about what had happened between her and Ty back at the wedding—which was where it had all started, really—would be about as far from keeping it to herself as it was possible to get. So she went with "Let's just say I stepped in it last night, and brought all that back up without meaning to. I wasn't nice about it, either. I feel terrible."

She was usually the first to sense when a client's frown came from more than just a bad hemline. And even though Ty hadn't exactly been turning on the charm, she knew what it felt like to have her supposed happily-ever-after blow up in her face, knew how much she hated it when Wyatt brought it up to make a point. Last night, she had wanted to tease Ty, make him a little uncomfortable, so they'd be even. Not stick a knife in and twist.

Hen, always her staunchest supporter, came over and patted her shoulder. "It was an accident. You didn't know."

"Still. I wish I had handled it differently." She pushed herself off Bugsy's hood as a couple of pedestrians came into earshot, a mother and daughter strolling along Main Street hand in hand. "I'll have to . . . I don't know. Do something. Apologize, maybe." Or maybe not. What was done was done, and he had copped his attitude first. Still, she hated knowing she had poked a sore spot when she had been there, done that in the relationship department.

She didn't mind people thinking she was a little out there, but she never wanted to come across as mean.

7

By Friday near quitting time, with T minus one week and counting to the fashion show, Ashley's to-do list had slopped onto page three of her computer spreadsheet, filled with everything from "Ask Krista about borrowing chairs" to "Write script for radio spot" and something that had auto-corrected to "Blonde Cokes and cheese."

She couldn't remember what it was supposed to say, but had left it on the list, hoping she would have an aha moment.

The week had been mostly a blur, though a few moments had stood out in sharp relief—like when the elderly hot water heater had decided to burn through one of its rubber seals, filling the utility room with smoke and necessitating a visit by the Three Ridges Fire Department, plus an emergency call to Ed Skye. And when, later that same day, Feed Store Billy stuck his head through the front door and announced, "You know you've got a cat out here in the trap, right?"

Ashley had raced out with Hen at her heels, the two of them cheering at the sight of the black cat crouched in the back of the live trap, glaring at them through yellow slits. Nick had picked her up, cage and all, and promised to do what he could with the injured leg, and do his best to find the stray a home.

Meanwhile, Ashley worked late each night, got up at the crack of dawn to tweak the window display, where the volleyball game changed every day and the score inched up, and she existed mostly on microwave popcorn.

And she was having a blast.

Sure, it was work, but it was *her* work, her choice. Her reward, sitting bright and shiny at the end of it all—not just the payoff, but proving that she could handle the life she had chosen for herself. *Hey, Ma, look at me. I'm a grown-up!*

Not that her mother would necessarily agree. As far as she was concerned, Ashley wasn't a fully functioning adult until she caught herself a good provider and wrangled him down the aisle.

Sigh.

"I'm off!" Hen announced, bustling through from the back room. She paused at a mirror, smoothed the wisps that had escaped from the single thick braid that ran down her back, and tugged at the tie-dyed sundress she had paired with a blue velvet blazer and steel-toed work boots. "Wish me luck."

Ashley gestured, sprinkling fairy dust with an imaginary wand. "Go forth and get lucky."

"You sure you don't want to come?"

"On your blind date? Pass. Unless you want me to sit at the bar with my phone and bail you out if you give me the high sign."

"It's not going to be like that. It's more like a block party. You could totally come. Burgers, beer, and everybody from Mystical Myrna from the tarot place to Great Uncle Bob and his ancient beagle. One of them passes gas that can clear a room, and nobody's really sure which one." She beamed. "You'd fit right in."

"I'm going to take that as a compliment." *Maybe?* "I can't, though. I've got a billion things to do for the show, and the store has been so busy that I'm way behind." The week's numbers were going to be on the high side, and they had already sold half the tickets, but if Ashley didn't get cracking on lining up models, there wasn't going to *be* a show.

"You're going to burn out," Hen warned. "Tell you what. I'll wait out the last fifteen until closing time, and we can go over to the BBQ together. You can even take your own car and bug out early. Who knows? Maybe Gerald has a friend."

Yegad, no. "Thanks, but if I don't have time for a hot dog with your Great Uncle Bob and Farty the Beagle, I definitely don't have time to date." Heck, she hadn't even found five minutes to ovary up, call Ty, and apologize for her gaffe the other evening.

Correction: she hadn't *made* the time.

"Your loss. I'm out of here. See you tomorrow!" Hen practically danced over the threshold and out onto the sidewalk. There, she gave a startled, "Oh, sorry! I didn't see you there. Did you want to come in? We're still open."

Through the plate glass, Ashley saw a bulky, dark-clothed figure hesitate. *That would be a no,* she thought.

But then, to her surprise, the newcomer came through the door.

Shapeless beneath a heavy sand-camo army jacket that had J. DOLANS stenciled on the breast pocket, the dark-haired teen had big brown eyes, a snub nose, and a hunch-shouldered posture that made her look even shorter than her five feet plus a bit. She got a few steps inside the store, caught sight of Ashley, and stopped dead, doing a good impression of roadkill-to-be, pinned in a set of headlights.

"Hey there," Ashley said. "Welcome to Another Fyne Thing."

"I, um . . ." The girl trickled off to miserable-looking silence. The kind that said she didn't belong there. Maybe didn't belong much of anywhere.

Ashley's heart tugged. "I don't think we've met before, have we? I'm Ashley."

"Gillian." The girl looked down at her boots. "My mom and I moved here a few months ago."

Ashley had a million things to do and wasn't even sure Gillian had meant to come into the store—it wouldn't be the first time a pedestrian had gotten shanghaied by Hen's enthusiasm. But the hunched shoulders tugged at her. "How do you like it so far?"

"It's okay, I guess." A pause. Then, reluctantly, "There's this dance coming up . . ."

"The Summer Dance." A long-held tradition, the high school's off-season prom was a few weeks away, and the store had been doing brisk business off the racks labeled FUN AND FLIRTY, OLD HOLLYWOOD, and RED CARPET. "Are you looking for a dress?"

"No! Well . . . no. I just want something . . . um, girly." The last word was close to a whisper.

Oh, honey. Ashley knew what it was like, getting dropped into a new high school and not really fitting in. "Well, you've come to the right place. We've got girly, but we try to lean toward unique and a little funky at the same time." She figured that was a safe angle to take, given the teen's mismatching earrings—one a skull and crossbones, the other a simple sterling stud. "Are you looking for a small pop, like jewelry or a hair comb, or something that makes a bigger statement, like a whole new outfit?"

Gillian tucked her too-hot coat tighter. "Hair, maybe? I'm, um . . . There's this boy."

Ashley risked a woman-to-woman grin. "Gotcha. Come on. Let me show you a few things, and we can see if we're on the same page." Who cared if it was five minutes to closing and she had the to-do list from hell? This was what Another Fyne Thing was all about.

Forty minutes later, as Ashley rang up Gilly's purchases, she knocked off fifteen percent and threw in a couple of pens. "Promise me you'll report back in a few days? I'm dying to know what happens at the next Drama Club meeting."

She hadn't gotten the girl to trade out the camouflage coat—or even take it off—but the turquoise-and-silver earrings and hammered necklace they had zeroed in on really made Gilly's blue-green eyes pop, and trading her chunky white sneakers for pointy-toed Justin boots had slimmed things down and added an inch to her height. Better yet, she was making fleeting eye contact now, and the faint flush in her cheeks came from pleasure rather than embarrassment. "I will," the girl promised. "And, Ashley? Thank you."

"Hey, you're the one spending your birthday money. And you're welcome. It was my pleasure—truly." More, she had managed to sneak in a couple of asides about how there was nothing wrong with Gilly wanting to look her best, but if she couldn't be herself with the guy she liked, then he wasn't the right guy.

Otherwise known as the sort of thing Ashley wished her mother had told her, rather than spinning stories about true love conquering, when all the evidence in front of them both said otherwise.

"Still. Thanks." Gilly touched one of the dangling earrings and looked at herself in the gilt rococo mirror that hung off-kilter near the hats. "I'll let you know how it goes with Sean."

"You'd better. If you don't, I'll hunt you down and swap out those boots for the white pleather gogo knockoffs with the platforms and all the fringe."

"Ewww!" the girl said with satisfying animation. "Not happening, because I'll be back." She said the last three words in a passable Terminator impression. Wearing a smile that would have seemed impossible when she came in, she headed out the door, looking several inches taller than before, and not just because of the boots.

As the door jingled shut behind her, Ashley snagged her phone off the counter, took a second to find the number she wanted, and made the call. A minute later, when it went to voice mail, she said, "Hey, Barb? It's Ashley over at Another Fyne Thing. We're holding an event here next Friday, and I'd love to hire some of your Drama Club kids as servers. If you think they might be interested, give me a buzz back in the next day or so. Thanks!" Lips curving, she rang off. Then, to herself, she said, *"There's this boy . . ."*

Okay, maybe she was letting herself get distracted, just a little. But it was for a good cause, and she had the rest of the night to knock stuff off the list.

Heading for the front, she killed the neon OPEN sign, flipped the door sign to CLOSED, and locked up. On her way back to the counter, she announced to the empty sales floor, "I hereby swear that I will do the things on the Big List in order, even if I don't want to."

Which meant that first up was . . . She tapped her laptop to awaken the spreadsheet from hell. Ugh. Writing the radio spot.

She shouldn't complain—she was getting the airtime on the cheap, thanks to Jenny's contacts—but the assignment felt an awful lot like homework. *In a hundred words or less, tell us about your event. Make it fun! Exciting! Make it POP!!* She could practically see the exclamation points in her head. She couldn't see the paragraph, though. She was a far better artist than copywriter, and even her art was questionable these days.

Lucky for her, she knew a slogan goddess who no doubt dreamed in pithy paragraphs rather than big, chaotic splashes of color. Even better, Ashley had a pair of high-heeled bronze boots in the store that had Shelby's name written all over them. Figuring they could work out a deal—she'd rather do that than ask for yet another favor—Ashley reached for the phone.

Just as her fingers brushed the handset, it gave a cheerful ring.

"Ha! Kismet." Figuring it was Barb, she answered. "Hey, thanks for calling me back. What do you think? Can I rent a couple of your kids and put them to work?"

There was a moment of startled silence. Then Krista said, "Well, I've only got the one and she's a bit young for hard labor. But if you're in the market for a great smile and questionable oozes from both ends, she's your girl."

"Whoops!" Ashley clapped a hand over her mouth, stifling a laugh. "Sorry about that. I thought you were Barb MacIntyre."

"So, you don't want to put your niece on the payroll?"

"Not quite yet, no." Reorienting, she tucked the phone against her cheek. "What's up? Everything okay?"

"Everything's fine. Better than fine—I've got a lead for you on some free wood. Old Man Plunkett just fixed up his sheep shed and he's got some leftover supplies he's looking to get rid of. They're yours, if you want."

"Heck, yes!" Lumber wasn't first on the Big List, but it was close to the top and weighed heavily in her anemic budget. "Anything I don't have to buy is money back against the bottom line. I can be there in— Wait. I'm going to need a truck. I love Bugsy dearly, but he's not much of a cargo hauler."

"I've got you covered. My dad said he could head over there now with one of our trucks and pick everything up, then run it down to you at the store."

"I can meet him at the Plunkett place and help load."

"Honestly, I think it's better if you stay put and let him hustle over there and get it done. Plunkett is on the other side of Mustang Ridge, and sooner is better than later, given those storm clouds."

"What storm clouds? It's beautiful out."

"Not up here, it's not. Though I'm not going to complain, as the grass could use a drink. It looks like it's going to be a soaker, though, and Dad doesn't want the wood getting wet. If you give the go-ahead, he can be down to you in a couple of hours."

"What, like I'm going to say no? Heck, yes! Tell him to pull around back—I'll have the loading dock wide open for him."

"Will do. Maybe we'll get lucky and this storm will dump a couple of inches on us, but give Main Street a miss!"

The rapidly darkening sky had sickened from gray to yellow-green by the time the twenty-some dudes and dudettes of Singles Week passed the marker stones at the top of Mustang Ridge, swaying in their saddles as the horses started down.

Riding at the back with a stray cow in tow, Ty patted his horse's neck. "There it is, Brutus. Home sweet home." The valley below unfolded like a grass-covered songbook, with a river for a spine, the notes and lyrics etched out in fence lines and buildings that spelled safety from the incoming storm. Thank Christ.

Relationship columnist Denise—square-jawed, with bristle-short hair and lovely brown eyes—reined back so her horse fell in step with Brutus, and shot Ty a thumbs-up. "Looks like we're going to make it back in time to stay dry, thanks to you. And we even walked the last mile."

It was a horseman's adage and a ranch rule to walk the first and last miles, but Ty would've run the dudes down into the valley if the storm had gotten much closer or if he'd started seeing lightning strikes. Better to have to cool out the horses than be the tallest thing out on the prairie with thunder and lightning closing in.

He hadn't let the guests see him sweat it, though. "I was more worried about getting back in time for the farewell barbecue."

"I can't believe this is our last ride of the week." Denise looked along the wide track, where the rest of the riders were clumped in twos and threes. Some had their heads tipped together, deep in conversation, while others snapped pictures with their phones, locking the memories into pixels. "It was fun," she added. "Maybe it started off rough, but it was a good reminder that I talk a better game than I've got. I don't think this singles stuff is for me."

"Amen," Ty said, laying his rein on Brutus's neck when the gelding eyed her mare, warding off a nip, or worse.

Denise laughed. "You're not a fan of Singles Week?"

"I don't mind trail-bossing it, but you can bet I'm making myself scarce when it's time for strip bingo." He glanced around. "Besides, of all the couples who've met here, there have been only six or seven weddings over—what, eight, nine years, with two or three Singles Weeks each summer? Seems to me that's a reminder that you can't force a relationship to work—it either does or it doesn't." And in his experience, it mostly didn't.

She tipped her face up to the threatening clouds and said, "I'd rather think of it as a reminder that you never know when or where you're going to meet your soul mate. Take the Skye family—Krista and Wyatt had a fling in college and then hooked up again at a horse auction, Jenny and Nick found each other because of a stray dog, and Rose and Ed met when she backed into his truck. Face it—you never know when or how you're going to cross paths with The One. It could be online, through a friend, at a wedding—"

"At a fender bender," he put in. "I never heard that story about Ed and Rose before."

"Women talk about those things more than men. Which is fortunate for me, as it would be a very long two hours of airtime to fill without my callers." She tapped her stirrup against his. "Think about it, though. You never know when you might meet your perfect match."

"Thanks, but I'm not looking."

"That's usually when you meet someone, isn't it? Oh, hey. There's Krista!" Diverted, Denise waved and hollered down to the barn. "Hey, Krista!"

"Hallo!" The rain-coated figure lifted her hat and beckoned them in. "Hustle up—we've got weather coming!"

Tipping his hat in acknowledgment, Ty set about herding the horses and riders through the gate and into the dirt parking lot, with the horses prancing more than usual and the riders' voices sounding unnaturally loud on the storm-deadened air. The weather was getting close—that was for sure—and it promised to be rowdy.

He had done his job, though. The horses and riders were home safe and sound.

As the barn workers came out to help the guests dismount and get their horses safely inside, Krista grinned at him. "Nice job, cowboy. Looks like you got them all back in the nick of time."

"Plus one." He reined around so Krista could see the old black-and-white cow at the end of his rope. "I believe this belongs to you?"

It wasn't the first time he had come across a stray critter out on the trail—horses got loose, steers wound up on the wrong side of fences, cows and calves could get split up. It was, however, the first time he had caught one wearing a neck strap that read, BEWARE: TROUBLEMAKER. IF FOUND, PLEASE RETURN TO MUSTANG RIDGE.

Krista's mouth fell open. "Betty Crocker! Ohmigosh, where was she? What did she do?"

"Couldn't say. She was on the main trail up in the high pasture, all by her lonesome and jogging on in like she'd heard the dinner bell. Took me ten minutes to get a rope on her"—all with the storm coming in and Brutus getting jiggy—"but once I did, she led just fine. What's her deal?"

"She's a troublemaker, just like it says." Krista patted the bony head, then bent to run a hand over the cow's ribs and legs, saying, "One of Nick's customers found her wandering in the backcountry one day. I took her in, thinking she was just another castoff, too old for milk and too skinny for steaks, but in hindsight she probably ambushed her old owners and took off. We try to keep her penned up in the high country with the rest of the rescues, because when she makes it back down here, she likes to let herself into the kitchen and trash the place."

"She . . . hmm." Picturing Gran and Dory in full-on Friday BBQ mode, rainy-day version, and then adding a cow to the mix, Ty tightened the lead rope on his saddle horn. "Right, then. Where do you want me to stash her?"

"Find an empty stall," Krista decided. "I'd like to have Nick take a peek at her before we turn her back out, as she's skinnier than I like. In the meantime—and changing the subject—can my dad borrow your truck?"

He shot a look over at where the farm vehicles were parked. Wasn't like his rust bucket would win any prizes next to her dually, especially after being garaged in a leaky barn while he was on tour. The funky smell was mostly gone, but so were the shocks, and the brakes weren't far behind. "Sure, but why would he want to?"

"It's got the cap on it. He needs to pick up some

freebie lumber for Ashley, and wants to keep it as dry as possible."

Ashley. Damn it.

The name went through him, kicking life into the embers he had spent all week trying to stomp out. Not that he was interested. Annoyed, more like it. He didn't like the way she had gotten stuck in his head, under his skin. Flirty, flighty, and constantly talking, she didn't have a filter or any concept of personal space. She had touched him too often while he'd sketched, leaning across to point to this detail or that, and reminding him that it had been a long damn time since he'd held on to a woman.

Not that he was looking to get his hands on one now. Especially not her.

Krista looked at him quizzically, warning that he had been silent for too long. "If you've got plans, you can drive one of the farm vehicles," she offered, as if his hesitation had anything to do with his POS truck.

That was exactly what he should do. He should hand over his keys, warn Ed that the brakes were iffy in wet conditions, grab a spare set of wheels, and head out, maybe shoot some pool or hustle his way through a couple of games of darts.

Instead, inwardly cursing himself for a fool, he said, "Tell your dad not to worry about it. I'll do the lumber run."

8

The storm clobbered Main Street with a one-two of pyrotechnics and a sharp rain that blew sideways, blurring the world beyond the open loading dock doors and muffling the usual sounds beneath a freight train roar of wind and water.

Perched on a packing crate, Ashley folded her knees up to her chin and stared out, caught between the part of her that loved being out in the rain and the part that winced every time a gust rattled the building.

Having lived there through the long, cold winter storms, she had figured she knew what she was getting into. Turned out it was a whole new ball game now that the insurance policy had her name on it.

"Hang in there, baby," she urged. "Mama can't fix the roof right now." The building inspector had said she would probably get a few more years out of it, but that she should start setting aside the money. And she would, along with saving to expand the sales floor and redo the Web site. Starting in thirty-five days. Almost thirty-four now.

Look at me—thinking about the long-range to-do list. Too

bad she really needed to focus on the shorter-term stuff, like lining up models, crafting decorations, finalizing the outfits and giveaways, and helping Ed build the stage that Ty had designed for her.

Ty, who she really should have called days ago. Maybe she should—

Nope. No distractions. In fact, get him out of your head. She knew all too well how good she could be at talking herself into new priorities. Pulling out her phone, she toggled over to the Short List, a subset of quick little chores that—like the Big List—she had vowed to knock off in order rather than doing the fun ones first. When she saw what was up next, she groaned.

Call Mom.

"Seriously? I didn't put that on here, did I?" But she must have, because there it was. And she had promised—one at a time, in order, no cheating.

Should've called Ty. As awkward as the conversation would've been, she'd bet money it would've been easier. But Ty wasn't on the Short List and her mom was, so she scrolled to the number and made the call.

She stared out at the rain while it rang on the other end, hating how phoning home had turned into a checklist chore.

There was a click and her mom said suddenly, "It's Ashley!" Her voice blurred a little as she held the phone away and called, "Jack, honey? Come and talk to Ashley! She's on the phone!" A pause. "Jack? Jack?" To herself, she said, "Where *is* that man? He was here a minute ago."

Used to the routine, Ashley wandered up the hall to

the break room, where she neatened the pile of catalogs and put away a couple of rinsed-out coffee mugs. She was wiping down the table when her mom finally left off hollering for her stepfather. Muttering, "He's probably out in the garden, back any minute," her mom lifted the phone, sharpening her voice. "Ashley, sweetie! It's so good to hear from you! How *are* you?"

"Hi, Mom. I'm good. Everything's good. The store—"

"Did Wyatt tell you that Jack and I are going to the Grand Canyon next weekend? He's even booked us on one of those mule tours. Do you know how long it's been since I was in the saddle?" She gave a girlish laugh. "But you know what they say. Once a rodeo queen, always a rodeo queen!"

"I hadn't heard. That sounds fun." So much for inviting her mom and Jack to the fashion show.

"And did Wyatt tell you that we're thinking about changing out the shutters on the house? I found the prettiest purply-blue. Jack?" she called suddenly. "Is that you? Ashley's on the phone!"

I didn't call to talk to Jack, Ashley wanted to say, *or to talk about Wyatt. I called to talk to you.* But why would today be any different? Her mom had always lived best through the men in her life. "I'm putting on a fashion show next week. Do you want me to send you some pictures?"

"You're modeling again? Oh, sweetie! That's wonderful."

"I'm not modeling—I'm putting on the event. For the store." *Remember the store I just bought?* A week ago, her mom had been all aflutter, not because it was a big step or because one wrong financial move could land Ashley in bankruptcy, but because she was tying herself to Three Ridges, and where did she expect to find a man in a place like that? A tic started up at the corner of her left eye as Ashley added, "The theme is Transformations."

"You're dressing like a boy? Oh, sweetie, don't do that. You're such a pretty girl."

"*Transformations*. Like from a caterpillar to a butterfly."

"Here's Jack! Jack, honey, say hi to Ashley. She's thinking about going back into modeling!"

There was a pause, a scuffle, and then her stepfather's voice said, "Ash?" The single slow word was enough to take her shoulders down a notch. "How's it going?"

She let out a pent-up breath, willing back the frustration. Jack wouldn't trample on her answer, she knew. He would wait her out, just like he had waited until her mother finally came to grips with the fact that Wylie Webb wasn't going to put a ring on it and she wasn't going to do better than a mild-mannered, slow-talking CPA who filled her fridge, took her daughter to the mall, and every three months on the dot asked her to marry him.

Thank God.

Cradling the phone a little closer to her cheek, Ashley said, "I'm good. I'm putting on a fashion show next week to bring in some extra business."

"Ah. The modeling." There was a gentle smile in his voice, because he loved his wife for exactly who she was. "I'm sure it'll be a huge success, sweetheart. How can it not be, with you behind it? Though I wish you didn't have to put this sort of pressure on yourself. I wish you'd let us help."

"We've had this conversation." Though the offer still wrapped itself around her heart. "I'm not taking your money, or Wyatt's." Jack was trying to retire, and she'd be darned if she gave her brother another reason to shake his head when he saw her. "But I love you for offering." Not that Wyatt had. Only Jack.

"I love you, too, sweetheart, and I'm rooting for you. Take lots of pictures of the show for me, okay?"

"Will do. Thanks, Jack."

"Do you want to talk to your mom some more?"

"No, I—"

But it was already too late. A rustle carried down the line, and her mother—practically caroling now that she had her preferred audience—said, "Did Jack tell you about the nice man we hired to fix the roof?"

"No, he—"

"He's something foreign. Polish, maybe? One of those countries that used to be Russian."

"I don't think Poland—" This time Ashley cut herself off. "Never mind. So, he's fixing the roof for you guys? How's it going?" Sometimes—most times, really—it was easier to go with the maternal flow than try to turn the tide. She opened up the silverware drawer next to the sink and did a little rearranging, putting the mismatched forks and spoons in order by size and giving an "Uh-huh" or "Oh, really?" when the pauses dictated.

"Jack said not to worry about it, though," her mom concluded. "He'll take care of it."

Having lost track of the complaint—something about the gutters?—Ashley went with "Mmm-hmm."

"Speaking of taking care of things . . . about this crazy idea of yours. You can't possibly be serious."

Heart sinking—*Should've hung up when I had the chance*—Ashley shut the silverware drawer. "You're talking about the fashion show?"

"No, silly! I love that you're getting back into modeling—a lady should always play to her strengths. I'm talking about you wanting to buy that whole big store with all the secondhand clothes and stuff."

Since her mom had never been to Another Fyne Thing—not even the Web site, as far as Ashley knew—that description had to have come from Wyatt. Drat him. Stomach tightening, she said, "I already bought it. Signed, sealed, and delivered. This is important to me, Mom, and I'm excited about it. I hope you can be happy for me."

"Jack thinks you should cut your losses and walk away. Better that than be dragged down by a business you can't handle. You're not a numbers person or a businesswoman, you know. You're an artist."

That one stung. Even though Jack probably hadn't said exactly that, or even close to it, there was almost always a kernel of reality at the center of her mother's mental constructs. "I can handle it. I've *been* handling it since last year, remember?"

"You should work for someone else. It would be safer. What happens if you lose everything?"

"I don't want to be safe. I want to be happy."

"Living by yourself in a little town in the middle of nowhere?"

"*Yes!* Why can't—" Ashley bit it off, knowing that snapping at her mom was pointless. Taking a deep breath, she leveled her voice. "I like it here. I can do this."

"Jack says—"

"I've gotta go," she interrupted. "Krista's dad will be here any minute with a lumber delivery, and I need to help him unload. I'll call you in a couple of weeks, okay? You can tell me all about the Grand Canyon."

"You're mad at me." The pout was loud and clear. "I'm just trying to help."

"I know."

"If you would just be reasonable—"

"Like I said, I gotta go. Love you." She ended the call, dropped the phone back in her pocket, and then just stood for a moment, pressing her fingertips into the break room counter hard enough to whiten the flesh beneath her nails.

Breathe. She's just trying to protect you in her own way. Just like Wyatt. Still, her mother's words echoed. *You're not a numbers person or a businesswoman.* Pinching the bridge of her nose, she willed them away, hating that they still resonated after all the hard work she had put in, the progress she had already made. "She's wrong." She said it out loud, willing herself to believe. "You can do this."

Maybe if she told herself that another thousand times or so, one of these times it would ring all the way true.

Blowing out a breath, she pushed away from the counter and turned. And froze.

Ty stood in the doorway.

Her heart thundered, pushing hot and cold through her bloodstream. He was there. *Hot*. She really should have called him. *Cold*. He was soaked through, wearing a dark green T-shirt that was plastered to the bulging muscles of his arms and torso, and worn jeans that had gone dark from the rain and clung lovingly to his hips and thighs. *Hot, hot, hot*. But why was he there? He didn't like her, didn't want to be around her . . . did he? *Hot, cold, hot*.

"Ty, hey." *Keep it casual. Don't overreact.* "I didn't expect to see you here tonight." *Or, you know, ever again*.

"Got some lumber for you." His eyes were dark, his expression unreadable. "My truck has a cap on it, so I said I'd make the delivery."

"Oh. I— Thank you! And in the pouring rain. I'm sure that wasn't on your list of fun things to do on a Friday evening."

"I've had worse." He paused, studying her like he wasn't quite sure what he was seeing. "Didn't mean to eavesdrop, but I heard some of that call. Everything okay?"

"With my mom? Sure, yeah. We're fine." She grimaced. "That is, if by *fine* I really mean 'talking past each other like we usually do.'" Even saying that much just went to show how rattled she was by her mom's lack of faith. Squaring her shoulders, she said, "Anyway. Lumber. Your truck. The rain. All I can say is thanks a million. I owe you one."

His mouth flattened out. "You don't owe me anything."

"Yeah, I really do. Starting with the apology that should've been headed your way a couple of days ago." Stifling the temptation to fiddle with the catalogs on the break room table, she hooked her thumbs in the pockets of her jeans. *Just do it.* "I was bitchy to you the other night, and I apologize. I was just . . . Well, it doesn't matter what I was thinking, or why. You were helping me out, and I handled it badly. I'm sorry for saying what I did about, well, you know." *Broken hearts.*

The pause that followed went on long enough to make her wonder if it would've been better to keep her mouth shut after all. Then a corner of his mouth kicked up, though with zero amusement. "Somebody told you I got left at the altar."

"My assistant, Hen. And she said it was six weeks before the wedding." Why had she said that? Six weeks was plenty bad, and the details didn't matter so much as clearing the air. "Sorry," she said again.

"Don't be." His eyes were shadows, his voice a rasp. "Six weeks is more accurate than most of the versions I've heard, and what happened with me and Brandi is part of the local deal. I knew I'd be coming back to it when I took the job. But it's been a few years, Krista needed the help, and I needed to get off the road and get my priorities straight. So here I am."

She was pretty sure it was the most he had said to her at any one time, and it was definitely the most revealing. With any of her friends—Krista, Hen, even some of her customers—she would have pressed for more. With him, she said only, "Welcome to the getting-my-priorities-straight club. I'd like to say I'm a founding member, but I think I'm more the one who pays her fee every year and only shows up for the holiday party. I'm working on it, though. So . . . apology accepted?"

"Accepted, but not necessary. I was being a bit of a jerk."

Figuring it wouldn't gain her anything to agree with him, she stuck out her hand. "Truce?"

His hand came up and enfolded hers. "Truce." She barely had time to register the warm strength of his grip and the gentle rasp of calluses before he disengaged, stepped back, and tipped his head toward the loading dock. "So, you going to help me unload this wood, or what?"

The work went far quicker with two people than loading it up had done with one, though the weather was just as nasty. Which meant they both wound up soaked within minutes when Ashley insisted on being outside with him, not just waiting inside to stack.

He appreciated that, though, just as he appreciated her apology. Meanwhile, he was doing his damnedest *not* to appreciate the way her wet button-down clung to her curves, or the way the rain darkened the denim where it cupped her fanny.

Yes, she was hot, and, yeah, maybe there was more to her than met the eye at first. Maybe they were even working in surprising sync, with her more than handling her end of things. But she was still off-limits.

"Coming at you." Having clambered into the back of

the truck to reach a pile of two-by-fours that had shifted on the drive, she gave a shove and sent the wood sliding along the bed in his direction.

"Got 'em." He loaded up and headed into the loading dock, where the air was damp and the concrete floor was doing the slippery-when-wet thing. "Watch your step."

"I'm good." She came in behind him with the last of the two-bys. "Plywood next?"

"A few of the sheets are pretty punky," he warned as they headed back out into the rain. "You won't want to use them for the staging, or anything that's going to hold weight."

"No problem," she said, grabbing one end of a sheet and sliding it out so he could grab a corner. "They can be butterflies."

"Excuse me?"

She grinned adorably from beneath sopping wet bangs as they schlepped the four-by-eight panel inside and set it on the grid of two-bys they had built to keep the plywood off the floor. "Decorations. I want to paint up these big butterfly cutouts for the walls, to add more color and make it look like a real party."

Seemed to Ty that the last thing her shop was lacking was color. This was her deal, though. "Want me to tell Ed, so he can add it to the project list?"

"Nope, I've got it under control. I borrowed a jigsaw from Billy, across the street."

"No offense, but you know how to use it, right?"

She wiggled her fingers at him. "Don't let the manicure fool you, cowboy. My stepfather, Jack, insisted that before he took me for my driving test, I had to be able to change a tire, jump a battery, top off the oil, and safely use a bunch of different power tools. I'm not sure what using a jigsaw had to do with getting my license, but once Jack gets something in his head, there's no dislodging it."

"Sounds like he was doing his best to look after you."

"He was. He still is." She squared up a two-by-four on the pile as they passed it on their way out, expression going from fond to rueful. "That's what they're all trying to do, in their own ways. Wyatt wants to protect me from myself, which means doing things his way, while Mom wants me to find a man to protect me, which—at least as far as she's concerned—means doing things *her* way. Meanwhile, I'm doing my best to figure out what my way of doing things is going to look like."

"Is that why you were living in LA?"

Look at the two of us, actually having a civil conversation.

She wrinkled her nose. "I'd like to say so, but the reality is that I followed a guy out there. Kenny. He was a decent drummer in a decent band that was always one lucky break away from the big time."

The rain blew sideways, sharp and cool, but the work was keeping him warm. "Let me guess. You got tired of footing the bills while he chased the dream."

"Ha! I see you've met him."

"I know the type."

Finished with the punky plywood, they started building a second platform for the drier wood without discussing the need. "I hate to admit it," she said, "but I was on board for that part, stuck it out for far too long. I didn't bail until the day he tried to sell my car on Craigslist."

"Your Bug?"

"Yep. He was trying to avoid eviction. Turned out, the rent money I had been giving him had gone up in smoke." She pantomimed inhaling. "So I left. You can mess with me, but you'd better not mess with Bugsy."

As they headed back outside, into the weather, he said, "Note to self. Trying to Craigslist your car is a dealbreaker."

"I've generalized that to grand theft auto. Since leaving LA, I've been adding to the list. For future reference, of course."

"Of course." Another piece of plywood went on the pile. "What's on the list? More felonies?"

"I'll look at that on a case-by-case basis. Who knows? Maybe Mr. Right has a really good excuse for that armed robbery pop. As far as I'm concerned, though, there's no excuse for walking out on your kid."

Ty fumbled his grip on the plywood as they lowered it to the pile. "Or hitting one. Hitting anyone smaller and weaker than you, in fact, with some exceptions. Case by case, like you said." Their shoulders bumped as they returned to the truck and grabbed the next slab.

"Stringing along a woman who loves you, promising you'll marry her, buy her a house—the whole nine yards—only to spend your life chasing from one rodeo to the next."

He got the feeling she wasn't talking about herself

anymore. "Not Wyatt." He knew there had been some history between him and Krista, long before he came to Mustang Ridge. He didn't seem the type to string a woman along, though.

"Nope. Our father, Wylie. The day I came along, he pulled Wyatt aside, gave him some cash, and told him he was the man of the house now, and I was his responsibility. We didn't see much of him after that, though Mom waited for him a long time. Too long." She made a face. "Which brings us to the next on the list— breaking promises. That's a definite don't-let-the-door-hit-you-on-the-way-out for me."

"Agreed." As they schlepped in a good-size chunk of beam that would make an ideal support piece for the emcee's stand, he looked across at her—soaking wet and holding her own, and nothing like he had thought she was.

She lowered her end, then fisted her hands on her hips. "You're staring."

"I'm thinking." That he had misjudged her. That he could talk to her. That they had more in common than he would have guessed.

"Of?"

"Your list is missing a big one."

"Oh?"

"Infidelity." He heard his own voice go flat.

Her expression shifted. "Ah."

"Yeah." Needing to move, he headed back out into the storm for the last piece of lumber, another big beam that he yanked out of the pickup.

She followed, grabbed the other end. "I'm sorry."

"She wasn't."

"Then you're better off."

"I figure." He waited until she put down her end, then let the beam go with more force than necessary. "Still sucks, though."

"It's on the list."

They headed back outside into the storm together. The wind had died down and the rain had softened to fatter, warmer drops. "Storm's easing," he said, reaching out to close off his tailgate. "Good timing, too. We're all done."

She wrinkled her nose. "Well, jeez. Now we're all soaked down with no place to go." Then her smile flashed. "Seriously, though, I can't thank you enough."

Sleek and wet, her body was all curves, and his fingers itched to touch. The half-light had darkened her violet eyes, turning them smoky and mysterious, and the bow of her mouth had his eyes zeroing in. He wanted to kiss her, wanted to drink the rain from her lips and feel the water on their bodies turn to steam.

"You should go inside," he said instead. "Get dried off." Because anything else would be a really bad idea.

"Yeah." She looked up at him, blinking the raindrops from her lashes. Then she held out her hand.

"I thought we already called a truce." He didn't want to shake again. He wanted more.

Apparently, she was smarter than that. "This isn't a truce," she said. "This time, we're making a pact."

"Oh?"

Her eyes fired with resolve. "To learning from our

mistakes, sticking to our lists, and choosing better the next time, whenever that might be."

Yeah, that resonated. He closed his fingers around hers. "To choosing better." Which, right now, meant getting in his truck and going back to Mustang Ridge before he did something stupid.

9

The next evening, Ashley drove out to pick up the boxes of coupon books and mini calendars that Jenny had put together for the giveaway bags.

"I can't thank you enough." Ashley gave her friend a quick, hard hug. "I'm going to have some serious IOUs out there by the time this is done. You, Shelby, Krista, Rose, Ed, Gran, Ty . . ." She didn't mean to trail off after his name, but she had reached the end of the list. She'd be darned if she let herself blush, though.

Jenny's eyebrows went up. "Ty signed on to help?"

"I don't think he signed on so much as he got roped into dropping off lumber and helping me with some set design. I don't know if he'll be back." She hoped he would, though. The other night, talking to each other like grown-ups, about stuff that mattered . . . yeah. She could do that again.

"Well, don't be afraid to reach out to him. Or any of us." Jenny tapped the boxes. "We're all rooting for you."

"Thanks. I mean it." Ashley hefted the printed materials. "I'll catch you later."

"Before you go, Nick wants you to stop by the kitty room."

"Everything okay with VW Cat?" Last she'd heard, the vet had worked his magic, and the bedraggled rescue was on the mend.

"As far as I know. I think he just wanted you to have a chance to peek in on him."

"Him? I thought it was a girl."

"Guess not."

"Well, Nick is the cat expert, so we'll go with his ruling on that one. And I'll stop by to say hey to both of them on my way out." She wanted to talk to Nick, anyway, and get him locked into a payment plan—hopefully a deferred one—before he conveniently "lost" the stray cat's paperwork.

She was getting better at accepting help, but that would be taking it too far.

Downstairs, she let herself into the deserted waiting room, with its cutesy posters and cushioned benches, and through to an exam room. Skirting the stainless steel table, she pushed through the door at the rear, into the treatment area beyond, where rows of cages lined one wall and a hint of Eau de Litter wafted in the air. "Nick?" she called. "You back here? It's Ashley."

The only answer was a meow from one of the top cages, where a fat gray tabby rubbed up against the bars, and a couple of squeaks from two cages down, where a little orange paw reached through, attached to one of two blue-eyed kittens. The cage between them looked empty at first glance, but, like the other two, there was a name tag slid into a metal slot in the lower left corner.

Easing farther into the room, Ashley saw that the tabby's name was Princess, the kittens were Nutter and Butter, and their invisible neighbor had been dubbed Vintage Store Stray. The empty-looking cage held a clean litter box, food and water dishes, and a large carpet-covered canister, a foot or so high, with a cat-size cut in the side and gnaw marks around the edges.

A pair of slitted yellow eyes peered from the darkness within, unblinking.

"Hey, kitty," she cooed. "Remember me?"

From the carpeted enclosure came a low-throated growl.

As the far door opened, admitting both the white-coated vet and the "Ah-woo-woo-woo" of a dog who didn't sound happy about being kenneled overnight, she asked the cat, "Was that *Thanks for the upgrade* or *Bite me*?"

"Hard to tell," Nick said. Rumple-haired and rugged, the vet looked like Indiana Jones had thrown on a lab coat instead of his leather. "Most days, I wish we had a gizmo that could do animal-to-English translations, as that would make my job a whole lot easier. With this guy, we might be better off not knowing. And, hey there. Thanks for stopping down."

"No problem. Thank *you* for fixing this guy up. Got a 'tude, does he?"

"Let's just say he's not the friendliest feline I've ever met."

"Why do I get the feeling that's an understatement?" She stuck out a finger to the next cage over, and got a gentle *pat-pat* from a fluffy orange paw. From the dark depths of the carpeted cave came an unblinking silence. Kind of eerie, really. "Do you think he'll come around?"

"It's possible, if somebody wanted to take the time to gentle him. As it is, the best I've got lined up for him is a warm, dry spot in a barn that's got a few too many mice." He shot her a sidelong look.

She held up both hands, knowing how Jenny's husband worked. "Oh, no, you don't. I'm not a bleeding heart like Danny." Who had "fostered" a stray for Nick last year as a favor, and wound up a dog owner. "I like my apartment just the way it is, thank you—or, rather, I've got plans for the stuff I don't like, and those plans don't include litter boxes, stinky tuna, and shredded upholstery."

"Did I say you should take him home?"

"I did my good deed with the trap." To the cat, she said, "We're done. Finished. Good luck with the mice."

"*Rrrrrrr.*"

"See? He doesn't even like me."

"Still not telling you to take him home." Nick nodded to Nutter and Butter. "If you're thinking of adopting a pet, these guys are sweet as pie. And you know what they say about two kittens being less work than one."

"I've only owned my own place for a week. Cut me some slack here!" She couldn't help it, though. She stuck a finger through the bars and rubbed a soft head, getting a ridiculously loud purr in response. *Awww.*

"Granted," Nick said, "they'll be dead easy for me to place in a safe indoor home. An adult black cat? They're like the green Jell-O salad of the pet shelter world—always the last ones left over, and often tossed aside. It'd be a stretch for me to find this one a safe pet home, even without the grumpy factor."

Guilt prickled. "He'll be okay in the barn, though, right?"

"They'll cage him for a few weeks, so he'll hopefully imprint on the location, and then they'll release him and see if he sticks around."

Pat-pat went the little orange paw. *Prick* went her conscience. "Why wouldn't he?"

"He might not like the barn or the other cats, and the backcountry has its share of predators."

"Don't tell me that. I don't want to know."

"Don't stress," Nick said. "You've already done more than most people would. Unless . . ." He reached down into the corner and came up with a plastic cat carrier. "What do you say? You could give him a couple of weeks in a nice house with his very own human, and see what happens."

Ashley felt herself wavering. Darn it.

The little orange paw batted at her again and blue eyes blinked innocently, as if to say, *Come on, give him a chance.*

She could do it, too. For the first time in her life, she had her own place and could make her own rules. And if she wanted to wear a big old SUCKER sign on her forehead, she could do that, too. Scowling, she said, "You were planning this all along, weren't you? And Jenny was in on it."

"I haven't a clue what you're talking about." He set

the cat carrier on the exam table, then added a big gift bag that said KITTEN STARTER KIT above an impossibly cute cartoon.

Ashley looked from the cage to the carrier and back again. "Well, shoot." It looked like she had herself a cat.

How bad could it be?

Sunday morning near their ten o'clock opening time, Hen came through the shop's front door and did a double take. "Whoa. What happened in here? Were we robbed?"

"Yes, that's exactly what happened. Thieves made off with all of the eighties-era stock, hangers, racks, and all." Ashley rolled her eyes. "No, I started rearranging last night. I couldn't sleep, and it was either move stuff around down here or stay upstairs and talk to the cat."

"What cat?" Hen looked around, eyes brightening. "*The* cat? You brought her back? Where is she?"

Ashley sighed. "Upstairs, I think."

"What do you mean, you think? You lost her?"

"It's a him. And, well, he's not lost, exactly. I just don't know where he is. Krista told me they can hide in the darnedest places." After she got done laughing at Ashley for letting Nick sucker her in. "She said to just leave food out and give him time."

"You should have put him in a small room for the first few days. A bathroom is good. Then there'd only be so many places he could hide, and you could go in there and make friends."

"Now you tell me."

"You could have called."

"Wish I had. Anyway, Petunia is upstairs some-where. I opened the cat carrier and *poof*. Like magic. Maybe I should've called him Houdini, instead."

"Oh, no. I like Petunia!"

Leave it to Hen not to give her grief for the name. As opposed to Krista, who had accused her of wanting the cat to never come out from under the sofa—or wher-ever the blasted thing was hiding—because he was so embarrassed. But, darn it, the cat had looked like a Pe-tunia to Ashley from the very beginning, and she was hoping he would sweeten into the name.

Eventually. Maybe. Hopefully. *Sigh*.

"So what do you think?" Refocusing, Ashley ges-tured to the empty spot on the sales floor. "Do you miss the eighties?" Most of the acid-washed jeans and fluo-rescent sweaters had gone into storage, while the nicer pieces were temporarily racked in the break room.

"It's like having our very own dance floor!" Hum-ming something dreamy, Hen swept into the open space, opened her arms, and did a *Sound of Music* twirl. "Quick, we need music. And a disco ball!"

"Music I can do." Ashley headed for the tuner they kept in the corner, cranking the volume just in time to hear Big & Rich implore her to save a horse by riding a cowboy. Raising her voice to carry over the music, she added, "We'll have to see about the disco ball, though."

Hen did a whole-body shimmy that looked like a holdover from her latest belly dancing class, and beamed. "Didn't there used to be one in the bowling alley?"

"I'll look into it." Or at least put it on a list. "We also

need to—" She broke off as the front door opened and the happy little bell jangled. "Welcome to— Gilly! Hi! I guess you got my message."

The teen was still wearing the camouflage coat, but she had on the boots she'd bought the other day, along with a touch of lipstick that was way too orange for her complexion. She started to answer, shot a quick look at Hen, and dropped her eyes to her toes. "Um, yeah. So I guess you really meant to call me? That wasn't, like, a mistake?"

"No way," Ashley said firmly. "I've invited some of my favorite customers to model." Including Froggy and Rose Skye. She wanted a range of shapes, sizes, and local faces. And given that several members of the Drama Club—including Gilly's crush, Sean—had agreed to work at the event, she didn't plan on letting the girl say no. "Will you do it?"

"Yes. I mean, I guess." Gilly's pause was both dubious and wistful. "Would I have to wear heels? I'm pretty bad at heels."

"You don't have to wear anything that makes you uncomfortable. Scout's honor." Ashley gestured to the try-on area. "Come on down. I set aside a couple of things to get us started."

The teen made it down the three short steps to the sunken sitting area, but then stalled, eyeballing the garments currently occupying the COOL STUFF I'M GOING TO TRY ON peg as if afraid the purple Grecian gown might suddenly animate and try to strangle her.

"Trust me." Ashley draped an arm across the hunched-in shoulders. "We'll find something you love and can't wait to show off." She gave the camo collar a tug. "We're going to have to talk about the jacket, though."

Instead of the *No way in hell* look she had gotten last week, now she got a resigned nod. "I figured." The girl stuck her hands in her pockets, though, pulling the garment tighter around her body. Tipping down her chin so her whacked-off hair obscured her face, she mumbled, "My brother left it at our old house the last time he visited. Right before he deployed." A pause. "A couple of weeks later, the truck he was in ran over an IED. He was thrown clear, but he went back for his friends. He got two of them out before . . . well, you know."

Ashley's heart sank, though she had suspected something along those lines. She didn't know, not really. Always before, she'd had a few degrees of separation from things like war and violence. Which made her lucky, she supposed. "I'm so sorry." It sounded so inadequate, and no doubt the teen had heard it a thousand times before, but what else could she say?

"It sucks. Mom didn't want to stay in the house anymore, so . . . well, anyway." She moved away a couple of feet, hesitated, and then shrugged out of the jacket. Beneath the heavy layer, she was boy-straight through the waist, with thick arms, rounded shoulders, and a long, elegant neck that wore a ball-bearing chain holding a single dog tag. Draping the camo over her arm, she placed her free hand protectively below the lettering that spelled out J. DOLANS. "I like to pretend that Bubba's here with me, like I can talk to him about everything that's going on. Which is stupid, because it's just a jacket."

Though her throat had gone tight and scratchy with emotion, Ashley managed, "It's more than that." Far more. "We can work it into the show if you like."

"Some days I want to leave it in my room," Gilly said, like she hadn't heard. "But then it's like I'd be leaving him in there, alone and bored. And Bub hated being bored. So I pretend he's looking over my shoulder and cracking jokes about the crap they serve for lunch, or how the trig teacher, Mrs. Merchison, needs to even up her bra straps." Her shoulders moved restlessly. "Which is stupid, I know, because he's not really there. He's dead, and he's not coming back." She blinked away tears. When Ashley started forward, the teen held up a hand. "Don't. Please. Just give me a second."

Sweetheart, you can have whatever you need. Blinking back tears of her own, Ashley stared at the COOL THINGS hook, wondering if the Grecian dress would be too much of a one-eighty.

She had been thinking it would be fun to go over the top with the makeover, but now she wondered if that would make Gilly feel like her usual style was wrong. Clearing her throat, she said, "What if we stick with the military theme, but turn up the volume? There are some great jackets on the steampunk rack, and we could play around with some pants and high boots—that sort of thing."

There was a pause, then a rustle, followed by the sound of boots on the hardwood, and Gilly came up beside her to gaze at the purple dress. "Would it be okay if I tried both? I think . . . Maybe it'd be okay if I wore something different, just for one night. My mom might like it." The last part came out wistful, like the girl didn't have a clue where she fit into the new world order.

Flashing back on those too-quiet years between when Wyatt left to rodeo full-time and send his winnings home, and when their mom had finally agreed to marry Jack, Ashley could relate. Maybe not all the way, but some. She gave the teen a gentle elbow bump. "You got it. In fact, I think that sounds perfect. The way I see it, you never get too old to play dress-up. You just get to a point where you need an excuse." And maybe Gilly needed more of an excuse than most. "You ready to give this a try?"

"I guess . . . yes." The rounded shoulders squared up a little. "Yes, I am."

"Do you want to leave Bub's jacket out here with me? Maybe over this chair?" Ashley patted a spindle-back. "There's plenty for him to see, and you can practice coming out of the dressing room and giving a little twirl for your audience."

Gilly's eyes narrowed.

"I'm not making fun of you, I swear. I talk to my car all the time." Okay, maybe that wasn't the best example. Digging deeper, Ashley added, "Look, I've never lost anyone close to me, but I imagine it helps to feel like you can still talk to Bub, and that he's answering the way he would have." Who knew? Maybe it was a good way for the teen to hash out stuff with her subconscious. "As for the coat, we've all got our symbols and good-luck charms. Yours just happens to be a big-ass jacket that doesn't for a second work with purple chiffon."

The silence that followed probably wasn't as endless as it felt. Until, gradually, Gilly's lips curved and she dipped her head in a shallow nod. "Okay, thanks. Sorry. I get . . . you know. Twitchy."

About how other people saw her, what they said about her. Yeah. Ashley knew how that went. "I don't blame you." But she held out a hand. "Pass it over and let's get this show on the road."

Slowly, and with a lingering brush of her fingers, the teen handed her the heavy jacket. Then she stepped back. "Okay. Where do you want me to start?"

Trust. Ashley felt it in the weight of the lined jacket, which was warm from stored-up body heat, and in the rare soft moment inside her brain, where it was suddenly quiet enough for her to hear a little whisper of *Don't screw this up.* Gilly wasn't her responsibility, and her problems were way out of Ashley's wheelhouse. But she was new to town, and Ashley knew what it felt like to live alone even though the house wasn't empty.

Besides, she was a customer. And every customer deserved the fantasy.

"With the purple," Ashley decided, seeing Gilly's eyes linger on it. "Let's see how it looks, and we'll take it from there."

She got a shy smile, followed by a fleeting moment of eye contact that made her feel like she'd just rung up a thousand-dollar sale. As Gilly disappeared into the changing cube, Hen shot Ashley a double thumbs-up from the other side of the room and mouthed, *You rock!*

Giving in to the temptation, Ashley did a little spin of her own in the cleared-out space at the center of the sales floor. She didn't know if she was going to be able to make the second payment, or even pull off the fashion show. But right this instant, it felt like she was exactly where she was supposed to be, doing what she was meant to do.

10

Monday night, Ty drove around the back of Ashley's shop to the loading dock again, not wanting to stop on the sidewalk and do the *Hey, what's up?* thing with the guy from the feed store or cross paths with one of the women Brandi had worked with at the bakery.

His ex was long gone, having cleaned out their shared apartment of everything but some large furniture and a few odds and ends in a way that hadn't made a lick of sense. Who the hell left the sofa but stripped the covers off all the cushions? She had probably meant it to be symbolic, but he'd be damned if he got what she was going for. And seeing how she and her we're-just-friends-now-I-swear ex had probably bounced on those cushions while Ty was working, he didn't much miss the covers, or the couch. Good riddance, and all that.

Still, Three Ridges had its ghosts for him. He and Brandi had eaten at the pizza place on the corner most Fridays, hunkering together over a large sausage-and-pepper while they talked about their future without ever really nailing down the details, except when it came to the wedding. They had bought furniture at Kitty's Kountry Kitsch and registered for a whole bunch of stuff that didn't make any sense to him but had put a shine in his fiancée's eyes. And he had done his time at the bakery, waiting for her to finish up for the night.

All in the days before things started going sour, of course. But still, the good times—and the life he had imagined—had carved echoes.

Fortunately, he and Brandi hadn't ever been to Another Fyne Thing. He never would've thought he'd be grateful that Brandi had preferred her designer labels crisp and new, but he was glad not to have memories poking at him as he climbed out of his truck.

He was already questioning the impulse that had brought him back into town. Didn't need any added complications.

The loading bay was closed, but the man-size door next to it was cracked open, and when he swung it further, music spilled out. Stepping through, he saw that the big space, which had been empty a few days ago, was jam-packed now. The newly built staging bumped shoulders with a worktable, and the walls were lined with leaned-up plywood cutouts of giant butterflies.

Ashley stood with her back to him and her hips bumping to the beat as she painted a slash of blue on a six-foot wingspan. She was wearing jeans and a faded pink sweatshirt with the hem and cuffs hacked off, and had her hair pulled back in a ponytail and flip-flops on her feet.

"If the seats sell out by next Fridee," she sang, keeping to the tempo and missing most of the notes, "then this store and I are really meant to be!" She added a bump and grind that notched his body heat up a few degrees and tempted him to move in close.

Instead, reminding himself that he was there to help, not do anything stupid, he tapped her on the shoulder. "Hey, Picasso. Looking good."

"*Aieeee!*" Ashley dropped her paintbrush and spun around, yanking up her hands into fists to defend herself against the big . . . *Oh, heck.* She whooshed out a breath, adrenaline kicking into her system at the sight of amused eyes the color of dark molasses. "Ty! Ohmigod, you scared me. I wasn't—"

"Expecting me. Yeah. I know. I'm hoping this will make up for it." He held up a paint roller, complete with a fresh, fluffy green cover. "Ed mentioned you could use some help painting the stage."

As she got a better look at him, her pulse bumped, and not because he had startled her. He was wearing battered jeans worn nearly through at the stress points, along with a dark green T-shirt that had seen better days. He smelled shower-fresh, though, and there were comb marks in his wavy hair.

He looked like a man who was ready to put in a few hours, and she was a woman who could use that kind of a man. She could appreciate him, she reminded herself through the thud of her pulse, even *like* having him around, without going over to the dark side of her DNA.

Stay casual. Keep it cool. Teasing, she said, "What, did Gran threaten to cut off your cookie supply if you didn't put in a couple of hours? Remind me to thank her."

"It was my idea this time." His lopsided grin deepened, reaching his eyes. "Guess that means I'm part of the team. Do I get a T-shirt?"

"See anything you like on the sale rack? Some sequins, maybe, or a crop top? Sorry—the lavender silk hasn't come in yet." His chuckle did quivery things to her insides, but she told herself not to go there. *Just give the man a gallon of paint and point him to the stage. Remember that whole deal about learning from your mistakes?* "Seriously, though, thank you for coming all the way back out here. A million times thank you. I want to get at least the first coat done on the staging tonight, and it was looking like it was going to be a late one."

"Especially when you've got butterflies to paint." He moved up beside her to study the one she was working on, where she had worked subtle human silhouettes into the black of the insect's body—a man and a woman, kissing. "Nice," he said, his voice a warm rasp coming from entirely too close. "You're going to make each one different?"

She tapped the copy of *Butterflies of Wyoming* she had gotten out of the library. "Different colors, species, you name it. Anything else would be boring."

"Hidden pictures, too?"

It gave her a buzz that he saw it. "Some will have pictures, some words. I want people to see something new every time they look around the room."

He quirked an eyebrow. "I don't think that'll be a problem. Fair warning, though—if you want anything more than monochrome out of me, you'll have to sketch it out. I'm a paint-by-numbers guy."

I highly doubt that. She had heard him play, after all. Still, if he wanted paint-by-numbers, she could more than work with it. "Then the staging is yours. I want people to focus on the models and the clothes, so I'm going dark gray for the stage itself and lighter gray for the display." She indicated four one-gallon cans stacked on the nearby workbench.

He leaned in, studied the cans. "Otherwise known as Dusky Charcoal and Lakeshore Mist?"

"Otherwise known as thank goodness Mrs. Applebee decided two-toned gray wasn't nearly as sexy a bedroom color scheme as it had looked on whatever DIY show she was watching, and returned two cans of each." She grinned. "Billy gave me a deal on them."

"Dusky Charcoal and Lakeshore Mist it is." As he reached across her to grab the first can, his arm brushed across hers, skin on skin.

Heat sizzled at the point of contact, the sparks all but visible. She sucked in a breath. He stilled. And suddenly there was a giant, rainbow-colored elephant in the room.

Attraction. Chemistry. Hormones. All the things that didn't listen to logic or better sense.

Ignore it, she told herself. *It doesn't matter.* But the sudden drum of her pulse said that it mattered far more than she wanted to admit. "Um," she said.

Yeah, because that was brilliant.

He drew back, expression dark, though not with any of the annoyance, frustration, or judgment he had been aiming her way last week. Now the heat that pulsed between them was something else entirely. Something more elemental, more compelling, and far more dangerous. "Sorry," he said, his voice a low rasp that skimmed across her nerve endings like an electrified feather. "Guess that doesn't count as keeping my distance."

Was that a question? She couldn't tell. "We'll have to watch that. Seeing how we're both coming off some hard knocks in the relationship department, and neither of us is looking for something serious." She paused. "Right?"

His eyes shifted away. "I've got some irons in the fire, and don't know where I'll be this time next year. Probably moving on. So serious isn't in the cards right now, likely won't be for a while."

It was dumb for that to bring a pang when she was in the same place—not because she was moving on, but because she was staying put. "Understood, which means we've got our answer. Neither of us is looking for something serious, and I don't do casual." At all. She lifted a shoulder. "I'm just not wired that way."

His eyes met hers once more, searching for something. "That's not a bad thing." A pause. "So, then. What now?"

She yearned to toss her better sense in the trash and lean toward him. Instead, she nudged a gallon of Dusky Charcoal in his direction. "We paint."

He hooked the wire handle and gave the can a liquid-sounding shake. "Bring on the gray-meets-gray."

Sniffing in mock affront, she said, "That's Dusky Charcoal meets Lakeshore Mist to you, buster."

"Better than lavender." His grin eased the tension in the air.

Some, anyway.

They spent the next few minutes getting their workspaces arranged—or, in her case, rearranged, as she shifted to the next plywood cutout in line and started sketching her concept, planning to bury the words *Girl Power* into the outer edge of the butterfly's wings. Across the room, Ty levered open the first can, dumped the paint into the roller tray, and got to work, starting at the bottom of the staging and rolling his way up with smooth, even strokes that made his muscles bunch and flow. His hands were big and capable, his movements steady, making him look like he could go on for hours.

She told herself not to stare, but even when she made herself turn away and focus on her butterfly, she remained elementally aware of his presence, his movements, and how the sticky sound of the paint roller was almost like a kiss, moist and intimate. Which made it darn near impossible to concentrate on her painting.

Stop it. You know where you stand. Unfortunately, rather than feeling like they had settled anything, it felt more like she was tippy-toe at the edge of a cliff and sorely tempted to take the leap, even though everything inside her was screaming, *Don't do it! Don't jump!*

She was going to listen this time, darn it. She *was*. Buying the store had been a leap, and she still wasn't sure if she was going to have a soft landing or go splat. Another leap—especially one involving him—could put her in some serious free fall, headed for a bunch of pointy rocks.

"Paint your darned butterfly, already," she muttered under her breath, and made herself mix a brilliant shade of purple.

"What was that?"

"Just talking to myself."

Sort of.

Quiet fell between them, not quite comfortable, but getting there. After a bit, he asked, "Have you always painted?"

It was a safe question. A let's-just-be-friends question. *You can do this.* She'd far rather be his friend than some sort of not-quite-enemy. Wiggling her paintbrush in a gesture of *yes/no/sort of*, she said, "I've always been into art. Paint, pencil, pastel, clay—whatever struck me. It used to drive my instructors batty that I'd rather be okay at a whole lot of things than really good at any one thing. My mother, too."

"She wanted you to be an artist?"

"She wanted me to be a prodigy."

He glanced over. "Oh?"

Shrugging, she said, "It's not that interesting."

"We've got a lot of paint to get through, and now you've got me curious. So tell me about being a prodigy."

"I wasn't. That was the problem. I was good, but not spectacular."

"Good is good."

"Not good enough." She could leave it at that, but something about being there with him, with the radio playing alt rock and the world outside going dark, loosened her hold on things. "After I came along and

Wylie faded out of the picture, money got real tight. Mom worked retail, while Wyatt watched me and picked up ranch chores where he could. From age eleven on, when he should've been being a kid instead of raising one. And the whole time, they had it in their heads that I was going to be the one to break the family tradition by actually being somebody."

"Everyone is somebody."

She only wished it had been that easy. "Tell *them* that." But she exhaled. "I take that back. I owe them so much." Which was part of the problem. "They were so convinced that I was something special, that when one of my art teachers used the *p*-word—prodigy, I mean—they took it and ran with it. Classes, contests, supplies . . . stuff I knew we couldn't afford, but they kept insisting, said it was an investment in my future."

"Lot of pressure to put on a kid."

"They just wanted me to be okay." Words emerged from the patterns on the butterfly's wings, not *Girl Power*, but *Stand Your Ground*. "It wasn't until I went off to art school—little fish in a big pond, you know—that it became painfully obvious that my version of good wasn't close to being good enough."

"Depends on your perspective." He nodded to the purple butterfly. "It suits you. As does the motto."

She stepped back and surveyed the finished product, feeling her lips curve.

It wouldn't have rated the back of the bathroom door at Iron Horse, the gallery that handled Wyatt's sculptures, and was admittedly more a craft project than a piece of art. But the sweeping swirls of purple and gold were so fluid it made the butterfly's wings look like they were moving, and the text disappeared and reappeared depending on how she focused her eyes.

Stand Your Ground.

Yeah. She was working on that one. Getting better at it, though.

"It's okay." But she smiled as she said it.

"Why butterflies?"

"One of my favorite parts of being at the store is seeing the glow a woman gets when she finds something that speaks uniquely to her, something that transforms her old look into something new and vivid. That's when she's a butterfly. Better yet, it's when she stops wishing she could blend in with all the other caterpillars, and spreads her wings instead."

"Like you're doing now."

"Trying to do, anyway." It mattered that he saw it. That he got it. "My family doesn't understand, but that's okay as long as I do." Throwing her arms wide, she did a little pirouette, letting her head fall back as she exclaimed, "I love this place. The town. The shop. My new life. All of it."

When she stopped her spin, her ponytail came to rest over one shoulder, but her head felt like it kept on going a moment longer, in a wonderfully dizzying sensation. Then she caught the look on Ty's face, and the spinning stopped.

Everything stopped as the naked hunger in his expression reached inside her and sparked the blaze that had been building since the moment he'd tapped her shoulder and called her Picasso.

Setting aside his paint roller, he rose to his feet. Came toward her. Held out a hand. "You're beautiful, Ashley. Inside and out. Don't ever let anybody tell you different."

Men had called her beautiful before, not seeming to care that it was a happy accident of genetics that her face was arranged the way it was, and nothing to do with what went on beneath. Ty, though, saw deeper. He saw what mattered.

Almost without conscious volition, her hand rose to his. Their fingers tangled together, the drag of his work-roughened skin sending new heat into her veins. She wanted those hands on her face, her body. It didn't matter that they had agreed not an hour ago that this wasn't going to happen—things were shifting now, changing.

Transforming.

She stepped closer, her eyes locking on his lips, on the way his throat moved when he swallowed thickly. His free hand came up to her waist, slipped down to settle at the point of her hip, where her jeans rode low, baring a strip of sensitized skin. As his thumb traced a maddening pattern, he said, "I don't want to do something you're going to regret."

"I won't." There was no hesitation.

One eyebrow quirked in what she was coming to recognize as not-quite-a-smile amusement. "You won't kiss me, or you won't regret it after?"

"I won't regret it. Not when I know exactly what I'm getting into." She flattened her palm on the solid bulge of his chest, feeling the powerful drum of his heart. "I said before that I'm no good at keeping things casual, but that's not exactly true. It's more that I've never gotten a chance to try." Not as a grown-up, with honesty on both sides. "I think I'd like to. With you."

His fingers tightened on her hip. "Why the change of heart?"

She glanced over at the butterflies, one purple, one blue. "Not a change, an evolution."

"I'd be an idiot to argue with that," he said in a low voice. "Especially after seeing what I've seen from you over the past few days." He lifted a hand to brush his fingers across her temple and down to her cheek, and when she looked back at him, he caught her lips with his.

And, for the second time, they shared their first kiss.

It started soft and sweet, then deepened incrementally—a slide of lips, a touch of tongue that said he knew what he was doing. She parted her lips and let him in, reveling in the sensation when his arms banded around her, tightening her against his body with delicious pressure. He changed the angle of the kiss, taking it deeper, and she followed him down into the whirl of pleasure. Oh, this was what *she* wanted, here and now.

His masculine scent cut through the odors of sawdust and paint, surrounding her as surely as his big body enfolded her, not making her feel protected so much as powerful. Their lips fused, their hands roamed, and Ashley lost herself to the moment, the magic. The man.

His kiss.

It went on and on but passed in a flash, and before she was nearly ready, he had eased back to look down at her, his eyes black with passion in the muted light.

She stared at him, breathing hard as a single word echoed in the sudden stillness of her brain: *yowza*. That hadn't just been a kiss, it had been *the* kiss, the one all others should be measured against. Or was that coming from the freedom of knowing that she didn't have to worry about the future with him?

The floor was solid beneath her feet, the world steady around her. She hadn't gone over the edge of the cliff. She *wouldn't* go over, not this time. Touching a finger to his lips, she said, "No regrets, cowboy."

One eyebrow lifted. "Another pact?"

"If you like."

"Well, then." He leaned in and brushed his lips across hers, once more, sparking greedy need within her. "Here's to keeping things simple and being good to each other. And to no regrets."

Far from regretting her decision, Ashley found that things between her and Ty got better and better as the week went on.

On Tuesday, he showed up at the store just past closing time, armed with more brushes and rollers, along with a memory stick loaded with music.

"You made me a mix tape!" She clutched it to her chest, playing it up so he wouldn't see that she had gone all mushy inside. Then she mock-frowned. "Or is this a comment on my choice in radio stations?"

"Gift horse," he drawled, "mouth. You want it or not?"

Of course she wanted it. She wanted all of it—the tunes, the help, the man. . . . But she would stick with the first two, at least for now. She knew that kisses soon wouldn't be nearly enough, but she wasn't ready to go any further with him. *Take it slow. Don't jump until you've got your spot picked out at the bottom and you're sure you'll land on your feet.*

They painted to rockabilly and the blues, argued the merits of her beloved alternative rock, and made up unlikely names for a new slate of appetizers at the Rope Burn—everything from Peeping Tom Frog Legs to My Eyes Are Up Here Chicken Breasts. And when the staging was its full two-toned gray and a dozen butterflies were propped up to finish drying, she walked him to the back door and they kissed to the sweet melody of a single guitar played so well she could almost hear words in the notes.

On Wednesday, he brought a giant picnic basket from the ranch, flourishing it as he came through the door. "I've got fried chicken, coleslaw, biscuits, and cookies. If I know Gran, there'll be a checkered picnic cloth, too, for fun."

Stomach tightening as much from the sight of him as the menu, Ashley grinned. "We'll take it up on the roof when we're done with the grunt work—the view is incredible. It'll be the perfect reward for us getting the rest of the floor space cleared and the racks packed away."

And it was, too. As was the precious half hour they spent nestled together after their picnic, staring up at the sky while he showed her the Boot, the Snake, and a few of the other constellations the old-timey cowboys used both as navigation and as company on the long, lonely nights out with the herd.

Then, later, after they kissed good night, she came through the door into her apartment with her lips warm and chafed and her body feeling feather-light. Spinning across the living room with her arms wide, she said, "Can you believe it, Petunia? I think I might actually be able to pull this off." The fashion show. The shop. Keeping things with Ty within bounds.

All of it.

On Thursday, Ty came to help her assemble the stage on the eerily empty sales floor, lugging the heavy sections in from the loading dock, one by one, while sweat beaded his brow and dampened his T-shirt, making it cling to his muscles.

The sight heated her blood. That morning, she had awakened with her heart pounding and the phantom press of his lips on hers. During the day, she had caught herself staring at something—a mannequin, an outfit for the fashion show, a sea of butterfly-shaped give-away bags—and seeing him instead. The powerful width of his shoulders, the glint that came into his eyes before they kissed, the lopsided grin that made her weak in the knees.

She didn't jump easily into bed with a man, but she wasn't any stranger to sex. Sex with him, though . . .

the thought brought a whole-body flush and a thrum of anticipation.

Hold off, warned her inner voice. *There's no rush. Better to let it build.* Which was true. Her body, though, wanted to charge headlong and see if the reality matched the fantasy. Or, better yet, exceeded it.

Come upstairs, she wanted to say as he worked the bolts into place, securing the first two gray-painted sections together. *Let's take a break together.* Instead, she said, "I'm going to order pizza."

They polished off a large pepperoni and a two-liter of high-test soda that she had picked on the theory that she needed the caffeine and sugar to keep her going. It made her jittery, though. So much so that she almost invited him upstairs after all, when their good night kisses suggested they both had more than their share of energy to burn.

She lingered in the kiss, held back by the sense that it wasn't time yet. She had to do this on her own.

Stepping back, she brushed her fingers across his chest, let them trail down his arm, and thrilled to the way his nostrils flared. "Sleep well." Her voice was husky, her breathing quick.

He gave a short, rusty chuckle. "Yeah, right. You, too."

"Yeah, right. I'll see you tomorrow?"

"Count on it." He brushed his lips across hers one last time, and said, "You're gonna do great." Then, settling his Stetson on his brow, he jogged down the stairs of the loading dock and made for his truck. He waved before hopping in, and again when he pulled out of the back lot, threading his truck along the alley and back out onto Main Street.

As the sound of the truck's engine faded, a church bell tolled in the still night air, saying it was midnight. Then past midnight. And, ready or not, it was Friday.

11

By midday, Ashley could barely remember her name as she buzzed around the shop, hanging butterflies and setting up her best mannequins. Later, she would dress the figures with the exquisite gowns Della had sent up from the city, along with a handmade card that looked like a ransom note and said, *Good luck! Wish I could be there—I know you'll kick ass!* Hen, meanwhile, had taken to screaming at odd intervals, mostly when she found things that she thought were done that weren't, or had somehow gotten undone, even though the shop was closed for the morning and they were the only two people there.

All in all, they were right on schedule. Ashley had even written it on the Big List: *Friday morning. Utter chaos.*

She had already checked it off. In fact, she was thinking of checking it off a second time, just because.

"T minus eight hours and counting," Hen announced, grabbing double handfuls of her long hair. "Aahhhh!"

"We've got this," Ashley assured her. "We're a team.

Speaking of which, can you help me with this?" She had gotten a killer deal on a bolt of polyester cloth printed with jungle-esque foliage that had the occasional pair of slitted yellow eyes peering through, and was using it to swath the bar and catering station.

Hen made a face. "Can we talk about that fabric?"

"What's wrong with it?"

"I'm pretty sure those eyes are following me."

"Last month you thought the mailman was following you. And the eyes add visual interest."

"I say they're creepy, but you're the boss." Hen snagged the staple gun off the top of the bar setup that the caterers had brought over first thing, and got to work, deftly pleating the fabric that Ashley held up and fastening it in place. "Speaking of beady yellow eyes that can see into your soul, how's your cat?"

"Petunia the Invisible?"

"He'll come around," Hen assured her, "especially when you've got more time to sit and talk to him."

Guilt pinched. "In the next decade or so, you mean?" Between the store and Ty, she didn't know how much sitting and talking was going to happen anytime soon. Not that Hen knew about the Ty stuff. Ashley had been keeping that to herself, for now. "How long do cats live anyway?"

"The teens are getting up there. How old is Petunia?"

"No clue. I'll have to ask Nick." She didn't put it on the Big List, though, as the darn thing was already too daunting. Instead, she crossed off *Hang fabric*. Next up? *Arrange chairs*. "Okay," she said, dusting her hands together like a gymnast laying on some chalk. "Let's dial up the girl power and—" She broke off as a knock sounded at the front door. "Hold that thought."

She headed for the door, muttering about the meaning of a CLOSED sign and the note below it that said, *Sorry, we're closed to set up for tonight's fashion show! Doors open at 7 p.m., the show starts at 8. For tickets, see Betty at the bakery.* When she saw who was on the other side, though, she grinned. Popping the lock, she swung the door open. "Gilly, hey there. Looking good!"

The teen was wearing a vivid green tee with jeans and boots, and had her brother's jacket slung over her arm, name patch facing up. And instead of staring at her toes, she peered up at Ashley through her bangs. "Hey. I know you're closed. Sorry to bother you."

"Is everything okay?" Ashley hadn't seen her since the other day, when she had sent Gilly home from their big try-on session with a ticket for her mom.

"Sure, fine. I just . . . I thought you might need some help. You know, setting up and stuff."

"Ohmigosh, yes. Thank you!" Ashley caught the girl's arm and drew her through the door. "Come in, come in. Hen? We've got a new recruit."

"Woo-hoo! Come on in, girlfriend. We've got work to do!"

The Big List took a beating over the next six hours, but it was like a movie villain—every time Ashley thought they had struck the killing blow, the darned thing dragged itself back upright and came at her again. And she was running out of time.

"Done and done." She crossed off *Hang curtains* and *Update window display*, as the front of the store was now swathed in rented sheers and the volleyball game was now a jumping-and-hugging celebration with a scoreboard that said EVERYBODY WINS!

The curtains had been Shelby's idea—a way to heighten anticipation by making everyone guess what was going on inside the store in the last few hours before the show. What Ashley hadn't anticipated, however, was how stuffy and hemmed-in the store would feel with the windows blocked off. *Hello, claustrophobia.* What if Three Ridges were hit with a zombie apocalypse while they were setting up for the fashion show? There could be a whole army of rotting undead plastered up against the plate glass, just waiting for her to unlock the door.

Meanwhile, back in reality . . . Sighing, she shook her head.

"Problem?" Hen asked from the lower level, where she and Gilly were setting up the folding chairs.

"Next up on the hit parade is *Pimp dressing area*, but I don't think we have enough time before the models start arriving for hair and makeup." The loading dock was crammed with outfits and dressing tables, one for each model. She had planned to fancy it up with curtains, butterflies, personalized touches for each station, but the clock was ticking way too fast. Bummed, she added, "I want them to feel like stars."

"They will," Hen said. "Don't worry."

Gilly nodded quickly. She hadn't said much, but she had worked her butt off all afternoon without complaint. Now she ventured, "Having someone do my hair and makeup is already more than I expected. But if you want to do something extra, how about special goody bags just for the models? I helped my mom with some yellow-ribbon benefits, and that's what we did for the VIPs."

"Brilliant!" Ashley bounded down from the upper level to give the teen a high five—which was probably totally uncool, but she wasn't sure what had come after the knuckle tap, and, hey, it was a vintage store. "You want to give me a hand? Grab a dozen of the nice paper bags with the handles and a bunch of tissue paper, and meet me in the warehouse. Hen? Can you come up with a snack station for out back? I've got nibbles and sodas in the fridge, along with champagne, sparkling cider, and strawberries."

"On it!"

They cranked out those tasks, knocked *Put programs on the chairs* off the Big List, and were just starting to schlep the boxes of stuffed-full goody bags—the ones for the ticketholders, not the special ones they had just made for the models—to the ticket-taking station at the front door, to be dispensed at check-in, when there was a brisk knock at the back door.

Startled, Ashley looked at the clock and got a serious adrenaline zap at seeing that the caterers, models, and hair-and-makeup people were right on time. *Flee! Escape! Run-run-run!* "Ohmigosh, is it really six thirty? Here. Take these!" She shoved her box at Hen, saw that her arms were already full, and froze as panic bubbled up. "It can't be time. There's still too much to do. We have to decorate the aisles, finish the catering stations, and disguise the garbage and recycling. And the sound system isn't working yet. Where's Jolly! I need—"

"You need to breathe," Hen said firmly. Setting aside her box, she appropriated Ashley's to stack on top of it. "There. See? Dealt with. And you know what? Even if those boxes are there when you open the doors in a half hour, it won't matter. Nobody is going to know that you didn't get to some of the finishing touches you had planned. I mean, get a load of this place." She slung an arm across Ashley's shoulders. "Look around you! Look at what you've accomplished!"

Ashley blinked, and in that instant, the shop floor transformed around her. She suddenly saw the butterflies on the walls, with their happy bug faces and subliminal messages; the colorful jumble of wire-hung clothes, frozen in playful little scenes; and the rows of chairs radiating away from the central display in concentric curves, as if the gorgeous gowns that swathed the strategically placed mannequins had caused ripples.

She swallowed thickly. "Oh. Hey, wow." It worked, really and truly. Not just the way she had imagined it, but even better. "This is . . . *wow*. Amaze-balls."

"See?" Hen nudged her toward the back. "We've got this. Go on and let the models in so they can get started in hair-and-makeup. It's almost show time!"

Oh, God. Showtime. She was totally going to throw up.

She didn't, though, and the next fifteen minutes were a whirlwind of people, noise, and laughter. The excited models—including Froggy, Rose and Gran Skye, Mayor Tepitt, and a half dozen other regulars of all shapes and ages—took a quick tour of the runway, exclaiming over the stage and cheering each other on as they took turns striking a pose or two. Back at their changing stations, they riffled through the clothes that had been laid out for each of them, and started a heated undies-versus-no-undies debate that had Ashley picturing all sorts of *Model Falls Off Stage into Crowd* moments of the sort that would get the store a gazillion hits on YouTube, but not in a good way.

Putting her index fingers between her lips, she gave a piercing whistle that cut through the buzz. Into the surprised silence that followed, she said, "Let's keep our undies on. We don't want any wardrobe malfunctions, do we?" Not sure she wanted the answer to that one, she hurried on, "We've got just over an hour before the show starts, so I'm going to leave you in the more than capable hands of my hair-and-makeup crew." Otherwise known as the Girl Zone, as all four of her besties had insisted on volunteering for this part, bless them. She motioned Shelby forward. "This is my beauty ringleader. Shelby, do you want to take this away?"

"Absolutely! You, you, you, and you." Shelby pointed to the four loudest members of Team No-Undies. "Hop in your chairs. We've got work to do!"

Ashley stepped back as the models milled, some heading for their chairs while others checked out the snack table and their goody bags. Coming up beside her, Danny said, "We've got this. You go nail down whatever last-minute deets need nailing down." She caught Ashley in a quick hug. "And remember to breathe!"

"Working on it," Ashley retorted, hugging her friend in return. But she felt more settled as she headed back up the hall to the sales floor. Shelby and the others would make the models feel like stars, even without their names on the mirrors and balloons tied to their chairs.

"How does it look back there?" Hen asked from up by the counter, where she was getting the register booted up and ready to roll. They weren't going to focus on making sales tonight, but they weren't going to turn them away, either.

"That depends on whether you like your grannies going commando."

"What?"

"It's under control." More or less. "How are things up here?"

"T minus ten minutes and counting until we open the doors. Want to say it with me?"

Ashley obliged by grabbing handfuls of her own hair, and was amused when Gilly did the same. All three of them screamed in unison, making the bartender jump.

Oddly enough, it made her feel better. At least until she took a gander at the Big List and saw two key line items that weren't yet checked off. "Has anyone seen—" She broke off as she caught sight of a tall, dark-haired teen stalled at the end of the back hallway, as if he knew he didn't belong in hair-and-makeup central but wasn't quite sure where he was supposed to be. "Well, there's one of them." Raising her voice, she called, "Hey, Sean. Over here!"

Gilly whirled around and let out a squeak.

Smothering a grin, Ashley caught her arm and drag-steered her to meet the newcomer halfway. "Hi, Sean. Thanks for helping out tonight! You know Gilly, right? She's going to get you up to speed on taking the tickets and checking everyone in."

"I . . . um . . ." Gilly's face was bright pink, her eyes wild.

Recognizing incipient panic, Ashley added, "After you're done with Sean, Gilly, I want you to skedaddle to the back room for hair-and-makeup. Not that you need much—you've got great cheekbones—but Shelby knows how to play up the drama of those eyes." Okay, so maybe she was laying it on a bit thick, but neither of the teens seemed to notice. They were too busy not staring at each other.

"You're modeling?" Sean asked his left shoe. "Cool. Janey and Erik are helping the caterers. Did Mrs. Mac-Intyre ask you to help out? I guess she tagged a few of us drama geeks."

"Yes. I mean no. I mean—" Gilly took a deep breath, made a visible effort to pull herself together, and said, "Yes, I'm modeling, but, no, it's not because of Mrs. MacIntyre. I shop here sometimes." She plucked at the shirt. "I got this the other day." Then she looked morti-fied, like she couldn't believe she was talking to him about clothes shopping.

He didn't look put off, though. If Ashley remembered her deets correctly—she had pumped Barb Mac for some info—Sean had two sisters, one older and one younger. Odds were, he heard plenty about clothes on a day-to-day basis. "It's nice," he said, glancing over at her. "You look . . . different."

Ashley was pretty sure that by *different* he meant "pretty." She hoped Gilly could translate the boy-speak.

"Um. Thanks. Come on, I'll show you the welcome station. It's, ah, nice of you to help out."

"Mrs. Mac said we'll get a thank-you letter out of it. For college apps and stuff."

Note to self, Ashley thought, fighting a goofy smile as she watched them head off for the front of the store. *Write glowing rec letters for the Drama Club kids.*

Hen came up beside her, nudged her with an elbow. "Playing matchmaker, are we?"

Ashley pantomimed innocence. "Just giving him an opportunity to see her in a different light. Or at least a different jacket."

"I didn't think you had it in you. Or are you moving past the *Men suck* phase of the postbreakup continuum?"

"I don't think that men suck."

"Oh?"

Not going there. Not yet, anyway. She and Ty were keeping things quiet for the time being. "Why are we talking about this, anyway? I'm supposed to open the doors in nine minutes, and my sound system still isn't up and running. You haven't seen Jolly, have you?"

"No, I haven't. But I can do you one better." Hen looked past her and waved. "Yoo-hoo. Tyler! Over here!"

A sizzle-zap raced through Ashley's veins as she turned.

And there he was.

She could've sworn she hadn't been thinking of him, but the sight of him—big, strong, and solid-looking, as if gravity held on to him extra tight, planting his boots on the hardwood as he strode toward her—brought a whisper of, *There you are.* As if part of her had been waiting for him, counting the minutes since he'd left last night. "Ty."

"Hey." He stopped a polite distance away and nodded first at her, then at Hen. "Henrietta. Nice to see you again. Looking good."

Touching the ends of her hair like she was fluffing her feathers, she beamed. "Why, thank you, Tyler. You're looking good, too. So much happier than the last time we saw each other. You know"—she lowered her voice, barely, to stage-whisper—"right after Brandi left."

Ashley smothered a wince. "Hen, can you stick your head in the back room and see if they need anything?"

"Sure thing. Be right back."

"Sorry about that," Ashley said, once she was out of earshot. "Hen is . . ." She trailed off, not wanting to be disloyal.

"No problem. It's comforting how little really changed while I was away. Henrietta included." But where his words were carrying on a polite conversation, his eyes were locked on her with a good bit of smolder in their depths, as if he was thinking about the last time they had been in the shop together. Alone, with the lights down.

The heat inside her gathered, expanded. "I didn't think I would see you until later."

"I'm here to do your sound check."

"I thought Jolly was coming."

"I told him I'd take care of it. Unless you object?"

"To having a pro do my sound check and help me cross off the last big to-do I need to get to-done before I open the doors? Not in a million years." She grinned at him, had to hold herself back from doing more. "Come on. I'll show you where—" She broke off as the timer on her phone did its annoying *ding-a-ling* thing. She glanced at the clock and winced.

Following her gaze, he gave a lopsided grin. "Guess we're out of time."

"For now," she said, then took a quick look around and went up on her toes to brush her lips across his. "For luck."

"Knock 'em dead, killer."

"You're supposed to say, *Break a leg.*"

The lines deepened at the corners of his eyes. "Not a horseman's favorite saying."

"Then *Knock 'em dead* it is." She shot him a sassy finger wiggle, hoping he couldn't tell how much she wanted to cling. "See you later."

"Count on it." Raising her voice, she called, "Hen? It's time."

She felt Ty watching her as she made her way across the store, pausing at the register to put away the Big List. She gave herself a moment to brush a couple of wrinkles out of the iridescent silk blouse she had worn over a tight black tank and narrow black pants, wanting to look the part but let the models shine. Then, taking a steadying breath, she headed for the curtain-shrouded front door.

Hen met her there, eyes alight with anticipation. "Ohmigosh! Can you believe we're actually doing this?"

With her hand on the dead bolt, Ashley hesitated. "Tell me there hasn't been a zombie apocalypse out there while we were in here setting up."

Hen, bless her, said firmly, "If there had been, Ty would've showed up with a shotgun and plenty of ammo."

"Have I told you lately that I adore you? Okay. Here goes."

The lock felt stiff under Ashley's fingers, the door heavier than usual. Even the bell sounded muted as she swung the panel open, letting bright evening light spill through. It brought with it a buzz of humanity on the other side, hushed with anticipation and a couple of hisses of "Here she comes!"

Not zombies, she told herself. Applause broke out as she blinked into the evening sun, which seemed so bright after spending the afternoon cocooned in the store. The noise swelled almost instantly, becoming deafening. She would have fallen back a step in surprise if Hen hadn't given her a little push, propelling her all the way out, where she almost collided with someone who shouldn't have been there.

Mouth dropping open, Ashley let out a squeal. "Della! You came!"

The store's former owner grinned like a maniac.

With her dark curls tamed in a single braid and her curvy body accented by a sleek bronze dress made stunning by its simplicity, she looked every stitch the successful designer she had become. "You didn't really think we would miss this, did you?" She hooked an arm through her husband's and cuddled close. "Besides, Max wanted an excuse to come back and look at the library, see how his renovations are holding up."

"Not even," he protested gamely. "I love a good fashion show." Square-jawed, handsome Max Ramsay was a hands-on guy, a top-notch contractor, and something of a techno geek. Which made him an interesting foil to Della's older-is-better battle cry. At the moment, though, he looked perfectly happy to be back in Three Ridges, in front of the store where the two of them had fallen in love.

"See?" Hen nudged her in the ribs. "Not zombies. Friends."

And that was exactly what they were, Ashley saw, looking beyond Della and Max as the applause died down and someone shouted, "Open the curtains! We want to see who won the volleyball game!" That got a ripple of laughter, and then the same someone—she had a feeling it was Feed Store Billy—started a chant of "Cur-tains, cur-tains, cur-tains!"

So many faces! Some she knew, some she didn't, some she recognized but couldn't place. All here for her show, her little store. And there in the back of the group, Wyatt stood with Foster, Nick, and Danny's fiancé, Sam, and behind them, Ed and Big Skye. Some of the manliest men she knew. Emotion tightened her throat, an upwelling of gratitude, nerves, and the sudden overwhelming urge to snap her fingers and disappear, *poof*, like magic. Because if she could do that, then she could go out on top, before anything went wrong.

Instead, she gave a huge wave and hollered, "You want the curtains down?"

She got a cheerful roar in response.

"Okay, you got it!" Glancing back, she saw that Hen had the pull-rope in her hand and was giving her a thumbs-up. "Help me count it down to Another Fyne Thing. Five . . . four . . ." A hundred-plus voices took up the chant. "Three . . . two . . . one . . ." They hollered it together: "Another Fyne Thing!"

Hen yanked the rope and the curtains came down, revealing the window display. The noise level dipped momentarily while the onlookers craned to see who won. Then that same voice—*Note to self: Kiss Feed Store Billy*—hollered, "Everybody wins!" There was another round of applause, and a chant of "Everybody wins" began in the back.

Della surged forward to wrap her arms around Ashley's neck. "It's amazing," she enthused. "*You're* amazing. But, then, I never had any doubt. I can't wait to see what you've done inside!"

"Then come on in!" Forgetting her nerves—or maybe just pushing them down for now, which was good enough—Ashley propped open the double doors. "Single line, one at a time, let's get everyone checked in and get this party started!"

12

If the shop was a vision, transformed for the night into a butterfly garden with leaves and flowers of fluffy, frilly clothes, then Ashley was the goddess at the center of it all—vivid, bright, and ethereal as she moved among her guests, greeting each personally with a touch, a word, a smile, and guiding them where they needed to be, whether it was their seats, one of the catering stations, or over to a mannequin that wore a particular outfit.

The longer Ty watched her from the back of the room, as he leaned up against the wall near the big blue butterfly—the one that had a man and a woman kissing, in silhouette—the more he felt a song coming on. Not a generic ballad that skipped from beer to women to patriotism, like the ones that had kept Higgs & Hicks on top for far too long. More a guitar riff that would stick in the ears and metaphor-heavy lyrics that talked about being in the right place at the right time, which he was starting to think he had finally managed, for once in his life.

Ashley wasn't anything like he had thought. Or,

rather, she was exactly like he had remembered in the months following the wedding, when things on the road had been going to hell and he'd needed something fresh and honest to hang on to. Only she was better, because she was real, she was here, and they were good together.

"Surprised to see you here," Wyatt said, claiming the chunk of wall beside him.

Ty didn't let himself tense up. Didn't have any reason to—Ashley was a grown woman, and had said she would talk to Wyatt when the timing was right. Her family, her deal. So he said only, "I did a bunch of the painting."

"In other words, the girls roped you in."

"Gran pulled the old *You don't have to if you don't want to.*"

"Ouch."

"I didn't mind. Good cause and all that." Ty's eyes followed Ashley as she whisked through the vivid purple curtains that led to the back.

"You're probably wondering why I didn't put in a shift."

"Your business." Not to mention that whatever got said tonight was going to look different to Wyatt in a couple of days.

"Krista isn't very happy with me." Wyatt rolled his shoulders. "She says I'm being a stubborn ass. Blind as a bat, too, if I can't see that Ashley is handling herself."

Ty didn't want to have this conversation, but it wasn't like he could suddenly pretend he needed to be someplace else—they were all there for the same reason. A check of the wall clock showed him that they had another ten minutes before the show started.

Almost like he was talking to himself, Wyatt continued. "She was so damn talented growing up. Me, I did okay in school, did better at the ranches. Ashley, though . . . she was meant for bigger things. You could see it from early on—she tested off the charts and had this wild imagination. Her art teachers loved her, had Ma put her in special classes, enter contests, the works . . . until she hit high school and discovered boys." It came out flat, frustrated. "Ever since then, it's been one thing after another—this huge burst of enthusiasm and total commitment, followed by the inevitable pop of the bubble."

Stay out of it, Ty warned himself. *Not your deal.* But at the same time, it seemed to him like she was overdue for someone taking her side. "She seems pretty committed to me. Also seems to me that she cares what you think." Maybe more than she should.

Wyatt's lips flattened out. "You got a sister?"

Now he did tense up. "If I did, I think I'd want her to be happy, even if she isn't doing it how I expected."

"That's what Krista says—and she should know, what with Jenny wanting nothing to do with the ranch. Thing is, Ashley thinks she knows what makes her happy—for about a month at a time. Then she's on to the next shiny, interesting thing."

"Maybe this time is different."

"I've thought that before. Got tired of being wrong."

Ashley slipped back through the purple curtains, looking excited, alive, and wholly in the moment. Kind of the way she did after they kissed. Clearing his throat, Ty said, "Either way, what she's done here is pretty darn impressive. And if I had a sister who pulled off something like this, I think she'd want to know I was proud of her." When Wyatt's eyes narrowed, he shrugged. "But what do I know?"

Stepping up onto the platform that was built into the display dais and held the mic and mixer, Ashley leaned in and said, "Everyone? Could I have your attention?" Ringed by richly dressed mannequins set on the multi-tiered display, she outshone the brilliant clothing in slim, understated black and floaty green. When the lights dimmed a notch and the crowd noise followed, a smile brightened her eyes. "If you'll make your way to your seats, please."

"Guess that's my cue." Wyatt pushed away from the wall. "You got a seat?"

"I'm good."

That got a nod. "Catch you later, then."

Yeah, Ty thought as Ashley's brother moved off. *You will.* He hoped for her sake that Wyatt would come through for her today, give her the support she wanted from him. Hoped it for Wyatt's sake, too, because if he didn't watch it, she might figure out that she was doing fine without him.

As the last few stragglers planted their butts, leaving Ty with the standing-room crowd at the back, Ashley gave a little finger wiggle and another set of lights went down, leaving the stage spotlit. The move threw her into the shadows, but Ty couldn't take his eyes off her silhouette. Didn't want to. "Thank you all," she said into the mic. "Thank you for being here and supporting the uniquely fabulous women of Three Ridges and Another Fyne Thing."

Applause rippled through the crowd as music started down low—undemanding techno that wasn't Ty's thing but had a solid backbeat that suited the purpose—and the room tightened with the electric tension that he associated with the moment before a big band hit the stage.

With impeccable timing, Ashley leaned in and said softly, "And now . . . I invite you to sit back and enjoy . . . *Transformation*."

The music kicked up, the purple curtains parted, and a tall, steel-haired woman swept through, wearing a silvery dress that fitted close to her body and trailed a few feet behind her. Ty blinked as he recognized Rose Skye—but not looking anything like the Rose he saw around the ranch, wearing jeans and a welcoming smile. This Rose walked like she was on a mission, with a fierce expression and a hip wiggle he wouldn't have expected from her. Whistles rose up from the crowd— maybe not the usual noise for this sort of thing, but, hey, this was Three Ridges, and Rose had been the public face of Mustang Ridge for many years.

"First up is Rose Skye." Ashley's voice wove in with the music, adding rather than distracting as she described the outfit.

Rose hit the end of the stage, struck a pose, and then did something with the skirt, which split and fell away in one of her hands, flashing a brilliant purple underside. Beneath was a trim knee-length skirt of the same material, and a pair of shapely legs that Ty felt a little awkward about seeing.

A piercing wolf whistle was followed by Ed Skye's shout of "Yeah, Rosie!"

She blew her husband a kiss, gave a little twirl as she tossed the skirt-turned-shawl over her shoulders, and strutted around the other side of the runway as the music thrummed a solid, insistent beat. There was more applause as she disappeared through the curtains. A pause, and then they swept again to let Gran through. Her white hair was a fluffy halo, and her brilliant blue eyes were the same shade as the bolero she wore over flirty pink and blue polka dots. The dress bounced as she walked and showed legs that were a generation older, still looked great, and for some reason made Ty grin rather than squirm.

He couldn't stop himself. He let rip with a wolf whistle and a whoop of "Work it, baby!" Gran dimpled and winked at him, then blew Big Skye a kiss as she sashayed past.

"I'm guessing this model needs no introduction," Ashley said with a smile in her voice, and then introduced Gran anyway, along with the clothes, which included a jeweled butterfly brooch that glittered in the spotlights, seeming ready to take flight. Ty listened to her voice more than the details, loving how the low end of her natural register had a soft vibrato. And as Gran gave the room a saucy wave and disappeared through the curtain, he found himself settling back against his chunk of wall to enjoy the show. And, more, knowing that when the lights came back up, he'd be sticking around to be there for the woman who might not be his for keeps, but was his perfect match for now.

Most of the fashion show was a blur to Ashley—the lights, the audience, her own amplified voice, the models' faces as they hit their marks and posed—but certain moments stuck with her.

Like when Froggy did an impromptu boogie-woogie because she loved the long embroidered coat Ashley had picked for her, knowing its lines would give her the illusion of height while showcasing her curves. And when Gilly peeked through the curtains, disappeared for a second, and then, before Ashley could worry that she had chickened out, pushed through, looking young, fresh, and lovely in pale yellow chiffon. Maybe she shuffled a little in her flats rather than strutting, and maybe her pose was more deer-in-headlights than really working it, but on her return trip, her face had been aglow.

Her expression had pretty much made Ashley's night. The rest—from the standing ovation when the models paraded together in their final outfits to how, after she took a bow and invited folks to look around, there was a stampede to register for the three-night Transform Your Tacky Thing workshop she and Hen were putting on next week—had been gravy.

Or maybe icing. It had been that sweet.

Finally, as the models' friends and family members swarmed the stage to exclaim over their loved ones and the register rang loud and clear even over the crowd noise, Ashley descended from the mic stand and into the midst of her own fan club.

"You freaking rocked it!" Danny held up a palm. "Gimme five!"

Ashley obliged. "Is that still cool?"

"Who cares? Look at this place! You knocked it out of the park!"

"It was a team effort." Ashley slung an arm around Danny's neck, grabbed Krista, and beckoned Shelby and Jenny in. "Thank you all so much! The models look fabulous." Which was totally inadequate, but she hoped the group hug conveyed how much their help had meant to her, every step of the way. "Where's your dad?" she asked Krista. "He should be in on this." And Ty, but she didn't want to push her luck. She had been very aware of him all night. More, even, than Wyatt.

"He's buying mom the silver Dior. And where did that gorgeous overskirt come from?"

"Della."

"Right here, Ash!" And there she was, hair wild around her face, eyes alight with enthusiasm, with Max a couple of steps behind her, the two of them a unit.

Krista squealed. "Della! I thought you said you weren't coming!"

"I lied. I wanted to surprise our girl here."

There was a chorus of her name, another group hug, and Ashley's heart felt like it was getting too big for her ribs to contain the pressure. All these friends. All this support. Even love.

Unbidden, her eyes went to where Wyatt stood at the edge of the stage with his hands in his pockets and his expression unreadable. His hair was too smooth for his porcupine look, but the vibe was definitely there. She hated that the sight of him put a knot between her shoulder blades and gave her the urge to say something she knew would annoy him. But being around Gilly and Ty had put the brother-sister thing into a different light for her, enough so that she crossed to him and socked him affectionately on the arm. "Admit it. This wasn't the disaster you thought it would be."

Okay, maybe it came out sassier than she had intended. *Baby steps.*

But his lips kicked up at the corners and his eyes warmed a notch as Krista came over to loop an arm around his waist. "Not a disaster at all," he said. "Good job, kiddo. I'm proud of you."

"Excuse me?" Ashley pretended to clean out an ear.

"You heard me."

"Say it again anyway."

"Oh, for—" He scowled and then winced a little, as if his wife had just nailed him with an elbow. "You did a good job, Ashley. I'm proud of you."

Laughter bubbled up on a wave of pleasure. She was tempted to poke him in the ribs and demand that he take back the part where he said she was out of her mind buying the store, that it was just another phase. But she liked to think she was wiser now, or at least a little more mature, so she went in for a hug instead, and said, "Thank you, Wyatt. That means a lot to me."

He hesitated, as if waiting for the *And another thing*. When there wasn't one, he gave her a fatuous pat on the shoulder, like he wasn't quite sure what to do with his hands. When she stepped away, he added, "This was a whole lot to pull off in ten days. You did a great job. Of course, you'll have a better idea of how success-ful it really was once you've tallied the receipts and seen how many people come back with their coupons in the next couple of weeks. A great party is one thing; an uptick in sales is another."

Krista groaned. "Seriously, Wyatt? You couldn't just leave it at *I'm proud of you*?"

"Well, it's true."

"Yes, it is," Ashley said, patting his cheek because she knew he hated it. "But I'm not letting you bring me down tonight. You said you were proud of me— twice!—and there's no takesies backsies on something like that."

"I'm not trying—"

"Nope! Can't hear you." She stuck her fingers in her ears—so much for the whole thing about being more mature—and danced away, laughing. "Sorry—gotta go hug some more people. Stay, though! Eat! Drink! Have fun!" She hooked an arm through Della's on the way by. "You're coming with me. I want you to meet Hen, and Froggy is dying to say hey."

Over the next couple of hours, it became clear that Wyatt was spot-on about one thing: it really was a great party. Not just because the caterers kept the nib-bles flowing well after the contracted time or because the cash bar was doing a brisk business, but because people were having *fun*. Especially after Ashley got the runway music going again and cajoled a couple of customers up onto the stage to show off their new purchases by walking the runway and striking a pose, and wound up with a big audience, lots of camera phones in action, and a line of ladies who wanted to be next.

It was past eleven by the time things slowed down at the register, close to midnight before Ashley finally shooed the last of the stragglers and all but shoved Hen out the door, swearing that she wouldn't start the cleanup until morning. She had her fingers crossed, though, because there was no way she was going to be sleepy anytime soon, so why not start setting the store to rights? Or maybe tally the receipts—she had a rough idea from the register, and the number was a good one—but Della had landed two special orders, Bakery Betty had brought in some ticket money, and the clinic registrations hadn't been added in yet.

The Big List is dead. Long live the next Big List.

Instead of panic, though, the thought brought a glow as she killed all but a single spotlight and bumped the music back on. There was something very satisfying about knowing what she had on tap for tomorrow and the next day, but also that there would be surprises along the way. And knowing that she could handle them. *Here's hoping, anyway.*

Heels making hollow echoes on the stage, she wiggle-thumped a few strides of runway walk and struck a hip-shot pose, finding that the muscle memory was still there, whether she liked it or not.

"Is this where I'm supposed to whistle and shout, *Work it, baby*?"

She whirled, gasping even though she immediately

recognized the voice. Make that *because* she had recognized it. "Ty!" Heat flooded her face, then washed lower down, bringing a whole-body tingle. "I thought you left." She had told herself not to be disappointed.

"I just stepped out to get some air and let the crowd thin. I figured I'd hang around and see if you wanted help with the teardown." A corner of his mouth kicked up. "I guess not quite yet."

Breaking her pose, she brushed at her clothes. "Tomorrow will be soon enough, and Ed is going to help. I was just . . ." She lifted a shoulder. "Playing, I guess. Maybe remembering a little." The initial rush of being "discovered" at an open casting call had been exciting, at least.

"Wyatt said you used to model."

"Oh? Let me guess—he said I was a prodigy at that, too, could've gone to Paris and done cover shoots." It came out more weary than bitter.

"Something like that. You didn't like the work?"

"I didn't get that far. I bailed when I figured out that the agent Mom signed me with had cameras in the bathrooms and a big couch in his office that saw a lot of use. And he liked to adjust our clothes. A lot."

Ty's expression sharpened. "Did you report him?"

"To the authorities?" A headshake. "Mom acted like I was making things up to get out of the contract." She held up a hand. "I know, I know. But she's wired a little off when it comes to men. I learned to adjust." She was working on it, anyway. "Not to mention that sometimes it's easier to let her and Wyatt think what they're going to think, rather than trying to change their minds." She dropped down to sit at the edge of the stage, patting the spot beside her. "Besides, they've got a point when they get on the *You can't just bail when the going gets tough* bandwagon. I could've stuck it out with art school, maybe turned it into a career. Same with modeling. Life in LA, too, though Kenny definitely had to go. So, yeah, maybe I've got a habit of cutting and running when things don't go my way."

He squeezed her hand. "Seems to me like you got the running part out of your system."

"Maybe. Standing up there with the microphone, though"—she nodded to the upper platform—"I pictured myself taking a flying leap into the crowd, donkey-kicking the bar, and racing out the back."

He grinned. "Thinking something isn't the same as doing it. And for the record? That might not have been the sort of advertising you're going for, but ten years from now, folks around here would still be talking about it. *Remember when Ashley Webb blew up her own fashion show? Yeah, that was a real trip.*"

"Gack! I'm not ready to think about ten years from now." Though she could see Feed Store Billy saying exactly that. "I'm just starting to get good at figuring out the next ten days or so."

"Nothing wrong with that." He tipped his head to look at the three butterflies opposite them. The painted patterns were muted in the shadows, but the instructions came through loud and clear. *Be Powerful. Take Control. Let Go.* "Especially seeing what you accomplished over the past ten." He slipped his arm around behind her, snugging her up against him. "This was a hell of a thing you pulled off here, Ashley. A hell of a thing. You should be proud of yourself."

How strange that he and Wyatt could say two things that sounded so similar, yet were really so different at their cores. Leaning into him, she let out a soft sigh as her brain went blessedly quiet for a moment. "Thanks, Ty." She didn't need him to validate the night's success, but it was sure nice to share it with him. "You want some champagne or something to nibble?" Now that she was starting to wind down, her stomach was reminding her that she had missed a meal or three.

"I should go. It's late, and you're going to have a busy day tomorrow."

Which was true, but she also knew full well that she wouldn't be settling down to sleep anytime soon. Restless, edgy energy coursed through her, coming as much from the feel of his arm around her as it did from the night's success.

She had dreamed of him, awakened wishing he was there with her, kissing her. Doing more. They knew each other, liked each other, were starting to respect each other. They weren't rushing a darn thing, and sex wouldn't be jumping off the edge so much as climbing a level higher on the cliff, and she already knew those dangers.

So, not letting herself turn it into a Big Thing when it was really the next natural step in their casual fun, she said, "You could go . . . but I'd rather you stayed the night."

*   *   *

Ty knew he was playing with fire by sticking around, but he was ready for the burn. She was in his head, under his skin. Tonight, tomorrow, Sunday—it didn't matter at this point. It was going to happen. *They* were going to happen, and tonight felt right.

Leaning in, he kissed her deep and slow, the way he'd been thinking about it all day. Then, against her lips, he said, "I'll help you lock up."

13

Anticipation hummed beneath Ashley's skin as she went through her checking-the-locks routine with Ty beside her. Excitement. If she had thought it was sexy as hell that he had waited behind to surprise her after everyone left—which she definitely did—it turned out it was even sexier to have him reach past her and run the cage down over the front door, then crouch down to set the lock.

If Kenny had been there, he would've been sacked out in the break room, working his way through the leftovers and champagne.

Annnd that's the last time we're thinking about HIM tonight. First because there was no real comparison, and second because she didn't want to think too much when there was so much to *feel.* Like the masculine roughness of Ty's palm as he drew her close. The intoxicating scent of his arousal and her own. The heat that gathered where their bodies brushed.

"What next?" His voice was an ardent rumble.

"Next?" Her mind blanked.

"More locks?"

She blinked at him, their eyes level, thanks to her an-
kle-breakers. Such a strange sensation, to have everything inside her go suddenly silent. She parsed the
words one at a time. *What. Next. More. Locks.* "No." The
word was barely a breath, but it kicked things back into
gear, bringing a new burst of excitement. "We're done
down here."

"So, what do you say? You want to show me your
apartment?"

Sudden amusement bubbled up. "Actually, I should
probably blindfold you. Between the fashion show and
a few other things"—like tearing closets apart in an effort to find her alleged cat—"the place should probably
be certified as a major disaster zone."

"Do you have a bed?"

"I do."

"Is it big enough for two, in the orientation of your
choice?"

Heat coursed through her veins at the sensory images that brought to mind. "It's plenty big for lots of
different orientations."

His teeth flashed. "Then I'd say we're good."

"I'd say we are. I'd also say that the last one upstairs
is a rotten egg!" She tore away from him and sprinted
for the back hallway, but made it only a couple of steps
before he scooped her up against his chest, cradling her
easily as she squeaked and kicked her feet.

"Let me," he said. "I'd hate for you to twist one of
those pretty ankles of yours, running on those shoes."

Relaxing against him, she looped an arm around his
neck and leaned in to nibble his earlobe, then whis-

pered, "I can do lots of things in heels. Running is the least of them."

"Annnd, we're going upstairs!" He carried her up the creaky treads more easily than she would have guessed possible, making her feel positively delicate.

She dealt with the door, let them through, and waited while he turned back so she could lock up behind them. Then she put a hand over his eyes.

"Hey, now," he protested, amused. "Don't know if you want me to do this blind. Seems like there's a bit of stuff laying around."

Not just *a bit*. More like everything she owned, along with most of what she had inherited when she moved into the apartment. Calling it a disaster area was an insult to disaster areas. "Trust me. This will be fun. Turn a little to your left and take three steps. More left."

His chuckle vibrated against her, but he obliged. "You sure about this?"

"We'll find out, won't we? More left. Then take six steps. Now three more, nice and straight." She coached him through the cluttered living room and down the hall to the bedroom, so they skirted a Tupperware tub full of art supplies and a bag of cosmetics that she could've sworn was in the bathroom, last she checked. Then, finally, into the bedroom. She nudged the door closed and took a look around. The warm yellow light coming from the bedside lamp bathed the tousled bed and piled pillows, and shone on the books piled haphazardly within reach. There was laundry and a bit of clutter, but it was nothing like out in the main room. "Okay," she decided. "You can open your eyes."

"Kiss me first."

She obliged. How could she not when he held her against his heart and kissed her as if she was the only thing that existed right then? Locking her arms around his neck, she let herself slide down his body, until her feet came to rest on the floor, supporting her weight. Then, easing the kiss, she stepped away.

His eyes came open, gone dark with a passion that had her inner muscles clenching with rhythmical desire. He reached for her, toyed with the hem of her soft green shirt, then started to draw it up.

Stepping back, she held up a finger in warning. "One second. Blinds." It might be late, but there was no need to put on a show. She put an extra wiggle in her walk, though, and heard his hiss of indrawn breath. And when she came back toward him, she loosened the floaty green silk and let it drift down her body, leaving her in the tight black clothing beneath, and the heels that were rapidly becoming her favorites.

She felt beautiful. Powerful. Ready to take the leap. All the things she had painted on her butterflies. *Girl Power. Believe In Yourself. Go For Broke.* She wasn't going to break this time, though. She had everything under control.

This wasn't intended to be forever, but it was going to happen right now. And thank God for that.

His hands came up to cup her waist, his thumbs rubbing maddening circles just beneath her tank as he looked into her eyes. "Sometimes I want to pinch myself when I'm around you, just to prove that you're real. You are, though. I think you're one of the most real women I know."

Men had told her she was beautiful before, but this was so much more. Because hadn't she been thinking the same about him? That he was real, solid, important. Warning shivered at the back of her consciousness. *Let's not go getting ahead of ourselves. This is fun, not important. Important* sucked her in, wrapped her up, tried to take over.

Fun, she reminded herself, and went to work on the snap studs of his shirt, popping them from top to bottom. "I wanted to do this down by the lake that first day. Now I want it even more, because I've gotten to know the guy holding the guitar. And I like him a whole lot."

He skimmed the tank up over her head, taking the built-in bra with it. Eyes heating, he cupped her breasts and drew his thumbs over her peaked nipples, wringing a groan from her. As her head fell back and she surrendered to his touch, he murmured, "Glad to hear it, as I like you a whole lot, too. Why do you think I stuck around?"

Eyelids fluttering shut, she whispered almost soundlessly, "I thought you wanted to see if I needed help breaking down the stage?"

His lips cruised along her collarbone and down. "I lied."

If she had been all *Rah, rah, let's get the store cleaned up*, he undoubtedly would have pitched in without complaint. This, though, was a much better plan. Fighting the sensual haze brought by his oh so clever hands and mouth, she pushed the shirt off his shoulders and tugged the cuffs free, one at a time. It was an effort to lift her head, another to force her eyes to open and focus on him. In the end, though, it was so worth it.

He was magnificent.

The warm yellow light buffed his workingman's tan to an all-over gold and caressed the ripple of muscles that flowed across his chest and down his abdomen, where a trail of sparse, wiry hair disappeared behind the plain silver plate of his belt buckle. With his bedroom eyes half-lidded and his jeans showing an impressive bulge, he could've been fodder for a sexy cowboy calendar photo. He wasn't model pretty, though—his body bore the signs of his lifestyle, from the long, narrow white line that ran along the top of one pec, to a tougher, gnarled scar that rode just above one hip bone and bore a ladder of healed-over stitches.

She moved in and touched the scar beneath his collarbone. "What happened here?"

His eyes met hers. "An accident. Just stupid kid stuff."

Was there a story there? She thought so, but this wasn't the time or place to ask. Instead, she skimmed down to the second, larger scar. "And here?"

Lips kicking up, he said, "Stupid cow stuff. She didn't mean it, though. I was just too slow."

Fingers drifting down, past his belt to the ridge of hard flesh behind his fly, she traced the outlines and murmured, "Here?"

He sucked in a breath, pressed himself into her touch. "That's not a scar, darlin', but it'll be an accident waiting to happen if you keep doing that."

A laugh bubbled up. "Should I stop?"

"Hell, no. Especially since I'm going to do this." He hooked a finger in her waistband, and a moment later her pants pooled at her feet. His hands settled on her bare hips and his thumbs slipped beneath the narrow swaths of elastic that held her panties in place.

She had worn electric-blue hip-huggers dotted with little gold butterflies, in honor of the evening. Now he chuckled and she flushed. "I wasn't expecting company."

"That wasn't a complaint." He brushed his lips across hers. "They're unique, just like you. Though they've got to go." The panties slipped down to snag at her ankles, hobbling her deliciously.

"My shoes. I should—"

"Leave them on." It was more an order than a suggestion, but the husky rasp in his voice put an answering heat in her belly. "They're sexy as hell."

The flames flared higher when he caught her by the waist and lifted her like she weighed nothing, leaving the clothing behind. Her feet had barely touched the floor again when he started walking her back toward the bed, crowding her with his big, warm body. Her bare legs brushed against his jeans, bringing a frisson of vulnerability at being so much more naked than he was.

There's an easy fix for that. She popped his belt buckle, undid the top, and dragged the zipper down inch by inch, cushioning the move with her fingertips and shaping his impressive length through the soft fabric of his boxer briefs. Groaning, he thrust himself into her touch. Then, suddenly urgent, he yanked off his boots and shucked out of the last barriers of clothing separating them, leaving him standing beside her bed, gloriously naked.

Wow. She didn't think she said it aloud—kind of hoped she hadn't. But, seriously. *Wow.* He was bigger all over than Kenny, with muscles that came from slinging hay bales and fixing fences rather than half-assedly lifting weights, and his hard manflesh jutted aggressively from a wiry nest of hair. Yeah, bigger all over.

Not that she was comparing. More like doing inner cartwheels.

Holding out a hand, he said, "Nervous?"

"Not even a bit." This was what she wanted, needed. Still. *Wow.*

"Then what are you doing all the way over there?"

"Taking in the scenery." But she crossed to him, feeling deliciously naughty to be naked save for her heels. She had known that the right shoes could make all the difference, but she'd never extended that to the bedroom before. When she stopped in front of him, they were eye-to-eye. "Is this better?"

"Getting there." He caught her by the waist, spun, and launched her onto the bed.

She squealed as she landed, and then bounced, laughing. "What am I, a bale of hay?"

He followed her down, the mattress dipping beneath his weight as he covered her, trapping her beneath the delicious warmth of his big body, the friction of his sparse masculine hair, and the sensation of his hard length pressing between their bodies. Cruising his lips along her jaw, he said, "Prettiest hay bale I've ever seen."

"Gee, thanks." She thought there was a joke in there somewhere—something about fluffing her or checking for mold—but then he dragged his hand down her body and urged her leg up in a bend that reminded her of the heels, and her mind fogged.

He shifted down her body, kissing a path lower and fanning the sudden blaze that erupted inside. "You were saying?" he asked, his breath hot on her skin.

Nothing. She arched into his touch. *Everything.* She had nothing left to say, but everything to feel. His hands on her hips, her legs, her center. His mouth, hot and avid. The sweet longing inside, the need to have him fill her, consume her. Digging her fingers into his shoulders, she whispered, "You're doing just fine."

He chuckled against her skin. "Well, then." And he kissed her, soft and enticingly, and Ashley lost herself to the pleasure.

Perhaps he said something more; maybe not. Her whole world coalesced to the way his hands bent her to his will and his clever tongue moved across her skin. Guilt stung, bringing the faint sense that she should be doing something, doing everything. But that was back to comparing, wasn't it? And, oh, how lovely to be with a man who took charge like this, who made her feel adored. Worshipped, even.

So this is what lovemaking feels like. The thought was a

passion-wisp in her mind, quick and fleeting. Not that she and Ty were in love, but that he was making love to her, wholly focused on her body, her reactions. How wonderful.

With her head thrown back and her mouth stretched wide on a long, low moan, she wasn't thinking about how she looked or if she was doing things right. She didn't need to—not when he whispered heated praise against her skin and then moved up her body, his skin sweat-slicked against hers and his eyes ablaze with passion as he kissed her belly, her breasts, her lips.

His body was heavy on hers, his jutting flesh hard and urgent, enticing her to spread her legs and invite him inside, even though a warning chime said they had skipped a step.

Breaking the kiss, he said, "Hold that thought." He found his pants, dug out his wallet, and pulled out a zigzag of three condoms accordioned together. Snagging one, he tossed the others on the nightstand.

"Props for preparedness," she said, aiming for casual but afraid that the passion-rasp in her voice said otherwise. "Note to self: Buy condoms." On Main Street. Where everyone would know.

Instead of making her want to squirm, the thought brought a grin. She wanted this, wanted him. And wanted everyone to know she had him, at least temporarily.

"I wasn't ever a Boy Scout, but I know what happens to spare kids." He rolled the barrier into place, then returned to her, rising over her and letting his weight settle against her, into her. Looking into her eyes, he rumbled, "This way is better."

His words and the practiced ease of his moves put a quiver-bump in her belly, reminding her how little she knew about his past. But she liked the man he was to-day, and it would be dumb to blame him for having a life—and a whole lot of experiences—leading up to this moment. Nope, she wasn't going there. She was staying right where she was, deliciously trapped beneath him with her eyes caught in his as he poised himself at her entrance and then nudged inside.

Slowly. Torturously. Wonderfully.

Her thoughts puffed to mental confetti as he filled her, stretched her, setting off new bursts of sensation with each advance. Little inner fireworks sapped her ability to do anything but dig her fingers into the bunched muscles of his upper arms as he seated himself fully, his chest rumbling with a raw groan of satisfaction.

"Ashley," he said against her temple. "Damn."

It wasn't poetry or a serenade. It was better, because *damn* was right. Damn, he felt good inside her, against her. And, damn, it felt good knowing that she had brought him to the point of being buried inside her, with fine tremors racing through his body as he waited for her to adjust to his size, his very presence.

Opening her eyes—and not really sure when they had eased closed—she looked up at him, lips curving. "What do you say, cowboy? Let's ride."

His teeth flashed. "Move 'em out." And, suiting action to words, he withdrew in a long, smooth glide, then surged forward once more, setting off new and better fireworks.

Lids going heavy again, Ashley dug her fingertips into his haunches and breathed, "Yee-haw."

"Watch it. Your city girl is showing." He moved within her again.

She arched against him, breath thinning. "Oh? You don't say *yee-haw*?"

"Not so much." He set a slow rhythm, pulsing against her and tugging at her most sensitive spots.

"Then what?" She wasn't even sure what they were talking about anymore, didn't care as long as he kept doing what he was doing, and more of it. Moving beneath him, she urged him to pick up the pace, helped increase the length of each stroke. *Delicious.*

His breath quickened, rasped, and his voice gained a thread of tension. "How about *round 'em up*?"

"Like this?" She circled her hips, creating a new and intense friction.

"That . . . yeah."

Sweat gathered on his brow, coming from the effort of holding back, she thought, and set herself to break through his control.

"Or this?" She changed the rotation, angling to take him deeper.

He hissed in a breath, froze for a second against her. Then he bowed his head, let out a whole-body shudder, and began to move for real. And everything changed— the rhythm, the angle, the depth, all of it. Suddenly, her body vibrated like a plucked guitar string.

Had she thought it was good before? She must not have known the real meaning of the word, not with him. Because as he gave a raw groan and hammered home, she could do little more than dig her fingers into the heavy muscles of his back and hang on for the ride, feeling like she had straddled a wild stallion that bucked and plunged, untamed and elemental. Yet he was gentle, too—in the clutch of his hand at her hip, the brace of his other arm to take some of his weight off her.

Their scents mingled; their urgent cries mixed in harmony. Her body lit, burned. Unfathomable sensations filled her mind, spinning in a maelstrom of heat, noise, and color that blurred together to a gray roar and sucked her down. Tighter and tighter she spun, the surface pleasure going to numb tingles as a deeper and more urgent wave began to build.

Her head crowded the white-painted headboard; his hands found the spindles. Still, the wave built, drowning out the creak of the box spring, the thud of the bedframe against the wall, the fleshy collisions as he filled her again and again, his face etching with exquisite pleasure-pain.

She glimpsed the moment of *almost there*—beautiful in the gold-washed light—through fluttering lids that soon shut again as the maelstrom snapped tight and went brilliantly still—a moment of pleasure-paralysis, an eye in the storm. Then it exploded outward, a giant firework of reds, greens, and blues that lit the insides of her eyelids and had her bowing into him, her mouth opening on wrenching cries of satisfaction. Wondrous pleasure. Buckets of it, swirling around her, through her, and then spinning higher once more when he shuddered and came, with a groan rattling in his throat and her name on his lips.

"*Ashley.*"

The word went through her, kindling another pleasure surge and tightening her inner muscles around him as he jabbed his hips into her in a primal rhythm as he came. She wrapped herself around him and hung on for the ride, her body echoing his, accepting his. Reveling in an orgasm that went on and on and on.

Eventually, though, the waves slowed and stopped. He shuddered in completion. They both did.

Then they rested.

The whole world, it seemed, took a little break. There was no need to breathe, no reason to think, no purpose in doing anything except lie there beneath him and exist. And for a voice inside her to whisper, quite simply, *Wow.*

Wow. Ty had said it before, and he would say it again. In a minute. After he regained the feeling in his extremities and shook off the almost overwhelming urge to sprawl out beside Ashley and sink into a coma.

Because, damn. He had also said that earlier, but she did that to him—stripped him down to the essentials, like monosyllables and lying there as if he'd been electrocuted. Which, come to think of it, probably wasn't that far off the mark. Because, wow and damn, they were good together. He had figured they would be, but it turned out that this was one of those rare and wonderful times when the reality far outstripped his imagination.

And yee-haw for that.

Disengaging, he lowered himself beside her, trying manfully not to flop, and gathered her against his side. Her soft hair fanned out across his shoulder, clinging here and there to his sweat-salted skin.

Figuring he should really say something, he went with "Whoa." Which at least wasn't a repeat.

She grinned without opening her eyes. "Ditto."

And that, it seemed, was that. Apparently she didn't need a huge rehash or more ground rules.

Tightening his arm around her, he dropped a kiss on the top of her head and let himself breathe her in. Then, summoning the energy that was slowly beginning to trickle back into his limbs, he eased away from her. "I'm going to . . ." He gestured down at himself. "You know, bathroom."

"Across the hall. Sorry, no en suite."

"Hey, you've got indoor plumbing."

"You don't?"

"I do now." He stood, snagging his jeans on the theory that not all of the blinds were down. "You want anything while I'm up? I believe you mentioned champagne and strawberries?"

"If you don't mind running downstairs, then yes. I'd love some champagne and nibbles. And then, I believe I saw a couple more condoms in your stash?"

Though he would've thought it impossible a minute ago, his blood heated at the thought. "I'll be right back."

14

Morning came early, but there was no way Ashley could stay asleep when there was so much to do, so much to *feel*. Excitement. Anticipation. Satisfaction. Tucked in beside Ty, eyes still closed, she smiled into the early-morning light.

She'd bet anything that the store would be packed today, she and Hen running ragged. Even better, she had a couple of hours before she had to be downstairs, and a gorgeous cowboy in her bed. And surely she could think of something interesting to do with *that*.

Ty's warm weight beside her dented the mattress and created a gravitational pull that snugged her up against his side. His steady breathing was a gentle wave, his chest rising and falling beneath her cheek and the hand she had splayed across his heart without meaning to. She might have thought he was still asleep, except for the gentle drag of his fingertips across the point of her hip, soft enough to be on the edge of tickling her, and striking little desire-sparks instead.

"Mmm." She angled her face to kiss his throat. "A little higher, if you please. Or lower. Lower would work, too."

A chuckle rumbled in his chest. "I would, but it seems that we've got company."

Her eyes flew open. "What!?"

Yellow eyes stared back into hers, coming from a triangular black face that hung, buzzardlike, from a scrawny black body sitting at the edge of the mattress.

"I didn't know you had a cat." Ty's voice was blurred with sleep. "Is that *the* cat?"

"Yes, it's *the* cat. Trapped and vetted, and now living here because I'm a sucker and Nick is a sneaky bastard."

He kissed the top of her head. "You're good people, Ashley Webb."

"Be warned—he's not very friendly." She figured the understatement counted as positive thinking. "In fact, this is the first time I've seen him since I turned him loose."

"This is a good sign, then." His fingers curved around her hip. "What's his name?"

"Petunia."

"Oh, sorry. Her name."

"No, it's a him. He just seemed like a Petunia to me."

"No wonder he looks pissed."

"Shut up. He doesn't care what I call him."

"Says you. Why not just chop his balls off?"

"Somebody already did that. Which sort of sucks, because it means he used to have a home."

"Now he's got a better one. Even if he has to answer to a name like that." To the cat, he said, "You should give her a chance. Trust me—once you get past the prickles, she's all heart."

"Prickles!" She poked him in the ribs. "I don't have any prickles. I'm the least prickly person I know."

"Are you sure? Maybe we should test that out." He ran his fingers up her ribs, making her squirm. "Where were those prickles again?"

She squeaked. "Stop that!" She didn't really mean it, though. There was something wonderful about how easy he was making this, uncomplicated and *fun*. No pressure, no big discussions. Just taking things as they came.

His hands went to the back of her knee. "Maybe they were over here."

Twisting against him, she returned fire, tickling him and making him shout. The cat thudded to the floor, shot them a look of utter contempt, and trotted out the door, tail flicking like a conductor's baton. That only made them laugh harder as they wrestled, trying for each other's most sensitive spots. Ashley's breath quickened, and maybe there were even some prickles as her skin tightened and her nipples peaked beneath his touch. She rolled atop him, straddled him, danced her fingers up his ribs, and—

Crash!

The sound of shattering glass came from the kitchen, sounding like a rock had come through the window.

Ty bolted upright, then out of bed. "Stay here." He was out of the bedroom before she had her feet on the floor, but she grabbed the Louisville Slugger she kept in the corner and pounded out behind him.

"I've got—" She skidded to a stop at the sight of a shattered green saucer on the floor and the cat seated between the matching cups and plates in the open-front cabinet where she kept the dishes. "Oh, for the love of— Petunia! Bad kitty!"

Ty frowned at her. "I told you to stay put."

"This is Three Ridges, not LA, and I can take care of myself." She held up the baseball bat. "See?" She decided not to tell him how much it mattered that he had gone through the door first. "You, on the other hand," she said to Petunia, who sat on the shelf, flirting his tail and looking smug, "better watch yourself."

The cat studied her, reached out a paw, and tapped a green teacup. It slid an inch. Teetered. *Tap.*

"Hey!" Ashley took a step forward. "Don't—"
Crash!

As the noise reverberated, the cat took off like he'd been launched from a slingshot. He hit the floor halfway across the room and headed for the hallway at warp speed.

"Oh, no, you don't. Get back here!" Ashley started after him, only to pull up at the entrance to the empty hallway. "Darn it, where does he *go*?"

A warm chuckle sounded right behind her. "Looking at you, I don't blame him for skedaddling."

"What?" She turned to find Ty grinning at her. "Why?"

He plucked the baseball bat from her choked-up two-handed grip, set it aside. "No reason." Leaning in, he brushed his lips across hers. "Morning, sunshine."

"Don't you *Morning, sunshine* me. Did you see what that beast did to my teacup?"

"It was clearly premeditated," he said solemnly. "Murder one, twenty to life."

"Shut up." She wasn't ready to laugh about it. But she could heave a sigh. "Well, I guess it's progress. At least he came out in the open. Twice." Turning, she headed for the kitchen.

"What are you doing?"

"Feeding him."

"I don't—hmm."

"I know, I know. I'm reinforcing bad behavior, giving him attention, blah, blah. But I like those dishes!"

She dumped some Happy Moist Kitty in Petunia's bowl, determinedly ignoring Ty's amusement—yes, she was naked and, yes, she probably sucked as an animal trainer, but everything she had read online suggested it wasn't about training a cat so much as arranging your life around them. Well, except for that Jackson Galaxy guy on TV, who seemed to be able to fix even the orneriest feline with a feather-tipped wand and a tall scratching post. *Note to self: Get a really tall scratching post.*

Lifting her chin, she swept back to the bedroom for some clothes.

She half expected Ty to follow her, give her more grief, but he didn't. *Probably still out there laughing at me,* she thought, but with more amusement than real annoyance. Okay, maybe slapping down a bowl of wet food hadn't been her finest moment. But really? Did the cat really have to go for the green ones? She liked them best.

"Fine," she said, emerging from the bedroom in yoga pants and a soft gray T-shirt. "Go ahead and laugh at me, but keep in mind that I don't have a clue what I'm doing. I've never had a pet before."

He wasn't waiting to give her grief, though. He was cleaning up the broken glass. And she was pretty sure she had never seen anything hotter than a naked guy wielding a dustpan and a broom.

He straightened—all muscles and hair-dusted skin, with the sun filtering through the kitchen window behind him. "Me neither."

What were they talking about again? Oh, right. Pets. "Really? I would've pegged you for a dog guy."

"I like 'em. Haven't had one of my own, though. Never seemed like exactly the right time." He lifted the dustpan. "Where do you want this?"

"I'll take it. You go get dressed—or not, your call, and I'm not going to complain if you declare it Naked Saturday—and I'll deal with this and get some breakfast started."

"You cook?"

"I can handle French toast."

"Got coffee?"

"Do you like toothpaste flavor?"

"What?"

"My coffeemaker has issues. We've been trying to work things out, but you know how it goes."

He handed over the rattling dustpan and claimed a kiss. "You're adorable."

"You're naked." And adorable. Sweet. Charming. And willing to sweep up broken glass. Her heart gave a silly little flutter.

"Back in a minute." He shot her a leer. "I like extra syrup."

"I'll bet you do." She watched him go—the rear

view was just as good as the front—and gave her head a little shake, bemused by how quickly things could change, evolve, become important. Not too important, though. Sobering a little—*Keep your feet on the ground*—she dumped the glass in the too-full recycling bin and said, "Okay, cat. You won this round. Don't get used to it, though . . . I'll get you some toys and a perch, but I'm getting a plant sprayer, too." Thank you, Internet. "And fair warning—you go after the blue pitcher and we're going to have a problem."

Would it be needlessly stubborn or a good next move to leave the pitcher out rather than hiding it away? Debating, she propped the recycling bin on her hip, unlocked the back door, and swung it open.

Wyatt stood on the landing with a fist raised to knock.

"Eee!" She jumped back.

"Sorry." He grinned. "Didn't mean to scare you. I guess you didn't get my message?"

"I was . . . I, um, didn't hear the phone ring." Pulse pounding, she set the recycling bin aside and shoved her hands in her pockets. Her heart tightened at the simple pleasure in his face and the shag of rusty-tipped brown hair that flopped across his brow, making him look like his younger self—back when he'd been her champion and she had been his princess.

Oh, hell. This wasn't going to end well.

Last night at the show, it had felt like she and her brother were on the verge of reconnecting. Now, as Ty's footsteps crossed the kitchen behind her, she knew they were teetering on the edge of something else entirely.

"A little slow on the French toast, darlin'? Want me to start warming things up for you?" Ty's voice carried loud and clear, and Wyatt's expression blanked as he locked eyes with her.

She didn't look away. Couldn't. "We've got company."

"Who—" Ty came up behind her, wearing jeans and not much else, and stalled. "Oh. Hell."

Wyatt's face went thunderous. "Ty." He looked between the two of them and scowled. "Goddamn it, Ashley. Now what have you gone and done?"

Ty figured he should stay out of the first salvo—this was between Ashley and her brother, and his stepping in would only make it worse. But he didn't care for the look in the other man's eyes, and he didn't at all like his tone. Putting a hand on her shoulder—and seeing Wyatt's eyes follow the move—he said, "We should talk."

"You're damn right we should."

Ashley bumped back against Ty, trying to clear the door, but he held his ground and said, "We'll meet you at the diner in forty-five minutes."

A muscle ticked at the corner of Wyatt's jaw, and his balled-up fists said he was on the edge of taking a swing. Instead, he gave a short, tight nod. "Fine. The diner in forty-five."

"No, dang it. That's *not* fine." Ashley jabbed Ty with an elbow, pushing him back a pace, and turned to look up at him. She wasn't furious, though there was an edge of anger alongside her determination. "I appreciate you trying to get us to neutral territory, but this isn't your fight. This is between me and Wyatt."

Maybe, but he would need to clear the air, too. "You wouldn't be having it if I hadn't spent the night."

"You wouldn't have spent the night if I hadn't wanted you to." She nudged him back. "Go on. Please. I'll call you later."

"You're kicking me out?" It should have been surprising how much he wanted to stay. Family dynamics hadn't ever been his strong suit.

"For now. You're welcome to circle back around tonight after hours. Say, seven? I'll do better than French toast."

Wyatt growled low in his throat.

"Seven it is." He leaned in and brushed his lips across hers. "I'll get the rest of my clothes and leave you two alone."

A few minutes later, as the diesel rumble of Ty's truck faded from the back lot, Ashley pointed Wyatt to a stool at the breakfast bar. "Sit down. You're looming, and I want French toast."

Doing a not so slow boil, she turned her back on him and went to the fridge for eggs and milk, determined to hold it together, keep things civil. She loved her brother, but she wasn't twelve anymore. Even so, it sucked to get to this point so soon after last night, the nosedive from *I'm proud of you* to *What have you done?*

It was a long minute before one of the barstools scraped along the floor. Her shoulders came down a notch, but they still had a long way to go. She hated knowing he was mad at her, disappointed in her, but some days it seemed like that was all she could manage when it came to her brother.

Wyatt sighed heavily, and she knew if she turned, she would find him shaking his head. She cracked an egg into a mixing bowl instead.

"Talk to me, Ash. Tell me what's going on in that brain of yours."

She thought about it for a moment, then did a head-shake of her own. "No."

"What do you mean, no?"

"It's a complete sentence." But, as usual, she couldn't leave it at that. Not with him. "He's a good man. Admit it."

"He's an excellent cowboy." Which they both knew wasn't necessarily the same thing, as plenty of cowboys were piss-poor human beings. Like their father. Wyatt added, "I'm not trying to be a dick here, Ash. I'm trying to keep you from making another mistake."

She beat the eggs too hard. "I'm spending time with a smart, interesting, down-to-earth guy who plays a mean guitar. And who, for the record, helped me out a whole lot more over the past week than you did. Krista trusts him with her guests, everyone I know likes him, and we're on the same page relationship-wise—as in, neither of us is in the market to get serious. We're just having fun. Lots of it. How is that a mistake?"

Deciding he didn't rank French toast, she dumped the eggs straight in the pan.

"You know how you get." Wyatt sketched a hand around. "Today it's making him breakfast rather than getting a jump on things downstairs. Tomorrow it'll be cutting out early to go for a ride and watch the sun come down over the ridge. The next thing you know, you're hiring more help and leaving Hen to run the shop while you—"

"What, go out on trail rides with him and the dudes? News flash—I tried working for you and I didn't like it."

He gave her his patented *My logic is way better than yours* look. "That's not the point."

"You're right. It's not. The *point* is that you're acting like I've already done those things." The eggs were overdone, overbeaten, over-everything, and starting to smoke a little. She reached for a plate, grabbed air where the green one should have been, and pulled down the red one instead. Dumping the eggs, she banged the overloaded plate down in front of Wyatt. "You're not even giving me a chance to get this right."

He eyed the plate. "I think your eggs just bounced. And why are they black?"

She ground her molars. "I added lots of pepper." And, okay, maybe some soot. "This is the way Mom used to make them."

"Still does, when Jack doesn't get to the kitchen first." He nudged the plate away. "You go ahead. I already had breakfast, and you're going to need some fuel."

"For?"

"Long day at the store, right? Cleanup, sales, prepping for your clinic thing."

It mattered that he had paid attention last night, at

least a little. Still, she couldn't afford to let him off the hook. Not yet. "Right. For a minute there, I thought you were talking about needing my strength for later, when Ty comes over."

Under any other circumstances, his wince would've made her laugh. "You had to go there, didn't you?"

She propped her elbows on the counter and leaned in. "Look, I was going to pull you aside after dinner on Sunday and give you the heads-up about me and Ty. I'd apologize for the whoops-half-naked-guy-in-my-kitchen part, except that you were the one who just drove on over. Heck, if you'd been a few minutes earlier, you would've caught both of us in here naked, debating Fiesta ware with the cat."

He pinched the bridge of his nose. "Ashley . . ."

"Wy-att." She mimicked his put-upon intonation. "Look, you don't have to worry about me this time—I promise. I'm not going to follow Ty to LA for a record deal that never materializes, and I'm not going to work three jobs to keep a roof over his head and pay to record a demo. First, because Ty isn't that kind of guy, and second—and more importantly—because I've learned my lesson." Hearing her voice echo in the small space, she softened her tone to say, "So lay off. We're just enjoying each other. Since when is that a crime?"

"We're not talking about a felony here—don't be melodramatic." He sighed. "But do what you want, I guess." The *You always do* came through loud and clear.

She wanted to argue, wanted to say that wasn't fair, but it was what she was fighting for, wasn't it? For him to give her the room to do what was right for *her*, not what he thought she should be doing. Softly, she said, "I'm not trying to drive you mental, Wyatt. I'm really not."

A telling silence dragged out between them. Then one corner of his mouth kicked up. "That's just a bonus, right?"

"Something like that." She hesitated, told herself not to push it, but had to ask. "So. Are we okay?"

"Do I have to eat these eggs?"

"I guess not."

"Then we're good." He had that closed-off look in his eyes, though—the one that said he was agreeing with her because he didn't like fighting, either, but he wasn't totally buying what she was selling.

The bump of disappointment was what she got for pushing. *Don't ask if you know you're probably not going to like the answer.* "Well. I should get dressed and head downstairs." She slanted him a look. "I could use some help pulling the stage apart."

His chair scraped across the floor as he pushed back and stood. "No can do. I've got stuff back at the ranch."

What was that about not asking if she wasn't going to like the answer? Summoning a smile—it was her store, her responsibility, and maybe that was his point—she said, "No prob. I'll see you tomorrow?"

"For Abby's party, you mean?"

She hid the wince—mostly. "Yep. Exactly." *Yeowch.* She was the worst aunt on the planet. How had she forgotten that tomorrow was the kidlet's first birthday? And she had been planning on springing the Ty thing on her brother after dinner. Yikes.

Wyatt didn't quite snort as he headed for the door. "See you then," he said on the way through. But then he stuck his head back in and said, "And, Ash? Don't hurt yourself putting the store back together. You can't afford to be off your game. You've got, what, a month left before that next big payment? Better get cracking."

"Out!" she ordered, and he chuckled.

The door closed behind him; his boot steps went down the stairs. It wasn't until she heard a truck door slam that she let herself cross the kitchen and look out the window to watch him drive away. It was stupid to bother, stupid to feel, even for a second, the flash of panic that said she might not ever see him again.

"He's not Wylie," she said between gritted teeth. "You're due at the ranch tomorrow afternoon to blow out birthday candles." *Stupid, stupid, stupid.* Unhooking her fingers from the windowsill, she pushed away. "Time to get to work." But when she turned, her eyes lit on the counter where Wyatt had been sitting.

There was a piece of paper that hadn't been there before. It was the size and shape of a check—the kind that came with zeros that watched her like little eyes.

"Oh, hell." Stomach sinking, she approached it warily, hissing out a breath when she saw a five followed by three eyes.

Five thousand dollars from his and Krista's personal account. The notation line in the lower left was empty, like he expected her to know whether this was his way of saying he was proud of her and wanted her to have a cushion if she needed it, or whether he thought there was no way she could make it on her own, so he was bailing her out while shaking his head and muttering, *Again, blast her.*

Maybe he would've explained it if he hadn't found his head wrangler hanging out in her kitchen, half dressed. Now, though, they were back on opposite sides of the same old debate, and she felt like crap.

She and Ty should've had a magical morning to follow up their incredible night. They should've . . . Well, *shoulda, coulda, woulda.* Things rarely went the way she planned—she should be used to that by now. *Sigh.*

Picking up the check, she grimaced, wanting to tear it up, turn it into a satisfying confetti shower, and toss it in the bin with the broken cup and saucer. Or hand it back to him in person tomorrow. Strike a blow for independence.

Instead, she opened one of her junk drawers, pawed through, and found the old-school address book Jack had given her years ago, claiming not to trust technology. And though she wasn't sure what she thought about the check, it seemed right to open the book to the *W*'s, where two pages were filled with contact info for Wyatt, dozens of numbers and addresses she had dutifully added when he touched down, then scratched out when he moved on again, until he finally found his place at Mustang Ridge. Sandwiching the check between the pages, she shut the little book and tucked it away.

Then, sliding the drawer closed, she looked at the inedible eggs—*Hello, stress cooking*—and called, "Hey, Petunia! Do you like bacon?" She had a half hour before she needed to be downstairs, and she owed the cat some one-on-one time. "Here, kitty, kitty. Where'd you go, you little monster? I think we need to set some ground rules."

Ty got back to the ranch in the peaceful Saturday lull between when the shuttle bus left with one crop of guests and when it came back with the next. Figuring he should keep a low profile until he and Wyatt had it out, he hit his apartment to grab a couple of day-old muffins and a cup of instant, and headed back downstairs.

The barn was clean and the riding horses were turned out to graze, as Saturday was their day off, too. Only two of the stalls were occupied—fat little Marshmallow the pony was on a diet, and Betty Crocker, the cow that Ty had run in last week, wasn't doing well. With one prominent hip cocked, her ribs more visible than they should be, and her head low, she looked old and tired.

"Hey, Betty." He propped an elbow where the wooden sides of the stall stopped and the metal bars started. "How's it going?"

Instead of returning her to the high pasture, Krista had decided to keep her in a stall for a couple of days and stuff some food in her. The vet hadn't found anything really wrong with her, but warned that she was getting up there in age. Whether Betty was a pain in the ass or not, Krista wanted to give her a chance to rebound. If she didn't . . . Well, better to stuff her full of treats and put her down than let her wear out to the point that the coyotes or wolves started hassling her.

So far, there didn't seem to be much rebounding going on. If anything, she had lost even more weight since she'd been in the barn.

"You need to eat," Ty told her. "Either that, or learn how to photosynthesize, which I doubt is going to happen." Though Krista seemed to think the beast was some sort of cowhide-covered ninja, so maybe it was possible. He took a swig of his coffee, bit into his second muffin.

Betty's head came up. Nostrils flaring, she took a step in his direction.

"You want some muffin?" Why not? It was corn-flavored, with a hint of Gran's famous sourdough. Nothing in there a cow couldn't eat. Running open the door, he broke off a piece and offered it on a flattened hand. And darned if the old bossy didn't come right over to him and use gentle lips to take the muffin chunk.

Eyes a few notches brighter than before, she looked longingly at the rest of it.

"I'll split it with you." Heck, calories were calories.

"Watch that she doesn't get under your guard," a voice said behind him.

Wyatt's voice.

Okay. Here we go. Tossing the rest of his muffin in the shallow feed pan in the corner of Betty's stall, Ty ran the door shut and turned, bracing in case Wyatt was the sort to punch first, dialogue later. "You want an apology?"

He didn't get a haymaker, but he sure got a narrow-eyed glare from the other man. "You want to give me one?"

Ty had been going back and forth on that. He owned his choices, but he didn't want to undercut whatever Ashley had said to her brother. Not to mention, they were both consenting adults. "I'm sorry it played out the way it did, but I'm not sorry it happened. Your sister is an amazing woman."

Wyatt bristled. "As she reminded me in no uncertain terms back just now, I don't have any say in who she sleeps with. Never did."

The tone put an ugly twist in Ty's gut, but he hung on to his outer calm. "You want to take this outside, anyway, take a couple of shots at me?"

"Neither. I want to give you a friendly warning."

"I'd rather make my own call on things—thanks."

"I know, MYOB. Except this place"—Wyatt's wave encompassed the big barn, with its glossy mustangs and neatly ordered guest tack room—"is my business. Or one of them, anyway. And it's Krista's *only* business. Since she's mine, that makes you doubly my business."

Are you pissed because you want Ashley to do things your way, or because you're afraid I'll up and quit when things flame out? Neither option deserved airtime. "I've got a contract through the end of the season, and no intention of going back on my word. And that's all you're getting from me." At least until he talked to Ashley, made sure that Wyatt had left things okay with her. Maybe not even then.

Whatever happened between Ty and Ashley, it wasn't a family affair. It was theirs.

Wyatt scowled. "Krista warned me you play things pretty close to your vest."

"I'm not playing. Just keeping some separation between my job and my private life. Which isn't always easy around here."

"Look, Ashley means the world to me, and this place means the world to Krista. I don't want to see anything bad happen to either of them."

"Me neither." But he wasn't making any promises beyond his contract. Things happened. Plans changed. "If that's it?" When Wyatt didn't say anything, just kept looking at him like that was supposed to shake something else loose, Ty touched the brim of his hat. "I'll be on my way, then. Oh, and news flash? Your cow just sucked down my corn muffins. If you're serious about putting some meat back on her, you might want to think about a diet change. Pancakes might do the trick." He almost said *French toast*, but figured he'd better not. Wyatt might swing that punch, after all.

15

On Sunday, Ashley put in a long morning at the store before heading up to Mustang Ridge. As she drove between the big stone pillars that marked the main entrance, her ears were still ringing with a whole lot of, *What do you mean, you can't order it for me in pink?* and *Of course these super-skinny pants will fit me. I had a pair just like them in the eighties, and didn't you know that vanity sizing is a myth?*

She felt a little guilty about handing things off to Hen for the last few hours of the day, but maybe the traffic would taper off some. Or, you know, maybe not. *Fingers crossed.* Thirty days and counting. *Eep.*

With a stuffed-toy panther strapped into the passenger seat—she figured Abby had enough toy horses, and it had reminded her of Petunia—and several bottles of wine on the theory that a first birthday party was as much for the grown-ups as anything, she was no longer in danger of being the Worst Aunt Ever. Still, after parking in the main lot, she hesitated.

She and Ty were good—very good after last night—

and she thought she and Wyatt had left things okay, more or less. But . . .

The door to the main house flew open and Krista marched out, fisted her hands on her hips, and glared. Jenny, Shelby, and Danny were right behind her, making an imposing quartet, all of them wearing expressions that hit somewhere between *Well?* and *What the hell, girlfriend?* Which matched the texts Ashley had been getting for the past twenty-four hours, and hadn't been sure how to answer.

The Girl Zone knew she had been keeping secrets.

Oops.

Mouthing *Sorry!* and holding up both hands as if all four of them were toting shotguns rather than dirty looks, she got out of the car. "I can explain." Sort of. She wasn't really sure what had kept her from calling yesterday—the store had been busy, sure, but she could have made time. Clearly should have. She hadn't been ready to talk about her and Ty, though. She had wanted to keep it to herself for a day, hugging the memories close, taking them out one at a time to relish them, integrate them into an altered reality entitled *Ashley's Got a New Man*. She would have gotten that chance, too, if it hadn't been for Wyatt showing up.

Well, the can was open now, and the worms were having a party of their own.

Reaching back into the car, she pulled out the wine and the panther, which had a pink bow around its neck, affixed to a birthday card. Holding up the alcohol, she said, "I come bearing bribes."

Krista blocked the top step, tapping one silver-toed boot so it echoed on the wide boards of the porch. "We're not cheap, but we can be bought."

"Three bottles of that red you like with the creepy kid on the label." The too-solemn blond child of indeterminate gender was wearing an old-fashioned nightshirt and was probably supposed to look like a cherub, but the knowing eyes and weird smirk were more Chucky than Cupid. The wine was good, though. "And details. I promise."

Some details, at any rate. She hadn't realized until yesterday, thinking it through, how weird it would be to talk about Ty with his boss-slash-friend. Krista had known Ty for years, Ashley for only a couple of weeks. The whole idea took *It's complicated* to a whole new level, didn't it? But Krista and the others were the Girl Zone, darn it, and she wasn't going to back away from them—or anything else that was important to her—just because she had a new guy. Especially when the new guy was temporary and casual, and her friendships with Krista, Jenny, Shelby, and Danny were anything but.

When she mounted the stairs leading up, though, Krista didn't budge, except to hold out a hand. "I'll take the present in for Abby. Mom made a display in the dining room. The party starts in a half hour, so you'd better plan on talking fast, and making it good." Snagging the stuffed toy, she spun on her heel and stalked into the main house, followed by Jenny and Shelby. Who at least shot her little finger wiggles as they disappeared through the door.

Danny stayed behind, her expression a mix of sympathy and chiding. "You could have told us, you know. We're good at keeping the lid on things."

"It wasn't you guys I was worried about." Ashley stared through the door, feeling even more awkward than she had when she'd first arrived at the ranch, unannounced, ahead of schedule for the wedding and having just accidentally created a blowout between Danny and Sam. They had gotten past it—obviously, as they were engaged now—but she hadn't known back then how it would play out. Just like she wasn't sure how this was going to go. "How mad is she, really?" Either she had done more damage than she'd expected, or Krista was playing it to the hilt.

Danny lifted a shoulder. "Hurt is more like it. She didn't like hearing about you and Ty from Wyatt."

Who had probably been stomping around, bellowing like a newly branded bull. "Should I apologize?"

"Are you sorry?"

"That she's hurt? Yes. That I took the time I needed to get things straight in my head?" Or as straight as she could, anyway. "No. It was what I needed to do."

"Then don't apologize. She'll get over it, because that's what friends do. Especially if you stop hovering and come in already! Like she said, we don't have much time."

Ashley hesitated at the threshold, still not entirely sure of her moves when it came to the Girl Zone. "Is there cake?"

"It's Mustang Ridge. There's always cake."

*   *   *

With Gran and Dory busy in the kitchen, Rose fussing with the party decorations in the dining room, Ed entertaining the baby in the great room, and guests and family members to-ing and fro-ing everywhere, the girls ended up crammed into Krista's office with the door shut and two big bowls on the desk, one of cake scraps, the other of leftover buttercream.

Jenny took charge of the wine while Shelby and Danny cleared drifts of catalogs off the two spare chairs. Krista took her usual spot behind the desk, then spun her chair so she was looking out the window toward the distant mountains.

Ashley leaned back against the door with her hands in her pockets. "I'm sorry, you guys. Krista, you especially. This wasn't how I wanted it to go, how I intended for you to find out. It's just . . . well, it's complicated. Ty and I are . . ."

The chair spun and Krista fixed her with a gimlet stare. "You're sleeping with him."

"Yes, I—"

"Since when?"

"Friday night. We—"

"You're sure?"

"Excuse me?"

"It didn't start before then? Say, Thursday?"

"What the— No, it was Friday. Two nights ago. After the fashion show, he came back to help me clean up. And, well . . ."

"Touchdown!" Shelby did a boogie-woogie pirouette, then held out both hands. "Pay up, you guys!"

"Dang it!" Looking disgusted, Krista slapped a twenty on the desk. "Fine. You win." She wrinkled her nose at Ashley. "And for the record, I hate losing."

"Losing what?"

"The when-will-Ashley-and-Ty-do-the-deed? pool, of course." Danny handed her twenty directly to Shelby. "I had tonight. I figured you'd wait until the dust settled from the show, maybe give Wyatt some warning. Guess I underestimated the sparks."

Ashley choked on a laugh. "You guys were betting on me?"

"On the two of you, yes." Jenny handed out the wine in paper party cups emblazoned with Disney princesses. "I think this calls for a Girl Zone toast."

Face burning, Ashley took hers. "You guys are— Hey, wait." She eyed Jenny. "What was your guess?"

"Last Tuesday." When the others hooted, Jenny shrugged, grinning. "What can I say? Ty always struck me as the kind of guy who takes what he wants when he wants it. Given the hours he was putting in at your shop, we all figured he wanted it bad."

"And when Ty wants something bad . . ." Krista fanned herself. "Hoo, baby!"

Lifting her wine—somehow making the move look elegant, even when it involved a paper princess cup— Shelby declared, "To Ashley and Ty. The four of us would just like to say . . . *We told you so!*"

The others lifted their cups with a chorus of "Told ya so!"

Ashley laughed, tossed back her wine in two long

swallows, and banged the cup on Krista's desk. "Fine. You win. He's amazing. Barkeep? Another round, if you please!"

Jenny tipped the bottle over her cup, but didn't let the wine flow. "It'll cost you."

Ashley pursed her lips, already feeling the glow of friendship and alcohol. "I'm not reimbursing your twenty. Not my fault you thought I was easier than I really am." By only a few days, but still.

"Not money. Details. Tell us everything."

"I don't know." She looked around at the expectant faces. "Don't you think that's a little weird? Some of you guys have known him forever."

"Sure, but we like you better," Jenny said, still hovering the wine bottle over her cup.

"We love you both," Krista corrected. "But gossip is gossip, and what gets said in the Girl Zone stays in the Girl Zone. So start with the other night at the Rope Burn, when you said you were going to the ladies' room but followed him out back instead." She hooked a finger in the rim of the frosting bowl and pulled it toward herself. "Unless you don't want any of this?"

She did want it. She wanted the buttercream, the cake scraps, the wine. Most of all, she wanted to wrap herself in their friendship, in the feeling of belonging to them and them to her. "Okay, okay, you win. I'll talk." She waited while Jenny refilled her cup, then dipped a cake scrap in the icing, popped it in her mouth, and washed it down with a healthy swallow. Thus fortified, she said, "But I'm going to have to go back further than the other night at the 'Burn. Lots further."

"Back further . . ." Krista's jaw dropped. "Ashley Webb!" She nearly screamed it. "Tell me that you did *not* hook up with my wedding singer!"

As the others roared, Ashley hung her head in mock shame. "Sor-ry." Then she grinned sidelong at her friends. "Except I'm not sorry, really. For any of it." So, starting with the wedding, she told them everything.

Most of it, anyway. She confessed to having fudged her identity when she and Ty first met, and then convincing him to pretend they were strangers. She told them about unloading lumber with him in the rain, and about talking to him while they painted. And she told them how, after she invited him to stay the night, he had carried her upstairs. She left out the specifics on what had followed, but they seemed okay with that. Her head was doing a wine-and-sugar spin by the time she got to Petunia murdering her dishes the next morning and the look on Wyatt's face when Ty strolled into the kitchen half naked. And by the time she finished describing how she had cooked rubber eggs while telling Wyatt to stay out of her business, the others were whooping and wiping laugh-tears from their eyes.

"So there you have it," she said. "Ty came back last night for French toast and stayed for nonrubbery eggs this morning. And now I'm sucking down cake with you guys."

"I'm so happy for you." Danny slung an arm around her neck in a strangle-hug. "These guys have really been singing his praises, you know."

"It's easy to do," Krista said staunchly. "Trust me— there were times I used to wish there was a spark between us, because he checks all of the other boxes. He's smart, loyal, easy to talk to, and even easier on the eyes. He can ride a horse like nobody's business—hello, even Brutus likes him, and Brutus doesn't like anybody. The guests love him, Abby loves him—heck, *I* love him."

"And he's musical," Jenny put in with a nod in Ashley's direction.

"Not to mention," Shelby added, "he was engaged before and it wasn't his fault things broke up—I heard she cheated. Which means he's up for the home-and-hearth thing, and all he needs is to find the right woman."

That put a thorn-sharp pang in the vicinity of Ashley's heart. "It's not like that."

"No pressure!" Krista said quickly. "If it works, it works. If it doesn't, it doesn't. We just want you to be happy." She lifted her cup. "To Ashley!"

"Hear, hear!" the others chorused, and drained their little cups, not seeming to notice that Ashley was half a beat behind.

As if on cue, there was a knock on the door, and Rose caroled, "You-hoo. Are you guys ready for a party?"

"We sure are!" Krista swung open the door to her mom, who had an armful of bright-eyed baby girl. "There she is!" Krista swooped up her daughter into her arms and gave her a giggling bounce. "Yay for more cake! But presents first, right? And pictures. Lots of pictures!"

There wasn't just cake at the party—there was Cake with a capital *C*, courtesy of Gran and Dory. Delicately

piped and ringed with cutouts of galloping cartoon po-
nies and cows, the brightly colored two-tiered affair
was topped with a fat candle in the shape of the number 1, and had Abby's eyes getting impressively big
when Gran carried it in and lit the wick.

"Ooo!" The baby clapped her pudgy hands. Then
again, she had made a pretty easy audience, having
gone wide-eyed over everything from her presents to
the sight of Wyatt's scruffy gray dog, Klepto, wearing
a party hat.

Now she squealed with delight as friends and family linked hands around the big dining table and
launched into "Happy birthday to you . . ."

At the far end of the table, sandwiched between
Danny and Shelby—and far from Wyatt, who had
given her a gruff "Glad you could make it" when she'd
come into the room and had ignored her since—Ashley
sang along with gusto, figuring "Happy Birthday" was
one of those songs where if enough people joined in,
the bum notes canceled each other out and it sounded
kind of nice. Which it did, at least to her ears, as she
yodeled, "Happy birrrrth-day, dear Abby . . . Happy
birthday to you!" She finished on an unlikely warbling
note, then added a, "Woo-hoo! Go, Abby!"

"Come on, sweetie," Krista coached, puffing out her
cheeks. "Blow!" Abby produced a tiny puff of air, Wyatt snuffed out the candle with his fingers, and everyone cheered.

As Gran set about cutting the cake, the couples
turned to each other for hugs, kisses, and some *Remember when ours were that little?* Standing alone at the edge

of the crowd, Ashley suffered an uncharacteristic pang that she was the only one who wasn't part of a family unit within the larger sprawl. Most of the time, being at Mustang Ridge made her want her space. Today, the whole friends-and-family thing was making her downright sappy.

"Here." Gran appeared at her elbow with two perfect slices of cake on a plate. "These are for you."

"I can't possibly eat both!" She was stuffed, still a little buzzed.

Crinkles appeared at the corners of sparkling blue eyes. "Then you should find someone to help you with them." Two spoons appeared, wrapped in a HAPPY BIRTHDAY PRINCESS napkin. "Might I suggest looking in the barn?"

16

Most days after the riding was done and the guests had gone off to their cabins to get washed up for dinner or down to the lake to splash around, Ty put in a couple of more hours with the horses, checking for bumps or sore spots, going over their riggings for worn places, or doing a little extra training to bring along the newer mustangs and keep them happy working in the guest string.

Sometimes, though, it wasn't the horses that needed the extra training.

"That's right," he said, keeping his voice even and his energy low. "You want to take nice, easy brush-strokes in the direction of the hair. See how Marshmallow is moving his mouth, kind of licking and chewing? That means he's relaxed, but he's still paying attention to you. Good job."

Okay, maybe that was pushing it, seeing how the fat gray pony was looking longingly at the pile of hay in the corner of the big box stall, over near where Geoff's foster mom, Marybeth, was standing. Pretty and comfortable-looking, she had her hands in her pockets, and her expression was the same sort of neutral Ty tended to use the first couple of times he worked with a fresh-caught mustang. It was a mix of cautious optimism and readiness to act if things went wrong, glossed over with a whole lot of *What will be, will be.*

Marybeth and her husband hadn't had the boy long—only a couple of months—but it was clear that they cared. Which was more than a lot of kids like Geoff had going for them.

"I want a real horse. Not a stupid pony." Small for his nine years, reed-thin and stark-looking, with jet-black hair and skin so pale it was almost gray, even after a half day out in the backcountry sun, Geoff wore the scowl of a much bigger, older boy. Which wouldn't have been so much of a problem if it hadn't been paired with a whole-body jitter and a quick temper that had flared up out on the trail today.

Ty had nipped it in the bud, but didn't plan on subjecting Marshmallow to a repeat. "Show me that you can handle yourself with this guy over the next couple of days, and we'll see about letting you try Duke. Right now, though, what is Marshmallow telling you?"

A half hour before, Geoff would've told Ty to go do something anatomically improbable. Now, though, the kid actually took a couple of seconds of almost still-ness, and looked at the pony. "His head is up and his ears are back." The moment of clarity was followed by a sulky grumble. "I told you he doesn't like me."

"He liked you just fine a minute ago. What changed?"

"Nothing. He's just a dumb pony."

"Really?"

Silence.

When Marybeth shifted, looking like she was going to do a *Mr. Reed asked you a question, Geoffrey*, Ty gave her a little headshake. As with a new mustang, there were times you just had to wait things out, give the connections a chance to form on their own.

Horse or human, the lesson stuck better when the pupil figured it out for himself.

After a minute, the brushstrokes that had started getting harder and faster slowed down, eased up, and the boy's feet stopped making impatient patterns in the shavings. More, the simmering anger drained from the tense lines of his arms and shoulders, which were so thin beneath the Mustang Ridge T-shirt. Huffing out a breath, the boy said, "Maybe I was starting to get mad. It wasn't at him, though."

"Horses don't know the difference. They just know that something's upsetting the person who's supposed to be protecting them, and they worry about what's going to happen next. They think that maybe it'll be something bad, something that hurts, and they won't be able to get away. That would be pretty scary, don't you think?"

Marybeth drew a shallow breath. She had confided to Ty that while Child Services hadn't given her and Lawrence much information on Geoff's background, what little they had gotten suggested a pattern of profound neglect, maybe even abuse. From the way Geoff had flinched away the first couple of times Ty reached out to correct his position in the saddle, that seemed like more than a *maybe*.

When anger stirred, though, Ty tamped it down. Wouldn't help the pony, definitely wouldn't help the kid.

He figured Geoff was going to fall back on the *Stupid pony should know better* refrain, but the kid surprised him. He actually stopped brushing, moved to the pony's head, and crouched down off to one side the way Ty had showed him, making himself low and soft, and staying in full view of the pony's side-set eye. Holding out a hand, he said, "I'm sorry, Marshmallow. I wasn't mad at you."

Eyes softening, the pony stretched his stubby neck and blew on the boy's fingers. Geoff darted a look toward the adults, then reached up to ruffle the thick, silvery mane.

If the two had been alone, the kid might've said more to the pony—about what it was like to have CPS take him away from his junkie parents, stick him in a new school, then foster him out and move him to yet another town. Or maybe how sometimes he didn't even know why he was mad; the fury just took over and made him want to lash out, break something. Hurt himself. Hurt someone else.

Ty wasn't ready to leave him on his own yet, even with Marshmallow, so he hunkered down to the kid's eye level and said, "I'm proud of you, Geoff. It takes guts to recognize that you're angry, and a whole lot of toughness to rein in the mad and level yourself off."

The boy avoided his eyes and shrugged. "Whatever."

"Still. Good job." Ty straightened, his knees giving

the creak-pops that said they'd had too many rough landings over the years. "How about you say good-bye to Marshmallow and gather up the brushes for me? It's getting on toward dinnertime."

Pleased with Geoff's progress, he let himself out of the stall, turned toward the main barn doors—

And caught sight of a goddess coming toward him, bearing a plate of birthday cake.

Backlit by the sunlight showing through the open barn doors, Ashley was wearing a floaty skirt that showed the shape of her legs in tantalizing silhouette. Her hair flowed around her, warm honey against the soft white of her shirt, and her silver-tipped boots rang on the concrete surface of the aisle. She looked like a country girl on the way to a square dance, only better, and the sight of her did something strange to his insides.

He had left her bed some eight hours earlier, but it could've been eight seconds, the way she had stayed at the edge of his mind all day. At the same time, it could've been days since he had touched her, kissed her, the way his body revved at the sight. He had only known her—what, a couple of weeks? But she was definitely under his skin.

"Ashley." He crossed to meet her. "Hey." Giving in to the urge, he leaned in and brushed his lips across hers, catching a fleeting impression of her generous warmth and the smell of springtime. "Things go okay at the party?"

She gave a *so-so* wiggle with her free hand. "About as well as I expected."

"That bad, huh?"

"He'll come around."

"I don't want to make trouble between you two."

"He should be the one worried about making trouble." She looked past him. "I'm sorry. I'm interrupting."

"We're just finishing up. I was doing a little extra with Marybeth here and Geoff . . ." Ty gave the aisle a quick scan. "Geoff?"

"I'm in here!" the boy called from a half-open doorway farther down the way.

It was Betty Crocker's stall.

Hell. Picturing a one-cow stampede, with little Geoff trampled and Betty hightailing it for Gran's kitchen, Ty double-timed it toward the door, with Ashley right on his heels. "Come on out of there, Geoff," he began, but then stopped, rocking back on his heels at the sight of the boy standing there with his arms wrapped around Betty's neck and a huge grin on his face.

What was more, standing there with her lips doing a little *nuzzle-nuzzle-nuzzle* against the tail of his T-shirt, Betty didn't look anything like the depressed, dispirited animal he'd been dealing with, or the fire-breathing demon-cow Krista had warned him about.

She looked . . . normal. Sweet, even. And Geoff had gone still, intense. And very, very gentle.

"Awww," Marybeth cooed. "What's his name?"

"*Her* name," Ty corrected. "It's Betty Crocker." He studied Geoff for a beat as a suspicion that'd taken root the other day gelled to a near certainty. More, he had an idea. "You know, Geoff, she could probably use a friend like you. She's had a pretty hard life."

Brown eyes flicked to his. "Yeah?"

"Yeah. However it happened, she wound up wandering out in the middle of nowhere, all by herself, until somebody saw her and called Animal Control. They're like Child Services, only for animals. And they called us."

Geoff studied the big head that rested so close to his own. "So she's a foster, too?"

"Of a sort. But lately she hasn't been eating much, and we've been worried about her. I wonder if she might eat if you asked her to, though. In fact . . ." He glanced over at Ashley, and nodded to the cake. "Do you mind?"

"She likes cake?"

"Worth a try. She sucked down one of my muffins the other day, and I figure that if Gran did the baking, it's all-natural, or close to it." He shrugged. "Big cow, little cake, can't do much harm and it might do some good."

"Then let her eat cake." Ashley handed over the plate.

Using one of the spoons, he busted up the two generous slices of birthday cake into thumb-size pieces, then held out the plate. "Here you go, Geoff. Give her a piece or two. Flat hand, like we talked about, and keep your fingers away from her teeth."

Betty's ears flapped, and she let loose with a mournful-sounding "*Moooo.*"

Bracing himself to jump in there if things went south, Ty cautioned, "If she gets grabby, just let her have . . ." He trailed off. Because darned if the big cow didn't lip a small blob of icing from the kid's palm as gently as he'd ever seen, then wait, with her eyes bright, her ears up, and her stringy cow tail flapping like she was a brand-new calf that'd just gotten its first taste of its mama's milk. "I'll be damned," he said, then, "Sorry."

"Go for it," Marybeth said, grinning. "Look at you, Geoff. You're a regular cow whisperer."

And darned if the kid didn't shoot them a big, beautiful smile. "She likes me!"

"Okay," Ty said, "next step. Try tossing a couple more pieces in that pile of hay over there. See if she'll eat it."

The cow butted him gently, but Geoff nudged her away. "No, Betty. Ty says you need to eat some hay, too." He led her to the corner and tossed a blob of cake into the pile.

As Betty considered the hay with little enthusiasm, two new sets of bootfalls sounded in the aisle.

Ty craned around and caught sight of Krista coming toward them, with Abby propped on her hip, clutching a stuffed toy. Wyatt was right beside them, his eyes going flinty when he caught sight of the other man standing beside his sister. Ty put a warning finger to his lips. "We're having a moment here." *And if you want to start something, let's take it outside.*

"You're— Oh!" Taking in the scene with one quick glance, Krista started forward. "I don't think that's such a good . . ." Her steps faltered, though, and her expression took on a hint of wonder as Betty nudged Geoff's leg with her head, then condescended to forage for the treat he had just tossed, getting a mouthful of hay in the process.

Ashley caught Ty's hand and squeezed. "Look! She's eating!"

Wyatt just scowled at her. "Hmph."

Shifting closer to Ashley—*Yeah, that's right, deal with it*—Ty said to Krista, "Seems like you guys had it wrong, trying to keep her penned up in the high country." He nodded to Geoff, who had started alternating bites of cake—one for him, one for the cow. "Look at those two."

"I'm looking," Krista said. "I'm just not sure I believe what I'm seeing. We talked about trying her in the pet enclosure with the goats, but we were afraid to have her that close to the main house. And given the way she was behaving with adults, we didn't want to try her with kids and risk them getting hurt." A headshake. "She must've been raised around kids, though, probably went in and out of the house with them when she was little. I wish we had known sooner. We could've— I don't know. Handled things differently."

This time, when Geoff stuck a bite of cake in his mouth, Betty grabbed a mouthful of hay. Watching them together, Ty said, "Hey, Marybeth, would it be okay if Geoff helped me with Betty for the rest of the week?"

She nodded quick permission. "Fine by me."

"What do you think, Geoff?" Ty asked. "You'd need

to be here at seven in the morning, before your break-fast, and then again after the riding is done for the day. She would be your responsibility."

Glancing shyly at Marybeth, the boy asked, "Would Lawrence mind, do you think? He said we were going to go fishing tomorrow morning, early."

You would have thought he had just run across and thrown his arms around her, the way her face lit. "I don't think he would mind at all, Geoff. You two could have your guys-only time after that. He might even like it if you brought him in here and introduced him to Betty."

"Okay." The boy looked sidelong at Ty. "I'll do it. And, um, I'm sorry for going into Betty's stall without permission. I won't do it again."

He probably would, Ty knew, just like he'd get mad again, get frustrated with himself and the people around him. The animals. Maybe even with Betty. But it was a start, and a good one. "Want us to give you a few minutes to tell Betty that she needs to finish her hay like a good cow, and you'll see her in the morning?"

At the boy's nod—maybe even with a hint of grati-tude in those wary brown eyes—Ty tipped his head and gestured for the others to give them room. It was also a test of sorts. At least this way, if Betty decided to make a run for it, they could head her off pretty quickly.

She didn't, though. She just kept picking through her hay for the last of the cake scraps while Geoff scratched her shoulder and spoke to her in low, serious tones.

As they moved out into the aisle, Ashley hooked her arm through Ty's and gave his forearm an approving pat. Seeing Wyatt's eyes narrow, he slipped an arm around her waist, then offered a finger to the baby. "Hey, Miss Abby. How does it feel to hit the big one-point-oh?"

The kid gave him a drooly smile.

He wiggled the stuffed toy. "Who do you have here? He looks a little like your aunt Ashley's cat, Poltergeist."

Ashley sniffed. "The cat's name is Petunia, which you very well know."

"You should cut the poor guy a break and try again with that one. Poltergeist works, don't you think? You pretty much never see him, until suddenly stuff is flying off the shelves."

As they grinned at each other, Wyatt cleared his throat.

Ty looked over, locked eyes. "Problem?"

"Nope," Krista said, hooking her free arm through her husband's. "In fact, I think I hear Mom calling from the main house. We should go see what's up."

Wyatt looked from Ty to Ashley and back again. Then, as if the words were being dragged out of him by a good cow horse and a long rope, he said, "There's more cake in the kitchen, since yours went to the cow. Pulled pork and corn bread, too, if you want to join us for dinner."

As peace offerings went, it was pretty grudging. But Ty figured it was a start.

*   *   *

Later, with her stomach full of good food and her head buzzing from the lively conversation, Ashley accompanied Ty back to his above-barn apartment, feeling a butterfly flutter of anticipation as she followed him through the door.

Up to this point, they had always been in her space, doing her stuff, and mostly talking about her world, her experiences. She was looking forward to getting to know him better.

Far from utilitarian, the apartment was elegant and thoughtful, with lots of exposed wood and a rustic log cabin feel. The open-concept main room was divided into kitchen, dining, and living areas by wooden partitions that mimicked the stall doors down in the barn, and a hallway led off, presumably to the bedroom and bath. The decor was sparse and unisex, with practical canvas and leather on the furniture and braided rugs on the wide-paneled wood floors, all in muted earth tones. The framed prints on the walls were Old West, the throw blanket on the big sofa was thick and soft, and the pillows provided pops of color.

Like the rest of Mustang Ridge, it smacked of high-end luxury, done the cowboy way.

"Nice," she said. "I haven't been inside since they finished renovating." At the time, Krista had been aiming it as an additional guest suite. Ty, though, had gotten it as a job perk.

"It's a big step up from the old bunkhouse I used to share with Foster—that's for sure." He hooked his Stetson on a rack near the door, tugged off his boots, and set them on a mat nearby. His socks went inside one, his feet into a pair of worn rope sandals.

The small actions put a quiver in Ashley's belly, feeling strangely intimate, considering that they were lovers. She had seen him wondrously naked, yet found herself staring at his feet, with their long, almost prehensile toes and sparse, wiry hair.

"Can I get you something?" he asked, seeming not to notice her sudden foot fetish. "Wine? Coffee? Or there's soda downstairs in the tack room fridge."

"Coffee would be good. Decaf would be better."

An eyebrow winged up. "Since when?"

"Since the fashion show is over. Time to detox and get some sleep." Not that she was tired just then—far from it. Quiet energy hummed beneath her skin, coming from the moment, the man.

"Decaf it is, then." He moved around the kitchen with the assurance of a man who knew his way around the high-end coffeemaker, reaching into a cabinet for a pair of heavy earthenware mugs and snagging creamer from the fridge, sugar from a small jar on the counter. His moves were powerful and precise, those of a man who was very comfortable in his own skin.

Aware she was staring, she turned away to study the space again, this time picking out the hints of him amidst the professional design. There wasn't much yet—some wet-weather gear hung on pegs near the door, a laptop open on the coffee table, a couple of dog-eared paperbacks by Louis L'Amour. He had been there only a couple of weeks, though. No doubt he would put his mark on the place in time.

"Madame's decaf." He handed it over, then leaned in to claim a kiss that curled her toes and made things go a little unsteady beneath her boots. "Let's take this out onto the back deck." He nudged the slider open and guided her through with a warm hand flattened at the small of her back. "There's a heck of a view, and a sofa that's perfect for two."

"Hey, that rhymed."

"I'm a poet and, well, you know." Her boots sounded on the thick wooden planks that made up the sturdy deck. At the far end, two chairs and a small sofa were thickly padded with pillows and clustered around a low table, all done in stained wood and waterproof upholstery the same blue as the sky.

Beyond the decorative iron railing, fences lined the sweep of green grasslands that rolled down from the barn and up to the ridgeline that formed the edge of the homestead valley. Horses and cattle dotted the landscape; the closest few raised their heads as the humans crossed the deck, then went back to cropping the grass. The sun was mellow, the air laced with the scents of livestock and baking earth. It was all very warm, very peaceful. With purple foothills in the middle distance and the loom of the craggy mountains beyond, the landscape seemed to go on forever. More, it seemed like it was theirs alone.

Ty tugged her down beside him on the couch and curled an arm around her shoulders, fitting their bodies together. "There," he said against her temple, following the word with a kiss. "That's better."

Sighing, Ashley relaxed into the thick cushions and the warmth of his body against hers. Taking a first sip, which was thick and rich and put Mr. Coffee to shame, she said, "It's gorgeous. I love that you can't see the main house or any of the cabins. You can almost forget that we're surrounded."

"By buildings, you mean?"

"Buildings, people, take your pick. Let's just say I've got huge respect for your ability to stay charming with the guests. If I had to ride out on the same trails day after day, year after year, answering the same questions over and over again, I'd go mental."

A chuckle rumbled in his chest. "How is that any different from what you do at the store? Except plug in *watching women try on the same outfits day after day.*"

She poked him in the ribs. "Most of my vintage pieces are one of a kind, buster. And even if they weren't, it wouldn't be the same at all, because the people would be different. Their stories are different. Take Gilly, for example." She told him about the teen, the family's loss, and how the girl was trying to put the pieces back together. "Her mother didn't come to the fashion show, which was too bad, but Gilly and Sean left together. Seeing her walk off with him, and the way he was looking at her like he'd never seen her before . . ." She grinned. "That was pretty special. And when I sell the dresses she wore at the show to someone else, it'll be an entirely new experience. Different woman, different story, you know?"

"Yeah." He toasted her with his mug. "I do know."

She huffed out a breath. "I just made your point for you, didn't I?"

He nodded. "Each set of guests brings something different to the ranch. Sometimes it's a bad attitude, the need to be a total pain in the ass, or the occasional lady fixed on getting a real-live cowboy into her bed. Most times," he continued before she could ask how often that worked, "they're fine people looking to get some miles in the saddle and have a good time, maybe even learn a thing or two. They're the ones that make it easy to give a little extra."

"Like today, with Geoff." Something soft and sweet moved through her. The look on the boy's face had been precious as he cradled the old cow's head. "You were good with him."

"He's okay. Or at least he will be, I think." His voice lowered, roughened. "He's got a better chance than most, got lucky with Marybeth and Lawrence. The foster system . . . it can chew up kids like him, spit them out tougher and meaner than they should've been." He stared out over the hills, but she got the sense he wasn't seeing the mountains beyond.

She hesitated, not sure if he wanted her to ask. But she wanted to ask, wanted to know where he came from, where he was going as he passed through her life. "Sounds like you speak from experience."

A sip of coffee bought him a moment, making her think he would change the subject. But then he nodded, and said, "I get Geoff because I *was* him. Except I didn't get a foster family. I just got the system."

17

The crapstorm that had been Ty's younger years—his personal song, as one overwrought music blogger had put it—wasn't a state secret, at least on the surface. Even a guy strumming a guitar in the background got some notice when you were talking about a name brand like Higgs & Hicks, and a handful of pseudojournalists had gone digging and latched onto his so-called tragic beginnings when he'd first joined the tour. That had died down quickly, though, and in the past few years he could count on one hand the number of people he'd told personally.

He had told Brandi everything, of course, when their whirlwind had started heading in the direction of till-death-do-us-part. He had figured she had a right to know what she was getting into, little realizing that the details would become ammunition when things started going downhill. And there had been a pretty, soft-eyed brunette who had sat down next to him at a bar in the heart of Vegas and asked what he was doing in town, not realizing that Weasley had canned him an hour before, and he'd had enough bourbon to loosen his tongue.

There wasn't any pressure now, no alcohol involved, but he found himself wanting to tell Ashley at least the basics. Maybe it was seeing her try to work things out with Wyatt, or the way his phone stayed stubbornly silent, with no word from Mac. Or maybe—probably—working with Geoff had brought the buried things far closer to the surface than they usually stayed.

Whatever the reason, where Brandi used to accuse him of putting up walls and shutting her out when it mattered most, now he found himself saying, "My mother was a user. People. Booze. Drugs. You name it, she used it." Including him, until he got big enough to go off on his own. After that, he had spent as much time as he could away. It didn't matter where, just away.

Ashley had sucked in a breath when he mentioned the system. Now she let it out slowly. "And your father?"

"I don't have a clue. Pretty sure she didn't, either. But it was all I knew, and she used to tell me how I should be grateful, that there were kids worse off than me in the neighborhood . . . until there weren't anymore." It was the truth as far as it went. As far as he wanted to take it with her just now.

She took his free hand and squeezed his fingers, but stayed silent.

"Child Services showed up one day—I don't know who called them or what changed. All I knew was that they said"—that nebulous grown-up collective *they* who were supposed to make life better rather than worse; it hadn't taken him long to figure out that was a crock, and that he was the only person really on his own side—"everything was going to be okay now, and then they gave me a cot sandwiched between two older boys"—one who had showed him a switchblade, threatened to cut him, and took his jacket, all within the first five minutes he was there—"and told me to mind my manners."

"Did your mother try to get you back?"

"If she did, I never heard about it. They were in the process of terminating Ma's rights when she died."

She made a soft noise of distress. "I'm sorry."

"Don't be. She was squabbling over a dime bag and lost the argument. And it was a long time ago."

"So were the days I used to imagine Wylie showing up for Christmas with presents for me and Wyatt and a diamond ring for Mom. But still."

Yeah. Still. It was why he had wanted to tell her, he realized. She understood more than most. "A couple of foster families tried to help, but I had a temper and was big enough to make them nervous. So back in the system I went, until I hit eighteen and they cut me loose. The caseworker wished me luck and said she knew I'd do great, but we both knew that was bull. A kid like me, with no foster family or outside ties, in and out of juvie and already with an assault pop on my adult record, thanks to a bar fight over another guy's girl and a judge who was already sick of seeing my face . . . Well, let's just say neither of us figured I'd be on the outside for long."

"I guess you beat those odds." She studied him over the rim of her mug. "Give yourself credit there."

"I got lucky." It didn't feel that way most days, though—more like he had failed the one person who had been counting on him back then. He hadn't gone looking for her like he had promised. Not until it was too damn late, after the system had swallowed her up. *They* had said it was better that way, that he was giving her a chance at a new life.

It wasn't until later that he had learned just how badly *they* had been lying.

He wasn't going there, though. Couldn't.

Draining his coffee, he set aside the mug and rose, still connected to Ashley by their joined hands. She was fresh and lovely in her pretty yellow skirt, surrounded by the backdrop of his temporary home. The sight of her there, in what was rapidly becoming one of his favorite spots, shifted something in his chest.

He wanted to be with her, lose himself in her, let things be simple, if only for a little while. It was strange, really, how uncomplicated things felt with her when they were surrounded by nothing but complications.

Here, though, now, there was just the two of them and the setting sun. "Can I give you the grand tour?" he asked, voice gone rough with the sudden thrum of blood through his veins as need surged.

For her. For the two of them together.

"I think I already saw most of it." She rose, though, smiling as though they shared a secret. Which maybe they did. "Except the bedroom, that is." *Thank you for telling me*, her expression said. *It's okay that you want to be done now.*

Did she know that was a gift?

He lifted their joined hands and pressed his lips to her knuckles. "I'll show you the way there. It gets kind of tricky. In fact—" Then, because he could, he swept her up in his arms and carried her, laughing, to the bedroom. There, he settled her on the big bed, came down atop her, kissed her, and lost himself to the night and the woman in his arms.

For tonight, at least, he was exactly where he wanted to be.

The next morning, full of energy and enthusiasm, Ashley blew up the volleyball game in the shop's front window, wanting something fresh, new, and really big. Once the space was empty, she hauled in a roll of chicken wire and got to work, not really sure what she was going to make.

She wound up building a giant bucking bronco with a cowboy astride. Which probably shouldn't have been a surprise, given where she had spent the night.

The wonderful, glorious night. Ty had opened up to her, made love to her, made her feel special, from the moment he told her about his childhood to when he kissed her good-bye out by her car early that morning, where all the world could see.

How bright and brilliant it was to discover that a casual relationship didn't need to be a superficial one. They could talk about things that mattered—far more than she and Kenny ever had, or the boys she had dated before him. It was like having a new member of the Girl Zone, only one who was wired with a very grown-up male brain. As for the sex . . . well, *wow* was just plain insufficient at this point. It was quickly becoming more like *wow* to the sort of exponential power she had failed to fully understand back in school.

"I can't believe we're using all this denim," Hen said from up atop the step stool, where she was attaching vintage 501s over the arching chicken-wire framework.

Tearing her thoughts away from Ty—no easy feat—Ashley looked at the mannequins she had propped up behind the bucking bronco, planning to make them look like a rodeo audience in a range of quirky cowgirl-inspired outfits. "Is it too much?"

"Oh, don't get me wrong. The concept rocks. I just wonder what we're going to do if someone comes in and wants to buy a pair of jeans." Hen shot a look toward the pillaged wall rack. "Please tell me you've got some stock out back."

"A little." *Make that a very little.* "Maybe this was a bad idea."

"Too late," Hen said cheerfully, coming down the ladder to stand next to her. "What do you think?"

"Here comes some foot traffic. Let's see what they do." That was their audience, after all. And in a month, their votes would be the make or break on the mayor's big contest.

Which she really needed to start thinking about now that the fashion show was in their rearview mirror. *Eep.*

The two women, one younger, one older, glanced up at the window as they passed. Their steps faltered, then slowed. Eyes widening, they looked from Hen and Ashley to the horse and back again . . . and burst out laughing.

"Well." Ashley looked up. "That wasn't what I was expecting. What did they—" She snorted, seeing it too late. "Whoops."

She and Hen were standing directly below the horse's streaming tail, which was intended to look like it was arched in midmotion, but on second thought could look like it was arched for an entirely different reason.

Clapping a hand over her mouth, Hen didn't do a very good job of stifling a giggle. "It looks like he just . . . Hmm." She skittered out of the line of fire, up to the front of the denim horse. Then she peered back at Ashley, eyes alight. "We've got those brown velour throw pillows. You know, the shaggy round ones? If we piled them up where you're standing, they would look like—"

"Don't you dare," Ashley warned, glaring. "If you do it, I'll—" What could she do? It wasn't like she would fire Hen, even if she installed giant road apples in the window display. "I'll tell Jolly you had a sex dream about him."

Hen gasped. "That was just a onetime thing!" Though her flaming face suggested that maybe it hadn't been so onetime as all that. "And I told you that in the Cone of Silence! I can't believe you would even consider—"

"So don't put poop in the window!" Ashley hollered just as the front door swung unexpectedly open. She clapped a hand over her mouth as the bell gave a cheerful *jing-a-ling*, and she sucked in a breath so hard that it sounded like a whoop. "Ohmigosh. I'm so—" The breath came whooshing back out as she saw a familiar figure on the threshold. "Oh, Gilly, it's you. Thank goodness."

Back wearing her brother's jacket but with the sleeves rolled up, a pair of narrow jeans on her lower half, and her shoulders square beneath the camouflage, Gilly looked from her to Hen and back. "Who pooped in the window?"

"Nobody!" Ashley shot Hen a warning look. "And nobody had better, either."

"Aye-aye, boss. Captain. Whatever."

Shaking her head, Ashley motioned for Gilly to follow. As they headed for the register, she said, "I'm glad you stopped in. I'm sorry I didn't get a chance to talk to you after the show. I wanted to thank you again for all your help. Seriously. You rocked the runway, and I'm not sure we would've gotten as far as we did with the setup if you hadn't helped out. I owe you."

Gilly hesitated, but then smiled shyly. "I'm pretty sure we're even. I wanted to thank you. You know, for inviting Sean. Mrs. Mac said you asked for him specifically."

Ashley grinned. "You're welcome. I know I said it's important for a boy to like you for yourself"—that got an emphatic nod from Hen—"but I also figured it wouldn't hurt for him to see you in a different environment." And by *environment* she meant *clothes*. Where the yellow dress and edgy styling had made the girl look like a hip urban princess, the later military outfit had made her look like a souped-up Amazon—wholly feminine, but ready to kick some serious butt. "Sooo . . ." She drew it out. "How did it go?"

The teen flushed brick red. "We're going to the movies on Thursday."

"Woo-hoo!" Hen did a little victory dance in the window, startling a couple of passersby. "Way to go, girl!"

"Ditto that." Ashley reached behind the counter to snag a tissue-tufted gift bag. "Which makes this perfect timing."

Gilly's eyes widened. "What . . ." She patted the pocket where she kept her wallet. "But I don't—"

"It's a gift," Ashley clarified. "Thanking you for helping with setup the other day." And a little because it had made her sad that Gilly's mother hadn't come to see the show.

The teen took the bag, new color flooding her cheeks. "But I just did it to help. I didn't expect—"

"I know you didn't." Which was why Ashley had wanted to give her something. "Go on, see if you like it. I'm thinking it might be just the thing for date night."

Gilly didn't need any further urging. She dug into the bag, neatly folding back the tissue paper as if it was precious. When she got to the inner layer, she pulled out the bundle that Ashley had wrapped in more tissue, and peeled off the foil sticker that read, I JUST FOUND ANOTHER FYNE THING IN THREE RIDGES, WYOMING. When the wrappings fell away to reveal a soft, summer-weight cardigan, her eyes lit. "So pretty!"

Ashley grinned. "It's the same color as your eyes, sort of caramel with almost metallic overtones. It's not quite military style, but it's got some asymmetry to it, and you can dress it up or down depending on what you put on under— Oof!" She rocked back on her heels as Gilly grabbed her, nearly knocking the wind out of her. Rallying, she steadied herself and returned the hug. "I guess you like it."

In answer, Gilly shucked off her brother's coat and tossed it on the counter, where it landed not quite name tag up. She pulled the sweater over her head, smoothed it down partway, and spun for the nearest mirror. "How do I— Oh! It's lovely!" It was snug across her bust and a little generous over her waist, with an angled hem and flared cuffs that created the hint of an hourglass figure. She stroked the soft nap of the fabric, face aglow. In the mirror, her eyes met Ashley's. "Until I met you, I never realized how much of a difference the right clothes could make."

"It's the attitude more than the clothes, I swear." Though the sweater was pretty awesome. "Promise me you'll swing by and let us know how your date goes?"

"Will do!"

Gilly bounced out of the store, looking young, eager, and so very different from the girl who had first come into the store . . . gosh, was it really a couple of weeks ago? Somehow it felt like forever and an instant, both at the same time. Was this what life was going to feel like from now on—a whirl of payments, deadlines, promotions, and sales, with a layer of fun stuff iced over the top?

She would be okay with that. In fact—

The burble of her cell phone drew her attention, and

she palmed the unit from her pocket. Her lips curved at the sight of Ty's name on the display. *Speaking of fun stuff on top.* She hit the button to take the call. "Ty, hi." A glance at the clock said it wasn't even noon yet. "Why aren't you out on the trail?"

"I am. I found a couple of bars of reception and wanted to hear your voice."

"Oh." Smiling foolishly, she cupped the phone closer to her cheek. "Hi." Which she had already said.

He didn't seem to mind. "I know we left things pretty loose for the week, but I want to see you."

And, oh, how she wanted to be seen. To see him, talk to him, be with him. She had the trash-to-treasure clinics to run, though, and didn't dare get behind on her paperwork. "I'm slammed until Thursday."

"Thursday, then. We'll borrow a couple of horses and go for a moonlit ride. You can ride, right?"

Anticipation bounced along her nerve endings. "I'd love to. And, yes, I can ride. Fair warning, though—I'm no cowgirl."

"We can work on that." His voice wrapped around her, warmed her. "I guess I'll see you Thursday, then."

"I'm already looking forward to it." It came out husky, as if they had just kissed.

"Me, too."

She held on to the phone a moment after they said their good-byes, aware that she was wearing a big, goofy smile. And that Hen had heard the whole thing. Face heating, she turned and said with as much *I'm totally cool* as she could muster, "So . . ."

Her assistant's smile was as big and goofy as her own. "So. You and Ty, huh?" She did a little dance. "Did I call it or what?"

Had she? "Were you in on the pool?"

"There was a pool? Darn it, I missed that one. I'm not missing out on this, though." Hen plopped down on the edge of the display. "Start talking, or I'm pulling out the furry brown pillows."

"Oh, no, you don't." Ashley grabbed her hand, hauled her up. "We don't have time to sit around and gossip. We'll work and gossip instead."

18

Thursday night was clear and lovely, with enough moonlight that the horses could see their way, but not so much that it drowned out the stars.

Ashley rode Justice, who was one of the ranch's most reliable beginner mounts, and did her best to remember to keep her head up and her heels down. Meanwhile, Ty sat astride like he'd been born in the saddle, atop a big, rawboned chestnut gelding whom he affectionately described as "always looking for an excuse."

"An excuse for what?" she asked.

"Anything he can think of." Ty patted the horse's arched neck as they came down off one gentle slope and started up the next. "Last week while Junior and I had twenty guests picnicking out in Keyhole Canyon, he untied the picket line—not just his tether, but the whole danged thing—and tried to sneak the herd out past us. Like we wouldn't notice twenty-two saddle horses making a break for it."

"Whoops." She grinned.

"Fortunately, Keyhole is a box canyon, so he didn't

have any other option than to go by us. He's that smart. In a thoroughly deranged, let-me-see-if-I-can-make-my-rider-look-like-an-idiot sort of way. I don't even want to think about the kind of grief I would've gotten if all the saddle horses had shown up back at the ranch without us."

"Maybe he'll grow out of it."

Ty shook his head. "He's been like this since Foster and I broke him out, five, maybe six years ago. He's mellowed a bit, sure—I only have to run the devil out of him a couple of times a month now, rather than two, three times a week. But the potential for mayhem is always there."

"Is that why he's your favorite?"

"He's not. He's a pain in my ass."

She slid him an amused look. "If you say so."

They rode out to a favorite spot of his, a little tree-sheltered hollow down by a slow-moving river, where they picketed the horses, lit a small camping lantern he had brought along, dined on melt-in-your-mouth pulled-pork BBQ sandwiched between thick slices of home-made sourdough, and passed a canteen of unsweetened tea between them.

"Don't look now," Ashley said in an undertone, "but I think your horse is thinking about proving your point."

The geldings had started out picketed about twenty feet apart, with enough slack to graze. Brutus had worked his way over to Justice, though, and had the other horse's tie rope in his mouth, up near the quick-release knot.

"*Hey* there," Ty said in a low growl, then followed it up with "Don't even think about it, meathead. You make us walk home and I'll put you in the dude string so fast that your honking big head will spin. On a *lead line*, mind you. And you don't want to be on a lead line, do you? That would be embarrassing."

The big chestnut dropped Justice's rope, looked at Ty for a beat, then gave a juicy snort and went back to grazing, sidling away from the other horse as if at random.

A laugh bubbled up in Ashley's throat. "He's like a giant cat. You can practically hear him thinking, *Nope, not listening to you. Just doing what I meant to do all along.*"

He leaned back against the slope that led down to the water, urging her down beside him. "Yep, that's Brutus. A thousand-pound redheaded cat."

She snuggled against his body, which was warm and soft, yet so solid underneath it all. "There's a terrifying thought."

"Speaking of cats, how is 'Tunia doing?" He had taken to shortening the cat's name, claiming it was a million times more masculine than *Petunia*, and that she should give the poor guy a break.

"As of this afternoon, the score was plates three, humans zero." She wrinkled her nose. "I finally gave in and hid the blue pitcher and the green vase. He seems to like the tall kitty-tree thing Nick found for him." The vet claimed a client had donated it after her kitty had spurned it for the arm of the sofa. She had a feeling he had ordered it himself.

"What about the feather-on-a-stick toy?"

"He dropped it in the toilet one night; then I swear he laughed when I poked myself in the butt in the dark." She sighed. "As pets go, he kind of sucks."

Ty chuckled. "I'll have to come over one of these nights, have a discussion with him about how us street kids need to be grateful when we get a soft landing."

"Please do. I'll even make spaghetti."

"Thought French toast was your limit?"

"Let's just say we're going to run through my repertoire pretty quickly."

"I can teach you to make a mean chuckwagon chili, if you like."

"Will it put hair on my chest?"

"We can tone it down to peach-fuzz level."

"Sold." She smiled against him, enjoying the banter, the night air, and having given herself permission to forget about the store, if only for a few hours. "How about you? Did you ever get a soft landing?" She hadn't missed the *us* when he was talking about street kids, or forgotten that she hadn't heard the rest of his story.

She wasn't surprised by the pause. After a moment, though, he said, "I guess you could say I did, though I don't know that I would call it *soft*."

"What, then?"

"Lucky," he said. "I'd say that when I headed out on my own, for the first time in a long damn time I got lucky. Because when I lit on down the road and stuck out my thumb, I didn't get picked up by someone looking to roll me for my money, or worse. Instead, the truck and trailer that stopped belonged to a stockman,

Jim Hess, who contracted bulls to the rodeo circuits, and was on his way to a job. He was big enough and tough enough that he wasn't afraid of me, and one of his guys hadn't shown up to work. He said he'd give me fifty bucks to help move bulls around in the chutes and load everything up when the show was over. Assuming, of course, that I knew how to handle myself around livestock."

"Did you?"

"Not a lick, which Jim figured out after about two minutes of talking to me. But he must've seen something he liked because instead of telling me to get lost, he let me in the cab and gave me a rundown on how to handle myself around bucking bulls—how to bluff them into thinking I was bigger and meaner than them, and how to tell when they weren't buying it."

"You started with bulls." It had taken Wyatt most of his teenage years to work up to handling the big, mean creatures he had dubbed "horns and hate on the hoof." Of course Ty had started there.

"At first I figured I'd just work the night," he continued. "I was going to add the money to my stash and catch a ride south. I'd had enough of being cold in the winter, figured I'd head where that wouldn't be a problem. Except by the end of the night, I was too damn tired to do anything more than climb into the truck with Jim's other guys and crash in a spare bunk back at his place."

He wouldn't have been much older than Gilly, she realized. And for him, an empty bed had counted as a good landing. "I take it you stayed on?"

He nodded. "I learned how to ride, found I had a decent touch with horses, and got along okay with all but one of the guys. Mason." His voice flattened. "There was this other cowpuncher, Bob—a little slow, but a good guy. Didn't deserve the business Mason liked to give him, and the others were too afraid to stand up for themselves, never mind him. So Mason and I went around once or twice. Three times, maybe. Some bruises and bad blood at first, nothing more. The last time, though, he went too far. And then, so did I." There was something dark and complicated in his tone.

Her heart gave a tug. He saw himself as the bad guy—for having a temper, liking to fight—when he'd really been standing up for someone who needed him. But that was Ty, wasn't it? He rescued people, and didn't even realize he was doing it. "What happened?"

"Mason wound up in the ER, getting his arm splinted and his face sewn up, and Jim yanked me into his office. I thought for sure he was going to fire me then and there, maybe worse. But he didn't."

"What did he do?"

She thought she caught a hint of bafflement, even all those years later. "He brought me to the pen where he kept this mustang named Slider—a big brute of a late-cut gelding that he'd gotten from some guy who couldn't afford to feed him anymore. Jim handed me a rope halter and told me break him on my off hours. He said I could take however long I needed, but to get that horse going under saddle, get him useful. As long as I was doing that, I could stay, but if I gave up, I was fired.

Turned out he had already given Mason a payout and cut him loose. I was on probation."

The ache got sweeter. "How long did it take you to gentle the horse?"

"Six months, three cracked ribs, and a whole lot of humility." There was a smile in his voice. "But damned if that jug-headed bastard didn't turn into one of the best cow horses on the property. He had good instincts. You just had to figure out how to make him think it was his idea to use them. Kind of like Brutus here." He glanced over at the gelding, who seemed to be minding his manners. Tone sobering, he continued. "About a year after that, Jim went to bed one night with a head-ache, and didn't wake back up. An aneurysm, they said. No hope for him, even if one of us had known to do more than tell him to take a couple of aspirin and a snort of whiskey." A heavy pause. "He didn't have any family, had a bunch of debts, so everything got sold off. The bulls, the horses, the saddles. Even the property, bunks included."

Which would've made Ty nineteen or twenty, and out on his own again, having lost his home, his horse, and the closest thing to a father—or at least a mentor—that he'd ever known. Ashley shifted to brush her lips across his stubbled jaw. "I'm sorry. That must have roy-ally sucked."

"Hard days, no question. But I came out with more skills than I had going in, and Jim's outfit had enough name recognition that it wasn't tough to get jobs for a couple of us with another stock company."

"You and Bob." It wasn't a question.

"He was a good guy. Good worker. When things slowed down, I moved on so they could afford to keep paying him. I bounced around, made some friends, made some enemies, broke some mustangs, learned to sit a bull for eight seconds and rope a calf in half that. Along the line, I won an old harmonica in a game of five-card stud."

Her lips curved. "And discovered that you had music in your soul."

He tightened his arm around her, brushed his lips across the top of her head. "I don't know about that. I do know that when I didn't have a rank mustang reminding me to keep my moves slow and my words even slower, playing a tune helped take the edge off my temper. I taught myself to play that harmonica, bought myself a guitar and a DIY book, and used them to keep myself in check while I worked for a string of rodeo bosses who'd cheat you as quick as they'd look at you. I was making enough money to live on, but not enough to live any different than I was. So I rodeoed and played the local bars, and told myself that if this was as good as it was going to get, it wasn't all that bad."

It wasn't the first time he had downplayed his musical talent. It was, however, the first time she thought she understood why. For him, it wasn't about pleasing the crowd so much as quieting his brain. That, she understood. "How did you wind up here?"

"Luck," he said promptly. "Doesn't happen often, but when it does, it matters."

"What happened?"

"I was at a rodeo and I had some words with a bull-dogger who was yanking his horse around, all pissed off. Nice horse, okay rider, snotty bull, not the horse's fault they lost. And even if it was, that's no excuse for treating an animal wrong."

Ty to the rescue. "You had words, huh?"

"Something like that. Anyway, afterward, I took myself off with my guitar, figuring I'd let things settle before I went back to the pens. I was senior enough by then that I could get away with taking a break. But then this guy comes over to me—not somebody I recognize, but he's got a bow to his legs and the look of upper management, so I figure he's coming to tell me to shift my rear, or maybe fire me for taking a couple of shots at the bulldogger. I set the guitar aside, and give him a *I was just headed back to my post* routine that we both knew was bunk. But he said he wasn't there to bust my hide for taking a minute to make damn good music—he wanted to talk to me about a job. He was the head wrangler at this new dude ranch, and he needed a second-in-command to wrangle some group trail rides, bonus points if he could carry a tune across a campfire."

"Let me guess. Foster." Bless him. She made a mental note to give Shelby's husband a big hug the next time she saw him. Which would no doubt horrify him, but in a good way.

Ty nodded. "Sure enough, Foster. I listened to him, listened some more, asked a couple of questions, and agreed to take a drive out there the next day. He's a smart man—first thing he did was bring me through the kitchen and introduce me to Gran." He chuckled. "I was sold before we got to the barn. Moved my stuff into the bunkhouse a couple of days later, and led my first crop of dudes the day after that."

And, she thought, *he had found his home*. "You love it here."

"It's Wyoming. What's not to love?"

"Not just the location. The Skyes, the horses. Even the guests. This place works for you."

"I'm sure glad to be back. Turns out that life on the road isn't for me anymore. A place like this is far more my speed."

"Then why not stay?" It was out there before she thought it through, not really realizing how it would sound—needy, and like she was hinting around for something they had already agreed wasn't on the table. "Never mind. Can I rewind that question and request a do-over?"

A chuckle vibrated in his chest, and he cruised his lips across hers. "No need. We're just talking. Besides, we should probably be heading back before we lose the moonlight and our horses turn into a couple of pumpkins."

"Yours is already the right color."

"Brutus?" Shifting away from her, he started packing up the remnants of their picnic. "He's more of a jack-o'-lantern. One of the ones with the crazy eyes and a fiendish smile."

"Here. Let me." She reached for the stack of empty Tupperware containers, one with a few carrot sticks left over.

"Save those."

"Bribing the jack-o'-lantern for good behavior?"

He grinned. "Something like that."

"This from the man who gives me grief for feeding my cat rather than letting him bust up the joint."

They kept the conversation light as they loaded their packs onto the horses, mounted up, and set out through the trees for the return trip. There was zero reason for the niggle of disquiet that had taken root in the back of her mind. He had let her in, shared more than she would have expected. She should be more than satisfied. She *was* satisfied, darn it. This was what they had agreed to, what she needed right now.

Still, as they headed back toward the ranch, she couldn't help wondering. Was he afraid to think about settling down in Three Ridges after what had happened the last time, or was there something more to the story?

For Ashley, the next ten days passed in a blur of workdays, work nights, and the occasional few hours of hooky with Ty. Or, better yet, more than a few.

It didn't matter what they did—anything from rearranging the racks to walking a colicky horse while they waited for the meds to summon the so-called "poop fairy"—she and Ty found something to talk about, something to laugh about.

Better yet, they decided to go out for sandwiches one night, and they didn't have to drive out of town to do it. Despite his earlier reluctance to embrace downtown Three Ridges, Main Street welcomed him with open arms. Bakery Betty all but leaped over the counter to give him a big hug when he came through the door, then called her daughters out to see him, acting like the prodigal son had returned.

Ty handled it with his usual charm, asking after mutual friends and avoiding the subject of his ex. Ashley, though, knew him well enough to see him loosening up as they talked, as if he had been dreading his first trip through the bakery's doors. Better yet, he kept hold of her hand through it all, leaving no question that they were together and earning an approving beam from Betty and a surreptitious glare from the middle daughter. Which was flattering, really.

They ordered their sandwiches and sat at a little table out front, with their knees bumping as they traded bites of turkey and spicy Italian subs and did some people-watching. Which, in a town as small as Three Ridges, involved lots of waving and *Hey, how are you?* exchanges.

It was all very simple and normal, and Ashley enjoyed every minute of it.

After dinner, as promised, he had a stern talk with Petunia, facing off opposite the black cat over the remains of a cartoon coffee mug she had unwisely left on the counter that morning. Instead of WORLD'S BEST MOM—it had been Della's—what was left of it read WO EST OM. They had decided that was Cat for *Damn it, human, my dinner is late.* Which was no excuse, really.

"Listen, Tunes, here's the thing," Ty began.

"His name is Petunia," Ashley put in.

Man and cat looked at her with near identical narrow-eyed expressions. "Please," Ty said. "This is guy talk."

"Ohh-kay." She held both hands up and backed off a step. "Sor-ree."

She sat on the sofa and pretended to do paperwork while she watched him put his head very near the cat's and explain, in a low and serious tone, that Ashley was good people, she meant well, and even if she got caught up in work stuff now and then, Petunia should really cut her some slack and leave the breakables alone.

"There," Ty said as the cat marched out of the room with his tail mockingly aloft. "I think we've got an agreement."

"You sure about that?"

An eyebrow quirked up. "What are you grinning at?"

"You." *You're adorable*. With kids, cats, horses . . . She didn't let herself go mushy, but the temptation was definitely there. He was the real deal—that was for sure. "You're a regular cat-whispering, singing cowboy, aren't you?"

"Don't forget incredible lover."

"Are you?" She tapped her lower lip. "I can't quite re—"

"Oh, really?" He crossed to her in three long strides and leaned down to scoop her up off the couch.

She squeaked as the papers went flying, but lost her weak protest to the ardent pressure of his mouth on hers, the grip of arms that wouldn't let her fall, and a body that was strong enough to lean on. And as he carried her to the bedroom and made straight for the window so she could deal with the blinds, she thrilled to his touch, his kiss, and the way he made her feel when he touched her, like she was his entire focus.

Life, she thought, *could be far worse.*

In fact, as Down Payment Day drew ever closer, there were only two real clouds on the horizon. The first was the hard reality that even with stellar sales and a second round of the trash-to-treasure clinic, she would either need to win the window display contest or cash Wyatt's check. The second wasn't even a cloud, really—more like a wisp, a faint haze that she wasn't even sure was real. There were times, though, that she caught a shadow on Ty's face as he checked his phone, a faraway look that said he wasn't there with her anymore. He was somewhere else.

Let it go, she told herself each time it happened. They were together because they wanted to be, because it was fun. And if it felt like she was teetering at the edge of the cliff, that was her problem, not his, and she could handle herself just fine.

Until, that is, he called her that Friday night, with two weeks to go to D-Day and eight days until the Midsummer Parade, and asked her to ride out with him. He brought her to a waterfall beside a fast-moving river, where hoofprints said the wild mustangs came down to drink and a hollowed-out spot in the nearby cliff held a fire pit.

"Sit." He guided her to a spot where she could lean back against the stone and watch the waterfall. "Close your eyes."

She eyed him. "Why?"

"Trust me."

Her hesitation didn't last long. Then, nodding, she closed her eyes. With the visuals suppressed, she was far more aware of her other senses—the scent of the river on the mist-weighted air, the warmth of the fading sun on her closed eyelids, and the sound of him turning away, toward where the horses were tied. "Should I count to a hundred and go looking for you?" she asked archly.

"No." His answer came from closer than she had expected. "Just lean back, relax. And listen."

To what? she wanted to ask, not sure if he was talking about the burble of the river, or if there was more to come. She held herself still and quiet, waiting. *Trust me,* he had said, and she did, at least in this.

Then, moments later, a single guitar note sounded on the moist air, mellow and resonant.

"Oh—" She breathed. She hadn't realized he had brought the old acoustic guitar—he must have disguised the case behind his saddle, planning the surprise. Another note, then a chord. And then he began to play.

Notes flowed over her, shimmered into her, and put a sweet poignant pressure in her chest. She didn't recognize the song, but thought it must be old, something the long-ago cowboys would have played around the campfire. She was sure of it when he started to sing.

Unbidden, her eyes fluttered open, taking in the sight of him standing near the water's edge, with the sun setting behind him, creating burnished colors in the waterfall's mist. His eyes were closed, his body swaying to the beat, and his mouth shaping the words as he sang about a pretty piece of land and an even prettier woman, both waiting for her cowboy to come back. He looked peaceful, earnest. And like he meant every word as he sang to her.

Warmth flooded her, feeling more complicated than simple pleasure, and the edge of the cliff suddenly felt very unsteady indeed. But as she watched his clever fingers on the strings and felt the music inside, she thought that, for the first time, the mist was starting to clear. And that maybe, just maybe, she was starting to see the possibility of a soft landing at the bottom of that long, scary plunge.

19

"He serenaded you down by the waterfall?" Danny put a hand to her forehead. "Ohmigosh. I think I'm having a quarter-life hot flash. Please tell me you guys did the nasty right out there in the open, and it was awesome."

The Rope Burn was Thursday-night busy, with the noise level up and the mechanical bull whirling beneath a steady stream of tourists. Still, Ashley glanced around before she said, "It wasn't out in the open, and it wasn't nasty. It was . . ." *Perfect*.

"It was . . ." Krista prompted, eyes alight, and Jenny and Shelby leaned in. "Come on. You can't just leave us hanging—"

"Or we'll just make up our own details," Jenny finished for her. "And we've got good imaginations."

So does Ty. Ashley compressed her lips together so as not to say that aloud. After a short set of old-timey cowboy songs, he had wiped off the Martin and tucked it into its carrying case, then spread a doubled-up sleeping bag on the soft sand near the fire pit. Champagne and strawberries struck a perfect note, making her heart sing as he lay down with her. Kissed her . . .

Made love to her.

"Drinks!" The waitress appeared with a spur jingle and a loaded tray, and divvied up the three beers, one wine, and one happy pink cosmo in a blinky glass. "Your apps will be out in a few minutes."

As she bustled off, Ashley said, "Okay, you guys want the four-one-one? Here goes." She gave them an edited version with just enough steam to heat her face and have their eyes going round.

Krista sighed and fanned herself. "Gotta give him points in the romance department. Who would've guessed?"

The other three raised their hands, grinning.

"Good call," Ashley said. "Because, wow. Anyway, we stayed there for a bit"—*made love on a blanket beside the river*—"and then rode home. Back to Mustang Ridge, I mean."

"And . . ." Krista prompted with a wicked twinkle.

Ashley lifted her blinky glass in a toast, took a sip, and said, "I stayed over at his place . . . and we didn't get much sleep."

Shelby lifted her wine. "To good loving!"

Jenny followed with her beer. "To sunset trail rides and serenades down by the river."

"To wanting to be with your guy, wherever, whenever," Krista added.

Danny scoffed. "Wimps." Fixing Ashley with a gimlet look, she lifted her beer and pronounced, "To finding Mr. Right."

"Hang on there!" Ashley put up a hand that didn't do much to muffle her friends' good-natured cheer. "Whoa. It's not like that. We're just having a good time."

"Of course you are, because he's crazy about you. Why wouldn't he be? You're smart, funny, determined, loyal, and wickedly creative. You're the total package, girlfriend. He'd be stupid not to see that, and Ty isn't a stupid guy."

Was that how her friends saw her? God, she loved them, loved that *beautiful* didn't top the list by far the way it did for so many men, or even with her mother. That didn't mean they were right about Ty, though. "Look, I get that you're happily married"—she nodded to Danny—"or happily engaged, and all to wonderful men. And, yes, Ty is amazing." It was the sort of statement that didn't deserve to be followed by a *but*. "But he and I have been up-front with each other from the very beginning that things between us couldn't get serious."

Shelby studied her across the rim of her glass. "Is it just the timing? Because that's the sort of thing you can't dictate." One corner of her mouth kicked up. "Ask me how I know. Or talk to Jenny. She had a return ticket to Belize when she and Nick got together."

"It's true," Jenny confirmed. "Of course, I didn't just chuck the rest of my life because I fell stupid in love. I brought Nick with me when I went south, and we did the long-distance thing for a while. Eventually, though, I decided I'd rather be here with him than anywhere else without him. That wasn't timing, though, so much as my priorities changing."

"It's not the timing," Ashley answered, but then shook her head. "Okay, it's partly the timing, at least for me. I've got too much on my plate right now to be in a serious relationship."

"Says who?" Krista inquired. "Seems to me you guys are doing just fine. Maybe Ty has had a few mornings where he yawned his way through breakfast or drove in fifteen minutes before the guests were due in the barn, but there's no harm in that. Human beings aren't wired to exist on work alone—there needs to be some balance with fun and family, too, and love comes wrapped up in that."

"In the long term, sure." Ashley wouldn't let herself yearn, not now. She had too many plans in play, too much riding on them. "But there are times that your hypothetical human being—in this case, *moi*—needs to buckle down and focus on work. When that happens, she doesn't have time to juggle a real relationship."

"Hello, McFly." Danny reached over to rap a gentle knuckle on Ashley's head. "Don't you get it? You're already doing that. You're working killer hours at the store, sure, but you're making time for Ty, too. You guys are alternating a couple of nights a week at each other's places, doing chores together sometimes rather than just going on date-dates—"

Panic sparked deep inside. "That doesn't mean anything. We're busy people and we like being together even if it's not a date-date."

"Hello, functional relationship."

Those three words probably shouldn't have made Ashley want to hurl her blinky drink at the nearest table of loud-and-half-drunk guys, and use the ensuing commotion to cover the sound of Bugsy's tires peeling out. She and Ty weren't having a relationship. They were just having fun. "We're getting off track here. It's not just about my schedule—Ty has his own stuff going on, too."

"Like what?" Jenny demanded, no doubt ready to demolish each point with a reasoned argument and the desire to see her friend happily paired off with a double-date-worthy guy.

Ashley hesitated. When they came down to it, Krista was still Ty's boss. Choosing her words carefully, she said, "I don't think he sees Three Ridges as his final landing spot. And—hello—his fiancée cheated on him and broke things off. I think it's good that he's not looking to rush right back into things."

"He's been here off and on for nearly a decade," Shelby pointed out. "And Brandi was a spoiled brat who was more interested in planning a big wedding than working on her relationship, and who, when things started going downhill, hooked up with an ex-boyfriend because it was easier than fixing things with Ty. She didn't deserve him. You do."

"You may have to work at it, though," Krista pointed out. "Cowboys are a stubborn breed. Once they've got their mental hooves planted on a certain trail, it can be hard to get them going in a different direction."

"That's the thing. I don't want to have to work that hard." It wasn't until it was out there that Ashley realized how true it was. And how awful it sounded. "I didn't mean—" But that was the thing. She did mean it.

"It's okay." Krista patted her hand. "I get it. You want someone to chase you, not the other way around."

"Well . . . yeah." And put so much better than Ashley had done. "Is that so wrong?"

"Of course not. I've met your mother." Krista gave their joined hands a squeeze. "But the thing is, the two aren't mutually exclusive. Pushing for what you want and making the guy work to get you, I mean. Ty is a straightforward guy—left rein means go left, right rein means go right, and both reins means stop. You may have to spell it out for him that clearly one of these days, make sure he knows what you want from him, what you need. Then you can sit back and see if he's willing to deliver."

Her mouth dried up despite the drink in her hand. "What if he's not?" Not that she was going to ask.

"Then you'll have your answer," Shelby said. "I'm betting, though, that it will go the other way—that is, if you want it to. He adores you, and when it comes to Three Ridges, he was ready to settle down here once before, and he circled back around even after things went bad with Brandi. He's kidding himself if he thinks this isn't his home base."

Part of Ashley—a large part—wanted to agree, wanted to believe it. But she didn't dare. Pinching the bridge of her nose in an effort to squelch the sudden mental churn, she said, "I can't handle this right now. Not with the parade a week away."

"Here are your apps!" the waitress announced cheerfully, flourishing a loaded tray. "One order of Commitment-Phobe Buff Wings, and the Two Kids, A

Dog, And A White Picket Fence Nachos, hold the sour cream."

"Admit it," Danny said. "You make up the names as you go."

The waitress winked. "I'll never tell."

As she jingled off, Ashley took a deep breath, settling herself. *There's no pressure, no rush.* At least not where it came to Ty. They were riding along the same trail for now, but she knew there was a fork up ahead somewhere that would put them on new trails heading for different destinations. And she was okay with that.

Cowboy metaphors. Sheesh.

"Speaking of the parade," she began.

Danny blinked. "Were we?"

"We are now," Ashley said firmly. "Because in case you've lost track—trust me, I haven't—it's a week from tomorrow. I could use some help from you guys, brainstorming the perfect display."

"You don't have any ideas?"

Ashley whipped out her Window List, slapped it down on a tiny bare spot on the table. "Tons of 'em. That's the problem, and it's why I called you guys."

Danny pouted. "I thought you wanted to talk about Ty."

"We did that. Now we're moving on to the brainstorming part of tonight's entertainment. Because, short of a three-ring circus, I don't know how I can be sure my window will beat Betty's brownie bribes."

"Hey," Krista said, "that's got a ring to it." Pitching her voice to a singsong, she followed the beat of the bar music as she said, "Beating Betty's brownie bribes, beating Betty's brownie bribes . . . Say that six times fast!"

"Not helping," Ashley said quellingly. "What *would* help is for you guys to tell me which of these ideas make you sit up and go, *Oooh.*"

But as the others put their heads together over her list, she found herself wondering if a third drink would be too much, when one was usually plenty. She was churned up, riled up, and not really sure how to bring herself back down to reality. What she and Ty had together was working, and she didn't want to jeopardize that by buying into too much girl talk or losing track of her genetic predisposition to grab onto a man too hard and fast. There was absolutely no reason to mess with her and Ty's success, or risk complicating things with the sort of emotions they had agreed to avoid.

Right?

"This one." Shelby tapped the page. "It's perfect."

Reorienting, Ashley followed her fingertip. "You like the game show one?"

"Like it? I love it. It's got all the bells and whistles—pop culture, digital displays, and the opportunity for the audience to play along and win discounts."

"And," Jenny added, "the visuals could be super awesome if you put it together right. Which you totally will."

"You're darn right I will. Or," Ashley added with a grin, "die trying."

"Please don't do that. We like having you around. Okay." Shelby flipped over the list and produced a pen.

"Time for a new list. First item, funny trivia categories. How about Favorite Cowboy Sayings?"

"Bad Hair of the Eighties," Jenny put in.

"Things That Don't Rhyme with *Orange*," Danny offered.

And they were off and running.

Late that night, Ashley rolled down the drive to Mustang Ridge. She parked next to Ty's truck, waved at the main house in case anyone was looking, and let herself into the barn, closing the doors behind her. It all felt very natural, very right.

She might have credited the cosmos or the brainstorming session for the warm glow in her belly, but she was plenty sober and had a new Big List to go along with her window plan. Besides, the buzz of anticipation didn't come from alcohol or work-related stuff.

It was all for Ty, and the night ahead. She was determined to set aside the bar conversation and stick to her plan, to their agreement. To having *fun*, darn it.

He had called earlier and invited her to come on over after they were done at the 'Burn. "Don't worry if it's late," he had said with a low growl that left no doubt where his mind had gone. "I'll wait up."

Sure enough, that sounded like fun to her.

The stairwell lights were on, and the door to his apartment was cracked open in welcome. After pausing a second to run fingers through her hair and tug at the front of her shirt, she knocked gently and pushed open the door, calling, "Knock-knock? Hope I'm not too late!"

When she didn't get an answer, she stepped through into the main room, expecting to find Ty asleep on the couch. He wasn't there or in the kitchen, but the small flat-screen TV was on and turned down low, and a mug sat on the coffee table next to his laptop, which had a country music forum on the screen. It looked like he had just stepped out of the room. But to where?

"Ty?" She poked her head in the bedroom, then the bathroom, but she was alone in the apartment. She hadn't seen him in the main barn, suggesting that he was checking on one of the horses in the back barn, or maybe up at the main house, raiding the snack fridge.

Figuring he'd be back soon, she sank onto the couch, tucking her feet underneath her as she leaned forward to snag a catalog off the coffee table. It was Western wear, granted, but you never knew where you'd find something unexpected.

Beneath the catalog was a new-looking blue folder, only slightly worn at the corners. It was heavily paper-clipped across the top and unmarked save for the upper right-hand corner, where it bore a sticker from Pendergast Private Investigations and a name written in ballpoint ink: *Priscilla Reed*.

At the sight, Ashley stopped breathing. Reed was Ty's last name, but who was Priscilla?

"Ashley, hey!" He came through the door with a six-pack in one hand and a wrapped bundle in the other that smelled like fresh brownies. "I saw your car. Just ran up to the house to get us a snack."

The sweet scent had her stomach dropping. She hadn't heard him on the stairs, didn't know what to say to him now. So she said the only thing she could. "Who is Priscilla?"

His eyes went to the folder, and his expression shut down like someone had turned out the lights.

Tell me you're looking for information on your mother, maybe her family. An aunt. Tell me that being around the Skyes made you want to reconnect. But he didn't. He just looked at her as if she had just backed him into a corner, even though the door was still open behind him. Voice trembling, she said, "You don't have a *daughter,* do you?"

He would have said something, right? They had talked about it, about how there was nothing lower than a father who would walk out on a child. He knew about Wylie. He would have said something, then, if there was a child out there with his name, his face, but somehow so far gone from his life that he needed to pay for information.

Right?

"You didn't open it." His voice was flat, his eyes dead. But the not-quite-a-question wasn't a denial. Exactly the opposite.

Her chin came up; her hand hovered. "Should I?"

"I'd rather you didn't." There was no hesitation, no offer to explain. There was just the slamming of a mental door with her on the outside.

Had she thought before that she couldn't breathe? How wrong she had been, because it hadn't been anything like this—there was a vacuum in her chest, a sucking emptiness that made her want to curl in on herself. Not because of the folder or even what it might mean, but because of the cold deadness in his expression, the sudden loss of the easy affection between them.

Oh, God. What was happening? Who was the man standing in the doorway? It looked like Ty, but it couldn't be.

Except that it could. It was.

She stood, legs gone rubbery. "I should . . . I need to go." Away from him, away from there.

Something flickered in his expression. "Ashley—"

"No, don't. It's okay. I'm fine." But then she wrapped her arms around herself to ward off the sudden chill, chafing the gooseflesh on her arms. "Okay, that's a lie. I'm not fine, but it's not your problem, just like whatever is in that folder is none of my business. You never promised me full disclosure." He hadn't promised her anything, really, except that he wouldn't disappear on her the way Wylie had by walking out on his job at the ranch without warning. But while he might be physically present right now, he had disappeared nonetheless. "I'm going to go," she said again, heart drumming miserably against her ribs. *Please stop me. Please talk to me. Please help me understand what is going on here.*

How had they gone from making love beside a waterfall to this?

He didn't stop her, though. He shifted aside, so he was no longer blocking the door.

Vision blurring, not meeting his eyes, she hurried past him and down the stairs. The barn aisle seemed endless, like one of those dreams where she was in a long hallway and the door at the end kept getting farther and farther away as she ran. She passed Justice's stall, saw Brutus's zigzag blaze, Betty Crocker browsing on a thick pile of hay. Then she was through the doors and out into the night, sucking in huge lungfuls of air.

You're freaking out. Overreacting. All he did was refuse to share something private. But the look on his face . . .

Bugsy was a welcome sight, so bright and foolish with his spring-loaded antennae and lash-fringed headlights. She got the door open, dropped into the driver's seat, and closed the door, cocooning herself in the quiet space, the familiar smells. Then she sat there for a minute, figuring she should wait for the shakes to subside.

One minute stretched to more, at least according to the digital clock in the belly of the bobblehead troll mounted on the dashboard. At three minutes, her diaphragm loosened up and oxygen found its way back into her lungs. At five, her head cleared some, no longer replaying that cold, dark stare over and over again. At seven, she figured she was okay to drive. She turned the key, waited for the classic engine to catch.

There was a brisk knock on the glass beside her.

"Eep!" She jumped against her seat belt, adrenaline sizzling through her at the sight of a familiar silhouette. Her hand went to the stick shift and her foot hovered over the gas. She could drive away, run away, not look back. She rolled down the window instead. And even though it hurt, deep down inside, she met Ty's cool stare.

Only it wasn't cool anymore. His eyes were stormy in the darkness, his face raw. "Come inside," he said, his voice as ragged as his expression. "Please."

Ty hadn't meant to go after her. He had told himself to let her go, to leave it alone—he already knew how this one ended. She wasn't Brandi, it was true. But he was the same guy he'd been before. The situation was the same.

Except it wasn't. With Brandi, he wouldn't have had to fight the urge to yank open the car door, sweep her into his arms, and carry her upstairs. He wouldn't have wanted to keep her trapped in his space until they worked things out. He wouldn't have been holding his damn breath while he waited for Ashley's answer.

Until, finally, she turned off the engine.

The silence that followed seemed very loud, broken only by the squeak of the hand crank as she rolled up her window. Then she swung open the door and climbed out of the spotted Bug without saying a word.

He didn't carry her, didn't touch her. He just led her upstairs and gestured for her to take the same place she had just been on the sofa. He sank down beside her, not so close that they were touching, but close enough so that when he flipped open the blue folder, she could see the picture that was engraved on his brain.

In it, his rawboned nine-year-old self glowered into the camera from beneath too-long bangs, in stark contrast to the blue-eyed, white-blond little girl he held in front of him. She looked like an angel; he looked like a prepubescent thug.

Ashley reached out, hovered her fingers over his face. "She's your sister."

"Was. Is. I don't know anymore. I haven't seen her since she was three years old. But I've been looking for her ever since I made my first fifty bucks putting bulls in the chute at that rodeo."

20

His sister. Ashley wanted to touch the picture, but didn't dare, wanted to ask what happened, but was afraid to hear the answer. More, she was ashamed. She had jumped hard and fast to the wrong conclusion when she should have known better. There was no way a man like him, coming from the background he'd come from, would abandon a child. She knew that. More, she knew Ty.

At least she used to think she did. Now she was realizing she had barely scratched the surface. She looked at the man beside her and saw a stranger. Worse, she saw the shadows.

"Priscilla." He touched a finger to the very corner of the Polaroid. "We called her Scilla, though. Ma shortened it because she decided after it was too late that she didn't like the name all that much." His lips twisted in a smile that held zero humor. "That was Ma."

Shame and all the rest gave way to an ache—for the boy in the picture, who looked so fierce and afraid; for the little girl, who was smiling bravely for the camera while clinging to her brother's hand; for the man sitting beside her on the sturdy sofa, looking at the picture like he was losing his childhood all over again.

She wanted to touch him, but wasn't sure she was ready to. So she studied the Polaroid instead. "Tell me about the picture."

"It was at the group home, the day they took her away. I was nine. Scilla had just turned three. A caseworker snapped the picture—I don't think she was happy about them splitting us up. I heard her arguing with someone about it. Didn't change what happened, though." His fingers hovered over the little girl's smiling face. Retreated. "The lady gave it to me a couple of weeks later. She said she'd send one to Scilla, too, but I don't know if she ever did." His hand balled to a fist. "I promised I would protect her, that I would always be there for her."

Oh, Ty. "What happened?"

"They told me she was adopted by a perfect little family. Husband, wife, golden retriever, little house in the suburbs, the whole fairy tale. It was what was best for her. That's what they told me, what I told myself. But now, when I look for her . . . it's like she never existed." He cleared his throat. "I've done everything I can think of. Ads. Online posts." He set aside the photo and flipped through a stack of photocopies and printouts. "When I had a little money from rodeoing I hired a guy, then another, but they didn't find anything but dead ends. There was a fire at CPS, lots of records lost, so sorry, too bad. Until Mac came along."

"Mac?"

"Ian Macaulay." He shot her a sidelong look, almost

a grin. "Actually, your brother introduced us, back at the wedding. Small world, and all that. Anyway, Mac finds things. Money. Stolen art. People. And I figured, what the hell? It had been a few years, and thanks to Higgs & Hicks, I could spare the cash. I hired him six months ago, told him to get in touch when he found something. So far, there hasn't been much. A couple of weeks ago, he said he might be on to something, had a lead in Rapid City. I haven't heard from him since." Expression going faraway, he touched his pocket, the one where he kept his phone, in a habitual gesture that suddenly made far more sense than it had.

"I . . . don't know what to say." He couldn't have changed over the course of the past few minutes, could he? Because now when she looked at him, the shadows were pain, the chill a brittle layer of ice covering a huge well of resolve.

"Lots for you to take in."

"Lots for you to go through." But there was still a pang there, a twist of discomfort. "Why didn't you mention her before?" *What else aren't you saying?* This wasn't about her, wasn't about *them.* So why did it feel like there was a part of it that was?

"Habit." He avoided her eyes when he said it, though. After a pause, he added, voice slow and low, "Fear. What if she's not okay? What if she's out on the streets, or worse? The statistics—"

She reached out to him and gripped his hand. How could she not? He was hurting, worried, carrying the burden all alone. "I'm sorry," she said, though the words were entirely inadequate.

After a moment, Ty's fingers twined with hers and squeezed.

"The system chews you up and spits you out," he said. "Getting fostered is good; getting adopted is better . . . at least it's supposed to be. Doesn't always work that way—kids would get dumped back into the group home sometimes, and be glad to get away. They'd tell stories . . ." He cleared his throat. "Most sounded like lies. Not all of them, though. I just hope to hell she's okay. If not . . ." His expression hardened. It didn't go cool, though—it stayed hot and fierce, making him suddenly look very much like the boy in the picture. The one who had promised to protect his little sister, no matter what.

Ty to the rescue, she thought, chest tightening. "She got adopted by the perfect family, right? So she's probably fine."

"Maybe. I sure hope so." But his bleak expression said that he'd be envisioning the worst until he had hard evidence that said otherwise. After a moment, he glanced over at her, expression shifting, darkening. "You thought I was looking for my daughter. What did you think, that I walked out, then got to having second thoughts years later?"

"I'm sorry." Guilt stung anew. "I'd take it back if I could. It wasn't fair, wasn't right, and doesn't fit with anything I know about you."

"Then why say it?"

"I was . . ." *Feeling scared, vulnerable, not nearly so in control as I want to be.* Even now, she was teetering on the edge of the cliff with her bootheels hooked on a little ridge. She could stay there, *should* stay there. But she was suddenly so tired of keeping her balance, so moved by his story that she couldn't hold back from saying, "What we have is important to me, Ty. It matters enough to worry me some days." Most days. "So when I saw the folder and realized you were holding back, I immediately pegged you with the sin that would hurt the most." She did her best to stifle the tears, but one broke free, tracked down her cheek.

His expression shifted instantly. "Ah, sweetheart. Come here." He slipped an arm around her, lifted her onto his lap, and kissed her.

The feel of his lips on hers made her burn even as the pressure of his arms made her want to weep in earnest. It felt like it had been an age since the last time he'd held her. Or maybe it was that, deep down inside, she had been sure they were done, that she would never kiss him again.

She was kissing him, though. And she thought they were going to be okay. Better than okay, even.

He eased the kiss, tucked her head beneath his chin, and rocked them both for a moment, as if he was taking as much comfort as he was giving.

Into her hair, he said, "I'm sorry, too, Ash. I went dark on you, and that wasn't cool—you weren't doing anything wrong. I just . . . It happens like that sometimes. Instead of getting angry or upset or whatever, I just go blank, lock everything down. I always figured it was better than getting pissed—especially the way I used to do anger—but Brandi hated it. Things were falling apart long before she left, and I heard a whole lot about how I needed to share more, give her more. So there you were, asking me for more . . ." He eased away, tipped her chin up so their eyes met. "What we have here is important to me, too, Ashley. *You're* important to me."

His face was alive and alight, and the heat that radiated from his body into hers made her feel, for a second, like she was coasting in an updraft, her boots braced on nothing but air.

"I'm not staying, though." His voice was tinged with regret. "I can't promise you that."

"I didn't ask you to." She lost some altitude, though, felt the heavy tug of gravity.

"I just wanted to make sure we were clear on that. If Mac finds Scilla—*when* he finds her . . ."

"I understand." This was what put that faraway look in his eyes sometimes, what held him back. He didn't want to make a new family. He wanted to save the old one. She got that, respected it. But, oh, how she wished she could have been the one to put that determined look in his eyes, the one that he was waiting for, searching for, fighting for.

"So . . . we're okay?"

He was asking more than that, but it was already too late for her. She couldn't turn back now, couldn't deny herself the glide, even knowing that she would inevitably hit bottom. "We're okay."

His exhalation said without words everything that she was feeling. Easing her aside, he stood and held out a hand. "Will you stay with me tonight?"

Before, he had always caught her up, carried her, left

her breathless. Now he waited until she placed her hand in his, then led her down the darkened hallway to the bedroom. There, he undressed her slowly, reverently, as if seeing each piece of her for the first time. Stood still while she did the same, feeling like she was undressing an intimate stranger, someone different from before.

They lay down together, but didn't kiss, didn't touch, just held each other in the darkness. Their breathing synchronized; her pulse thrummed in time with his. *This,* she thought. This was what she had needed, what she wasn't yet ready to lose.

After a time—maybe a few minutes, maybe an hour—a lone wolf howled in the middle distance, maybe from up on the ridgeline. Maybe beyond it. The eerie sound raised the fine hairs on Ashley's arms, yet tugged at something deep inside her, wild and primitive. She snuggled closer to Ty, smiling when his arm tightened around her.

As the night wore on, they kissed, dozed, stayed very close together, absorbing the sensation of skin on skin and the knowledge that they had weathered a very personal storm. Later—or was it earlier?—as a new day pinkened the horizon beyond the dark teeth of the distant mountains, he turned to her, kissed her softly, slowly, and then made love to her as if they had all the time in the world.

Which, for the moment, they did.

Over the next few days, Ashley put in crazy hours at the store, running two more crafting clinics and getting together with Kitty and her Kountry Kitsch for an impromptu sidewalk sale that pulled in some decent returns.

She made time for extracurricular fun, too. On Tuesday, the Girl Zone convened out at the Rope Burn to watch Ty play behind another of Jolly's regulars. They whooped, hollered, and danced, and at the end of the night, when Ty pulled Ashley up onstage for a kiss, she got way too much satisfaction from the looks she earned from the crop-topped cowgirls who had been waiting around to see who the hunky guitarist would pick to go home with.

That would be me, thankyouverymuch.

On Wednesday, she drove out to Mustang Ridge to celebrate the official launch of the new petting zoo, which had Betty Crocker as its centerpiece, along with two crooked-legged goats, an elderly ewe, and a one-eared mini donkey, all rescues. There were cupcakes, too, and lots of little people scuttling around the enclosure, dribbling handfuls of grain and crawling all over Ty. He bore it with good humor and then invited Ashley back to his apartment to help him shower off the icing.

She was only too happy to oblige. Then, later, she talked him into showing her the online profiles he had posted on various Web sites geared to connecting adopted children with their birth relatives. The picture of Priscilla was heartbreaking, the write-up was terse and factual, and the post was too easily lost in the ocean of information.

So many pleas. *Looking for my sister. Missing: my little girl. Have you seen my mom?*

Ashley had to blink back tears. Then, having learned some tricks from Della when it came to searching out the coolest and quirkiest vintage pieces online, she made some suggestions for better headings and keywords, tentatively at first, and then with more assurance when he seemed appreciative of the help, grateful to be doing something other than waiting.

When they had submitted the last change, he turned to her and drew her in for a kiss. "Thanks, Ashley." His voice was rough, but there was nothing cold in him now. "Thanks for pushing. For understanding."

She cupped his stubbled jaw in her palm, let the kiss linger. Then she pulled away to say, "If things had happened a little differently—if Mom had gotten sick and Wyatt wasn't around to help—the same thing could have happened to me."

In fact, the realization dug so deep that she called home, just to wish her mom and Jack a safe trip to the Grand Canyon. Her mom's pleasure had made her think she should do stuff like that more often. There had been a couple of jabs, of course—a suggestion that she close "her little store" for the weekend and come along, and a reminder that she wasn't getting any younger when it came to finding a good man to take care of her—but she let it roll off, telling herself that her maternal unit meant well, in her own way.

Look at her, being all grown-up and stuff.

By Thursday, she was alternating between terror and euphoria, convinced that she wasn't going to be able to pull off the intricate window display for the grand unveiling on Saturday morning, but equally convinced that, if she managed it, she would kick bakery butt. Recognizing the sensation from the last couple of days before the fashion show, she switched to decaf and practiced the grab-hair-and-scream maneuver at regular intervals. And what do you know? It helped.

"Okay." Hen turned back to her as the door jingled shut behind a happy customer departing with a double dose of late-eighties shoulder pads and washable silk and a floppy hat that Ashley didn't get, but, hey, it took all kinds. Her assistant dusted off her hands to signal a job well done, then hitched up her calico skirt beneath a studded leather belt. "What's next?"

"We need to finalize the questions for the last two trivia categories and print out the entry blanks for the customers."

"Which categories again?"

"Strange History of Three Ridges and Famous Cowboy Quotes."

Hen's face lit. "I talked to Barb MacIntyre at hula class last night and got some strange history for you. Back in the late eighteen hundreds, the townspeople of Three Ridges voted in a horse as their sheriff."

Doing her best not to picture the Drama Club maven wearing a coconut shell bra and grass skirt—and of course picturing it—Ashley jotted down the info. "A horse? Seriously?"

"I guess it was a really good cow horse. I'm sure it

was to protest something, but Barb wasn't sure what exactly that might be."

Hello, oral history of a small town. "Right. Anything else?"

"The clam shack used to be a whorehouse, back in the day."

Ashley grinned. "There's a joke in there somewhere."

"Yeah, but do we want it in full digital on Main Street during the parade?"

"Not if we want to win. Good point. We'll use it for the contest sheet, though. Which do you think would be a better, *brothel* or *cathouse*?"

"House of ill repute?"

"That'll work. It—" She broke off as the door popped back open and the bell jingled. "Froggy! Hey, girl. How was your anniversary?"

"Amazing!" Looking like a human Super Ball—round, bouncy, and guaranteed to spark a smile—she bounded across the store and did a little twirl that gave the impression of a flaring skirt, even though she was wearing jeans. "The city, the hotel suite . . . you should've seen Martin's face when he got a load of me in that dress! We almost didn't make it to the show."

"Woo-hoo!" Hen applauded. "Let's hear it for the power of a great outfit."

"And a great marriage," Ashley added.

Froggy grinned. "It's true. We've had our ups and downs, of course—who doesn't? But it always comes back to wanting more or less the same things, or finding a way to compromise when we want different things. And speaking of wanting things, you wouldn't happen to still have those blue shorts with the embroidered pockets, would you?"

"Right this way." Ashley made a sweeping gesture. "They've been waiting for you. Try them on, though. You may need to nip them in a little at the waist."

"Music to my ears." Froggy patted her tummy. "Especially after eating one too many caramel peanut butter brownie bites just now. Or maybe six too many. But, ohmigosh, they're gooood."

"Brownie bites?" Hen asked, zeroing in. "Over at the bakery?"

"Mmm-hmm. Betty is testing out four new flavors. Double chocolate lava, raspberry-filled, and the caramel peanut butter ones. There was mint, too, but it wasn't my favorite. Mint only really belongs in toothpaste, don't you think? Anyway, they're giving away a sampler with every cup of coffee. And speaking of coffee, any chance I can use your bathroom?"

"Sure thing. You know where it is."

As Froggy disappeared down the back hallway—the EMPLOYEES ONLY sign was really just a suggestion, especially when it came to their regulars—Ashley turned to Hen. "Uh-oh."

"*Uh-oh* is right. Betty is upping the bar for Saturday. Not just brownie bites, but *raspberry-filled* brownie bites!" Hen gave a heavy sigh and squared her shoulders. "I think I should go on a scouting mission. For the team, you know."

"Ha! You just want a chocolate fix."

"I could bring you some back. And a latte."

Ashley tried to hold firm. She lasted about three seconds. "Okay. But no mint for me, either."

Hen saluted. "No toothpaste. Aye-aye, Cap. I'll be right—"

"Ash-leeee!" The wail echoed in the back hallway. "Come quick! I flushed, and . . . Oh, gosh. Hurry! There's water *everywhere*!"

21

Three hours later, Ashley stood over Charlie Moyer, not sure which sight was more unsettling—the torn-up subfloor and gaping hole in the wall between the bathroom and the break room, or the plumber's copious butt crack.

"Fifteen hundred," he said, rocking back on his heels. "And it's only that low because Ed Skye said he'd fix the floor and install the new flange himself."

"Fifteen hundred." Her lips had gone numb. *Oh, God.* "Do you take Visa?"

"Check or cash, half up front for materials."

"Half . . ." She swallowed a surge of chocolate-flavored nausea, making her think the second round of brownie bites had probably been a bad idea. But after seeing the damage, she had needed the sugar hit. "Okay. Do it. I'll get you a check." What choice did she have? With the water shut off, the sprinklers were down, and she couldn't run a business without sprinklers. Not in Three Ridges.

Back on the sales floor, she pulled the big checkbook out from behind the register, trying not to whimper.

Hen watched her with worried eyes. "How bad is it?"

"Fifteen hundred, half now, half later. Plus materials for Ed to do the structural work." She was so going to owe Krista's dad after this.

"I've got a little saved up. I can—"

"No." Ashley gripped her friend's arm. "I love you for offering, but no. I couldn't take your money."

"It wouldn't be for long. I know you'd pay me back."

"Not even then."

"Talk to Ty, then, or Wyatt."

"They offered. Wyatt even left me a check." It was still upstairs in her junk drawer. She couldn't bring herself to rip it up, but she'd be darned if she cashed the thing. "I'm not going to do it, though. This business needs to sink or swim on its own. And so do I." It was time.

Hen's expression softened. "There's a difference between being tough and being stupid, you know. This is an unusual situation, and you've got people who believe in you and want to help."

"You *have* helped, all of you. But I need to do this part on my own." She tore the check out of the book and folded it in half. "This means there's no way I can make the loan payment if we don't win the grand prize on Saturday. Second place ain't going to cut it."

"Want me to swap out Betty's cinnamon for dried ghost pepper?"

It surprised Ashley that she could laugh right now. "Don't tempt me."

"Ed could remove most of the screws from the big

display tiers she's got in the window. When they go to load it up Saturday morning—*splat*." She brought her hands together. "Brownie mayhem."

Ashley made shooing motions. "Go sell something, would you?" She was laughing as she headed down the hall, but even she could hear the edge of hysteria in her voice. There was too much to do, too little time, and no guarantees. As for the plumbing . . . well, fingers crossed that was it for today's drama. She didn't think she could handle another crisis.

Tired from a long day in the saddle, herding a group of computer programmers who didn't seem to get that horses weren't machines, Ty headed for his truck, juggling an armload of wildflowers. It didn't matter to him whether he wound up helping Ed with the toilet flange, painting props for the window display, or doing last-minute errands for Ashley—he just wanted to spend time with her, wanted to be there for her.

Yeah, he had it bad. So bad that he was starting to think about signing on at Mustang Ridge for next season.

Popping the driver's door, he propped the flowers on the bench seat and slid behind the wheel. The engine rattled to life and he headed off, looking forward to the night ahead.

He hadn't gone more than a mile when his phone rang. Thinking it was Ashley with an errand, he glanced at the display.

Macaulay Investigations.

Ty hit the gas too hard going into a turn, and the truck

wobbled. Cursing, he eased up, straightened out, and brought the vehicle to a shuddering halt on the verge. Grabbing the phone, he took two tries to answer it, hoping to hell it didn't dump to voice mail first. "Mac? It's me. I'm here. Do you have something for me?"

There was a pause before the familiar measured tones said, "Yeah, I've got something." For the first time, though, Ty heard a thread of something else in the investigator's voice.

He thought it might be sorrow.

The blood ran cold in Ty's veins and his brain went still and quiet. Lifeless. For a second, all he could see was big blue eyes, swollen and red with tears, and a pair of chubby hands reaching for him; all he could hear were Scilla's screams of *No! No! Ty-Ty, no!* as they took her away. Bile soured the back of his throat as he said, "I'm not going to like it, am I?"

"No. You're not."

The steel and glass of the truck pressed in on him, squeezing the words out of him. "Is she dead?"

"I don't know for sure, but it's not looking good."

By the time Ashley gratefully flipped the store sign to CLOSED and locked up for the night, she had a new downstairs toilet, a plate of double chocolate lava brownies, and three of the four game show podiums painted and drying in the curtained-off front window. Better yet, Charlie had roughed in enough plumbing to give her water upstairs, which meant that she and Ty wouldn't feel like they were camping out overnight.

The to-do list still loomed large, but at least he was

on his way. She felt bad putting him to work, but they would no doubt carve out an hour or so for themselves. And she had those brownies, after all.

She hated to admit it, but they rocked.

Not letting the panic overtake her, she pushed through the heavy curtains into the display area, which smelled of paint and looked like a bomb had gone off, with scrap lumber and mannequin parts piled on one side, the assembled podiums on the other. As she reached for a paint roller loaded with bright orange, her cell phone came to life, the display showing two very welcome letters: *Ty.*

"Hey there." She cradled the phone to her cheek. "Are you on your way?"

"I was, but now . . ." His voice moved away from the receiver and there was a rustling noise. Cloth, maybe, or paper. "I'm sorry, Ash, but I'm going to have to bail on you tonight. Something's come up."

Her dismay quickly gave way to concern. "Are you okay? You don't sound okay. What happened? Is it one of the horses?"

"I'm fine," he said, sounding suddenly distant. "Everything's fine, and you've got a ton on your plate already. I just . . . I'll call you later, okay?"

No, it wasn't okay. *Don't do this,* she wanted to say. *Talk to me! I want to help.* But she really, really didn't have time to help anybody but herself right now, not unless it was an emergency. Ty was a big boy; he could take care of himself. If he said he was fine, then he was fine. "If you're sure . . ."

"Positive. And, Ashley? I'm sorry."

He disconnected before she could respond, if she had even known how to. Because, all of a sudden, that apology had sounded like it was meant for a whole lot more than his missing out on painting and lava brownies tonight.

The knots in her stomach twined together in one big tangle, making it hard to breathe, hard to think. *Don't overreact. Don't make this into more than it is. He can miss a night now and then without it being the end of the world. You've got plenty to do here. Too much, in fact. Don't let this distract you.*

But his voice. Oh, his voice hadn't sounded good at all.

The tangles congealed to a certainty: there was something very wrong going on up at Mustang Ridge.

She lifted her phone, scrolled to Krista's number, then Wyatt's. Then she lowered her hand, blanking the screen. If there was a problem with one of the horses, they would already know about it. If the problem was with Ty, it wasn't any of their business.

It was hers, though, whether he liked it or not.

Moving fast, she wrapped the roller, covered the trays of paint, grabbed the brownies, and let herself out the front door, where Bugsy was parked facing the curtained-off window display, with a sign in his back window that read WIN BIG AT ANOTHER FYNE THING ~ SATURDAY 10 A.M. His headlights seemed to be giving her a look as she headed for the driver's door.

"I won't be long," she said, hoping it would be true. "But whatever's going on, Ty needs a friend right now."

She drove too fast, straightened out too many corners, but her faithful Bug got her to the ranch unscathed. Without waving at the main house, she let herself through into the barn and took the stairs leading up two at a time. The door was shut, but it wasn't locked, and she gave only a perfunctory knock before pushing through. "What is going—" She broke off, heart sinking at the sight of a bulging duffel bag on the sofa. Ty stood over it, typing something into his phone. "Where are you going?"

He looked at her, expression damnably cool. But whether it was because she knew him better now or because there were cracks in the facade, she could see through to the grief beneath. More, she heard it in his voice when he said, "They gave her back."

"What? Who?" Catching sight of the blue folder lying on the coffee table, she sucked in a breath. "Your sister?"

Pain etched his face. "The bastards traded her back in, like she was a puppy that piddled on the damn rug." His hands clenched spasmodically, making fists that had no target. "She was six years old. Didn't they know what that would do to someone like her? Didn't they *care*? And the thing is, I never knew. I was in juvie by then, cut off. They never told me. If I had known . . ."

"You would have done anything you could to get back to where you could protect her," she said softly, heart breaking for him. *Oh, Ty.* She crossed to him—the duffel didn't matter right now. Nothing mattered but the shattered agony in his dark eyes. Touching his forearm, where the muscles were strung so tight they vibrated, she said, "What happened after that?"

As if her touch had unlocked the rigidity that had been keeping him on his feet, he sank to the sofa. Pushing the duffel aside, she sat down next to him.

He opened the blue folder to reveal a new picture, printed from the investigator's e-mail account. "This happened." It was a mug shot of a gaunt, tired-looking bleach blonde wearing too little clothing and too much makeup, dated eleven months before. "And then after that, she dropped off the grid."

"Oh—" Ashley breathed. "Oh, no." Her heart sank—for him, for the woman in the picture . . . and for herself. Because this was going to change everything.

22

To Ty, the woman in the photo was a brittle-haired stranger, shockingly old-looking, as if his subconscious had frozen her at eighteen or so and this hard-ridden twenty-nine-year-old didn't compute. He saw his own eyes in his mother's face, though. *Christ.* He had promised to protect his baby sister, and he had damn well failed at it. He had failed *her*.

Ashley took his hand, squeezed his fingers. "Tell me everything."

He tried, but it wasn't easy to organize his thoughts with the chaos that was going on inside his skull. He did his best, though, and it wasn't like there was much to tell. "Mac found her adoptive family—the woman, at least. Alba Druse. It turned out that the adoption was one of those save-the-marriage things, only it didn't." Anger was an ugly twist in his gut. "When the husband moved out, Alba decided Scilla would be better off back in the system." What a crock.

"Did she get adopted out again?"

"No clue. The fire at CPS wiped out the records. We don't know anything again until this." He tapped the mug shot. "Mac was pretty cagey about his methods, but it's her." The name at the bottom was Priscilla Ricci, but there was no doubt about it, right down to the two little moles at the corner of her mouth.

"Why was she arrested?"

"Drug charges." The words tasted foul. "He'll have more on that in another day or so."

"Oh, Ty." She pressed her cheek against his upper arm. "That's awful for both of you. I'm so sorry."

He rested his jaw in her hair, needing the contact. "She was released—I'm not sure why. But since then . . . nothing. She doesn't have a license, doesn't have utilities in that name, no credit cards or bank account . . ."

"Mac will keep looking. He'll find her." She linked her arm around his and squeezed. "If Wyatt recommended him, then he must be very good at what he does."

"Yeah. He's looking."

Her eyes went to the duffel. "But you want to help him."

"I've got to try to find her." Save her. He only hoped there was still something to save. "She's out there somewhere. On the streets, maybe." Or worse. "I'll put up fliers, show her picture around. Somebody has to know where she is."

"When are you leaving?"

"In the morning, just for a day, maybe two. Foster is going to cover the dudes for me tomorrow." He slid an arm around her, cuddled her close. "I'll try to be back for the parade."

"It's okay. I understand." There was a quaver in her voice, though, and she avoided his eyes as she eased away from him. "Saturday is your day off, and Scilla needs you. I can handle the parade on my own." Her smile didn't quite reach her eyes. "It's not like I'll be alone. I'll have Hen, Gilly, the girls, the Skyes . . . my very own cheering section, really."

"I want to be there." He didn't promise, though. Couldn't.

"I know." She went up on her toes, wrapped her arms around his neck, and said, "It's okay. We're okay. Go find your sister, Ty, or at least sit down with Mac and put together a plan. The girl in that photo needs her big brother."

Heart clutching, he nodded, then dipped his head to kiss her. Her arms tightened around his neck, almost strangling him, and he found himself returning the grip, holding on to her too long, too strong.

He was breathing hard when they separated, and not just because he wanted to sweep her up and carry her to the bedroom. It was more that things felt suddenly out of sync, like there was an undercurrent he wasn't understanding. "Ashley—"

Her lips caught his in a fleeting kiss. "I need to get back to the shop. I'll be thinking of you tomorrow, though, and Saturday. Good luck. I hope you find her."

"I'll see you soon," he said, wishing he knew what else to say. Wishing he knew why he wanted to grab onto her, hold her tight, and not let go.

She nodded. "See you." There was nothing off about her tone, her smile.

So why did it feel like she was saying good-bye?

*   *   *

Ashley held it together down the stairs and along the barn aisle, digging her fingernails into her palms to keep back the tears. *Don't be a baby. Don't freak out. It's not the end of the world.* It wasn't even the end of her and Ty's relationship.

Not yet, anyway.

Nope. Still not freaking out. He was just going away for a couple of days. He'd be back. They'd be fine. She had the store and a life of her own. She didn't need his undivided attention.

But, oh, how she wished she could have it.

She paused with her hand on the outer door, breath hitching.

Not now. Not yet. She just had to make it to her car, back to the shop. Her space. She'd be safe there. Alone there.

"Ashley?"

The voice came from behind her. Ty's voice.

Oh, no. She pressed her forehead to the rough wood of the door. "Not now, Ty. Please. Just let me go." She was tired and stressed-out. Whatever reserves she might've had left over had washed away when the downstairs bathroom flooded and her internal cash register started doing its *ca-ching ca-ching ca-ching!*

"Not on your life." He caught her shoulders and turned her around. "Something isn't right. What is it? Let me help."

A ragged laugh caught in her throat. Of course he would want to fix the problem for her. That was what he did—he came to the rescue. Thing was, he couldn't rescue her from herself. "You've got your own stuff to deal with right now, Ty. Don't worry about me. I'm good. I'm fine."

"Why don't I believe you?"

"Because—" Her throat closed on a surge of anger, of grief. Her eyes filled. "Darn it. Let me go. Please. I don't want to do this right now."

"Do what?" His fingers tightened. "Is it about Scilla? Are you mad that I'm leaving?"

"No." She hung her head, shook it. "Not mad. Just . . ."

"Just what? Come on, Ash, talk to me."

"Sad." She exhaled it on a breath. "Jealous. And, yeah, maybe mad, but at myself, because how crappy is it of me to be upset right now?"

He shook his head. "I'm lost."

"Me, too. I jumped off the cliff, started gliding, and lost track of which way was down."

"Huh?"

She caught his hands, peeled them off her shoulders, and lowered them, but didn't let go, so they were linked by fingers and palms, but he wasn't holding her up anymore. "I know we said we were going to keep things casual and take it one day at a time. But we also said that what we have is important."

"It is." His eyes went intent. "Ashley, I—"

"Don't, please. Because the thing is, it turns out that being important isn't enough for me, not when it comes to you." Her throat threatened to close up as new tears stung her eyes. "I want it all, Ty, and I know I can't have it."

He tightened his fingers on hers. "You're more than

important to me, Ashley. You've got to know that." But he didn't say the words, didn't make any promises to her.

She shook her head. "It's not enough, Ty. Not anymore."

"Because of what happened today?"

"You've been waiting most of your life to find Scilla. Short-term contracts, on-property housing, tour buses—you've built your world so you could cut loose the moment you found her. You don't even have a dog to worry about, never mind a house."

He shook his head. "You want me to get a dog?"

"No. I want someone to love me so fiercely that he'd turn his whole life upside down to have me. I want him to argue with me, fight for me, and move heaven and earth to prove that he's the one for me and that I'm number one for him." She smiled through her tears. "I've never had that, you see. And I deserve it."

"Of course you do."

"Just like you deserve to look for Scilla without feeling guilty about it." Her voice broke. "The woman in that picture needs you, Ty. Odds are that if you find her—*when* you find her—she's going to need a whole lot from you, whether or not she's willing to admit it at first. I think you're going to have to fight for her, one way or another."

He went very still, save for the agitated pulse at the side of his throat. "What are you saying?"

Nothing. I'm leaving. We don't need to do this now, not after the days we've both had. "I think this is where the trail forks for us, Ty. I think it's time for us to cut each other loose."

The silence that followed was laced with barn sounds—the rustle of a muzzle in hay, the stomp of a hoof, the bang of a bucket. It was all impossibly normal, as if the world wasn't in the process of ending.

Finally, sounding as if the words were being dragged out of him, he said, "If that's what you want."

No, damn you! How can you not see that I want you to argue with me, fight for me, chase me across three states, lasso me, and carry me home tied across the back of your horse?

He didn't, though. He wouldn't. And that was the problem.

"I wish you hadn't come after me," she said softly. Then she went up on her tiptoes, brushed her lips across his, and took a big step back, letting go of his hands as she did so.

The loss of that contact was wrenching.

He studied her as he had in the bar that long-ago night, as if trying to figure out how she was supposed to fit into his world. "I'm sorry."

Her heart shuddered and broke. "Me, too."

He reached past her and rolled open the barn door, letting in the night. "Good luck this weekend."

Tears gathered in her eyes, spilled over. "Thanks. You, too." After that, there didn't seem to be anything left to say except good-bye, and she couldn't. She just couldn't.

So she walked away instead. And she didn't let herself look back.

Ty stood in the doorway while the Beetle's pinpoint taillights wound up the drive that led away from the ranch, flashed at the top of the hill, and disappeared.

And she was gone.

As in gone, gone. Not coming back, at least not to see him. How had that happened? Why hadn't he stopped her?

Because she was right. That was why. She deserved everything she had asked for and more—to be loved, chased, courted, won. And he hadn't done any of that, not even when he'd been free to try it.

Had he been holding back so he'd be free when Mac's call came? Maybe. He didn't know. All he knew was that as much as he wanted to go after her, he couldn't, because she was right about something else: Scilla needed him.

But, damn.

Scrubbing a hand across his chest—which ached like a bull had caught him square in the sternum—he fumbled for his phone and punched a couple of buttons. When the call connected, he cleared his throat. "Mac, it's Ty."

"Yeah, I got that from the ID. I don't have anything else for you. Told you I'd call when I did."

"I want to meet up with you in Rapid City. Tomorrow morning, first thing."

There was a pause he didn't mistake for startled. He got the feeling very little surprised Ian Macaulay. "You don't have to do that."

"She's my sister."

"Didn't say she wasn't. Said you don't have to haul all the way out here to prove that you give a crap. You hired me, didn't you? Can't promise when or how, but

I'll find her. When I do, *that's* when you need to hit the road. Not now."

Ty's jaw locked up. "I'll be there at first light. Where should we meet?"

"Not at dawn, that's for damn sure." But Mac sighed. "Suit yourself. Two p.m., outside the cop shop where your sister got pinched. I've got a face-to-face with the cop who grabbed her. I'm hoping he'll give us the where-when-who."

"I'll be there."

There was a pause. Then, "Word of advice?"

"What's that?"

"Don't come. Not yet. Stay home, take care of your business there. Folks like your sister don't always want to be found. They're not the trusting type, and maybe don't think they need family. Maybe don't even figure they deserve it, or know how to do it right."

"Hell." Ty scowled, hearing an echo of Ashley's voice.

"I know. It's hard to believe that sometimes it takes some doing, getting them ready to come in from the cold. And sometimes it never happens. They're just too broken. I see it more than you'd think. Anyway, like I said, stay home, deal with your stuff. There'll be time to mobilize."

My stuff? Cold fingers walked down Ty's spine. "Thanks for the warning, Mac. But I already cleared my schedule for tomorrow. I'll see you at two."

"Suit yourself."

When the line went dead, Ty found himself right where he had been a minute ago—standing alone in the barn, with a big, aching hollow in the center of his chest that had less to do with the woman in the pictures than with the one who had just driven away. He couldn't go after her, though. Not unless he was willing to give her everything she had asked for, and more.

"Come on, then." He crossed the barn aisle and ran open Brutus's door. "Let's ride."

The drive home was enough of a blubbering blur that Ashley considered herself lucky she made it back with Bugsy in one piece. But luck was the furthest thing from her mind as she stumbled up the outer stairs, feeling like all of Main Street was watching her fumble for her house key and fight to get it in the lock. "Come on, come on, come on!" She chanted it tonelessly, mindlessly, wanting nothing more than to get inside, where nobody else would see her coming unglued.

She had done the right thing. She *had*.

But, oh, how it hurt.

Finally, the lock clicked. She practically fell through the door, stumbling on legs gone to water.

"Reowwwr!" The sharp cry came from ankle level, and was followed by a swat of claws.

"Ow!" She lurched back, dropping her bag as Tunes shot off the floor, scrambled across the counter, and sent two of her random-stuff jars crashing to the floor, where they detonated like button-and-penny-laden grenades. Then the cat levitated to the top of the cabinet, where she had stuck what was left of her dishes, thinking they would be safe way up there.

Glaring down at her, the furry fiend tapped the pretty blue creamer close to the edge.

Her eyes burned with tears. With fury. "Don't. You. Dare. If you even—"

Another poke, and the creamer went over. She lunged forward, reached for it. And missed.

Crash! It broke like sugar glass, into hundreds of pieces.

Ashley. Snapped.

Fury roared through her—at herself for falling when she told herself she wasn't, at Ty for not wanting her enough to fight back, at the investigator for his timing. "Fine!" she shouted. "You want to break things? Let's break things!" She spun and snatched up a mason jar full to the top with marbles, beads, and pretty rocks.

The cat shrank back, poising to run, but she turned and hurled it into the bricked-over fireplace, imagining her father's face.

CRASH! The shrapnel spray reached the couch and peppered the windows, suffusing her with a rush of satisfaction.

Tunes's eyes bugged, but he stayed put, looking transfixed.

"You liked that? How about this one?" She grabbed a cheap plate, sent it winging like at a Greek restaurant. Her high school nemesis. "Or this!" A coffee mug. A dish full of quarters and old keys. An empty Grey Poupon jar she had saved because she liked the shape. The creepy modeling agent, the art teachers that had told her she could make it, Kenny and his band. *Crash, crash,*

crash! She was making a mess of her apartment, but she didn't care. It might as well look the way she felt—like a freaking disaster.

Blood running high, she grabbed the last breakable off the counter and drew back, but then looked down at the little gray ceramic rabbit. "Damn it. I like this one." And if she broke it, she would never see it again, at least not the way it had been. She'd never again smile at it the same way, never again touch it, never again come to see it there at the breakfast bar.

Just like that, the fury drained, leaving crushing grief behind. *Oh, Ty.*

This wasn't what she wanted, wasn't what she had intended when she drove out to Mustang Ridge. Exactly the opposite. She had just wanted to help, wanted to be part of his life.

Now she was out of his life. For good.

Breath hitching, she stuck the little statue in the refrigerator, next to the mayo, where her hell cat couldn't get at it. Then, as her breath hitched and her vision blurred, she stalked out of the kitchen and straight into the bedroom.

There, she threw herself on the bed. And wept.

Oh, how it hurt. Inside. Outside. Everywhere. Her eyes burned, her throat tore, and each breath was like inhaling hot needles. Worse were the images that paraded through her mind like an agonizing slideshow, each more painful than the next. Ty plying the paint roller, T-shirt stretching over the body she had come to know so well over the past six weeks. Ty quirking an eyebrow at her, smiling at her, kissing her, sweeping her off her feet and carrying her to his bedroom.

Ty, sleeping beside her in the bed she was lying in now, alone.

She let out a low moan, curled herself into a tight ball, and tried to make her mind go blank. Still, the snippets came, twisting the dagger in her wounded heart.

Tears scalded her eyes and burned her throat, and she let out a broken sob that sounded suddenly loud in the room.

Bang! The bedroom door bounced suddenly back from the wall like it had been kicked open. For a second—a brief, damning second—she thought that Ty had followed her, that he was going to argue with her, for her. But then a lean, black-furred body thudded onto the bed, a wedge-shaped head with evil yellow eyes appeared in her field of vision, and a low growl vibrated from the beast's chest.

Ashley was too stunned to recoil, too caught up in her misery to do anything at all except think that maybe he would rip her throat out and be done with it. Too baffled do to anything other than stare when she realized Tunes wasn't growling after all—the noise was a rusty, disused-sounding purr. He even went so far as to prod the mattress a couple of times, as if he wanted to knead but didn't want to get caught acting like a kitten.

"What the—" The rest of her ragged question got lost when he head butted her in the mouth. She uncurled a little in self-defense, and he settled right in against her, soft and warm enough to spark more tears, partly pent up and partly because she had been reduced to snuggling with her mean old cat. And darned if the black devil didn't stay right there, purring like a generator while she soaked his fur with her tears.

23

Ty woke at dawn with a burned-down campfire in the fire pit, Brutus tethered over by the waterfall, and the acoustics of the hollow making the rushing water sound like it was coming from all around him. And damned if he couldn't smell springtime flowers, even though there wasn't a bloom within a mile of the falls this time of year.

As he blinked fully awake, though, the scent faded, leaving an empty ache behind.

Well, hell. He had ridden too hard and too far before circling back to the waterfall where he'd played for Ashley, made love to her. So much for avoiding places that reminded him of what he hadn't been able to hang on to.

He upended his canteen on the cooled-down embers, then kicked dirt on the mess. Untying Brutus, he slung his reins around the gelding's neck, then went around the back to double-check his bedroll. "Okay, meathead. Time to head back." He had a meeting to make.

When he grabbed for the reins, though, the gelding

flattened his ears and shuffled back several paces, giving him a look of, *You think so, huh?*

"Don't start," Ty growled. "I'm in no mood." He made a grab for the reins, but the horse danced back lightning quick, snaking his head like he was cutting a rank bull. "Brutus, you snotty bastard. *Whoa!*"

The chestnut wheeled, trotted away twenty feet or so, then turned back. His ears were pricked now, his eyes gleaming wickedly.

"Son of a—" Rage hazing his vision, Ty started after the horse, hands balled into fists. "Stop right there. If you move one more hoof, I'll—" He stopped dead, hearing the ugliness in his own voice. The menace. What the hell was he doing?

He stood there, fighting down the mean as the dawn got pretty around them. Thing was, the anger didn't want to fade. It wanted to get bigger and nastier, tearing at his gut and burning in his windpipe, and making him want to lash out and hurt something the way he was hurting inside.

"Fine!" He bellowed it at the big mustang, backing up the volume with big, aggressive body language. He took a couple of steps, waving his arms like he was trying to turn a stray cow back to the herd. "Go on. Get!"

The gelding shook his head in the equine version of *Make me*.

"You want to run off on me, just damn well *do it!* Why the hell not? Everyone else has."

Ty. Stopped. Breathing.

Those last three words hung in the air a good long time, backed up by a stomp of the big gelding's forefoot.

COMING HOME TO MUSTANG RIDGE   305

It was true, though. Everyone else had run off on him, one way or another. His sperm-donor father and junkie mother. Scilla. Rodeo Jim. Dim, good-natured Bob. Brandi. And now Ashley. He had lost them all.

Ashley.

Pain ripped through him, dragging the breath from his lungs and driving him to his knees beside the river, in the place where he had taken her slowly, wonderfully. "Goddamn it," he grated. Was she right about him? Was Mac? Brandi, even? Pressing clenched fists against his burning eyes, he ground out, "You idiotic, chickenhearted, damn fool stupid son of a—" A blow caught him in the shoulder, nearly sending him sprawling. He shouted, surging to his feet to meet the attack. And found himself eyeball-to-eyeball with Brutus.

The gelding snorted and nudged him again, hard enough to send him back half a step.

A few minutes earlier, Ty might've taken a swing at the horse, even knowing he would hate himself for it after. Now, he just lifted a hand and rubbed the sore spot over his breastbone. "Well?"

Brutus didn't move. Just stood there looking at Ty like he was possibly the stupidest cowboy ever. Which was a distinct possibility. Because, all of a sudden, he got it. He darn well got it.

He didn't know what he was going to do about it, how to fix it. But he was damn sure going to try.

"No, no, no. Dang it!" Ashley sat back on her heels, scowling at a mannequin she was pretty sure was scowling right back at her. It had a snotty look on its face, no question about it, and the punk-era leather jacket and ankle-zip acid-washed jeans didn't say *I love the eighties* so much as *Kill me now*.

"Problem?" Hen called from the sales floor, her voice muffled by the heavy curtains.

"Oh, no, I'm having a great time," she hollered back. "Of *course* I'm having problems—what does it sound like in here, a party?" Okay, admittedly the mannequin wasn't the only one who had some snotty going on. But after all the work she and the others had put in on the game show, the concept had gone stale on her. Glaring at the fifties-era mannequin, who looked smug and condescending in her perfect housedress, and like any minute now she might start lecturing Ashley about being a good little housewife, she said, "Tell me again why I thought this was a good idea?"

"It *is* a good idea! The customers will love getting a discount for answering the questions. You just need to find a happy place." The curtains moved at the far end and Hen's face popped through. "You sure you don't want to talk about what happened with Ty?"

"Very sure." Ashley adjusted the fifties housewife so she was picking her nose. "There's nothing to talk about. I hate that it happened the way it did, but we would've gotten there eventually. I can't help the way I feel about him, and he can't help being who he is. The only thing I *can* do is refuse to wait around for him to change. I'm not my mother."

"News flash. Ty isn't your dad."

"No, he's not. He's Ty. And that's the problem." Because Ty didn't want her enough to let her in, work for her, or even meet her halfway. Blinking back fresh tears—why hadn't she run dry by now?—she made it look like the punk rocker was reaching over to strangle June Cleaver.

"Therapy," Hen suggested. "Get some."

"I don't need therapy. I need to stop falling for guys who take more than they give." She scowled. "But right now, I need to make this bloody window work."

Hen shot a dubious look at the homicidal mannequins. "Maybe you should call Shelby, get her opinion on things."

"I will." Later, when explaining the situation didn't make her want to tear down the curtains, roll herself up like a giant cocooned caterpillar, and wait for Penny to come deliver the bad news from the bank. *You failed. Probably shouldn't have even tried in the first place. Who do you think you are, anyway?* "Maybe I should rip it all down and start over. Because right now, it really sucks." The window. Her mood. Her ability to think about tomorrow as anything but a chore.

"Umm. Is this a bad time?" a new voice asked, sounding tentative.

Ashley winced as Hen's head disappeared back through the curtain. She hadn't heard the bell, hadn't realized they had a customer. She was off her game, off her rhythm, off her rocker. "Of course not!" she called, forcing a lilt. "And welcome to Another Fyne Thing!"

"Thank goodness," Hen said cryptically. "Go right on through."

The curtains moved, and Ashley sucked in a breath to tell whoever it was to get lost. But when Gilly came into view, wearing a T-shirt and jeans with her vintage boots and belt, she let that breath back out again.

The teen hesitated just inside the curtained-off space, looking from Ashley to the mannequins and back again. "You're busy."

"It's okay. Come on in, look around. It's kind of a disaster right now." And, unfortunately, more reminiscent of *A Clockwork Orange* than *Family Feud*.

But Gilly seemed more interested in the furball that was currently perched atop the hippie's game show podium, tucked into the shape of a cat-headed loaf of bread. "I didn't know you had a store cat."

As far as Ashley was concerned, she didn't have a store cat. She had a house cat who had snuck out after her that morning and ever since had stayed within a two-foot radius of her, except when she tried to grab him for a return trip upstairs. Whereupon he vaporized. "He's not a cat. He's the reincarnation of a Russian spy with a split personality."

"Cool. What's his name?"

"Tunes. No, darn it. Petunia."

"I like Tunes better." Gilly crouched down and held out her hand. "Hey, buddy. You're a pretty boy, aren't you?"

Darned if the creature didn't jump down and trot right over to her, whereupon he butted his head against her hand and proceeded to wrap himself around her legs like a furry eel.

"Oh, for—" Ashley shook her head. "Never mind. What's going on in your world? How are things with Sean?"

Gilly made a face. "Over and done."

"What . . . ? Really?" It was a double shocker, both the announcement and how casually it was delivered. "What happened?"

"Once I started getting to know him better, it was always *My ex this* and *My ex that.* I came right out and said it was bugging me, and when it didn't stop, I told him that I just wanted to be friends, and that he should really think about what it would take to get back with her."

"Oh. Wow. I'm sorry."

The teen's shrug was entirely philosophical. "I was, too, at first. But the thing is, if it wasn't for him, I might not have come in here that first time. Which means I would probably still be wearing Bub's jacket and spending most of my time in my room. I'm grateful to Sean for giving me that kick in the pants, even if he didn't really do it—I did."

There went those darn tears again, blurring Ashley's vision and making things in the window seem better than they had a minute ago. "Wow, kid. You're something else—you know that? I wish I'd had half as much perspective when I was your age." Heck, she could use some of it now.

"That's from my mom, I guess, and Bub. They always wanted me to be my own person, and I think I'm getting there. Starting to, anyway." She hesitated, then said softly, "Things won't ever be back the way they were, but I guess we're finding a new normal, me and Mom. And I think wherever Bub is, he knows that we still think about him every day." She pulled out her phone, tapped a button, and swiped through some images. "This was from his last visit. We're getting it blown up and framed."

In the photo, a grinning Gilly was wrapped piggyback around a tall, spindly man with a prominent Adam's apple and a smile that said whatever was going on, you could trust him to handle it. A dark-haired woman stood with her arm linked through his, wearing a deeply satisfied smile that said all was right with her world just then. There was a lakeside picnic in the background and autumn color to the leaves, and Ashley could almost smell the thin trickle of smoke coming from the campfire.

Or she thought she would have, if she could have taken a breath.

Instead, she stared, transfixed, as a whole lot of buzzing started up in her brain—a cacophony of *Look at them* and *Think about what happened* and *How would you feel if something happened to Wyatt?*

She would be devastated, of course. And, worse, ripped up with guilt because she hadn't fixed things all the way between them.

Kind of how she felt right now, with Ty gone from her life.

She was grieving, miserable, lashing out, shutting herself away.

Oh, no. She had gone and done it, hadn't she?

She had fallen in love. For real this time.

With a thud, she hit the bottom of the cliff. The impact knocked the wind out of her and sent shock reverberating—a whole lot of *What were you thinking? What are you doing?* and *How could you?* Not because she had fallen for him, but because she had pushed him away. She hadn't given him a chance to breathe after learning about his sister's plight, hadn't taken a day—or even an hour—to see how things were going to shake out.

Her mom had given Wylie decades to pull himself together, which was crazy. Ashley herself had given Kenny three years and more do-overs than she wanted to count. Then she had turned around and given Ty three minutes on what he probably counted as one of the worst days of his life.

Not because she cared less for him, but because she cared so much more. And because, deep down inside, she was pretty sure he was out of her league.

Thud. She must have bounced, because that had her hitting bottom a second time, along with the realization that she had lost Ty because she hadn't truly fought for him. She had asked him to fight for her, but she had been the one retreating.

"Oh." Her hand went to her throat. "Oh, no."

Gilly lowered her phone. "What's wrong?"

I'm in love with Ty. And when you love someone, you don't keep score. "Nothing. Everything. I just realized I made a huge mistake." She should have given it more time, given *them* more time. How was it that she had dithered on the edge of falling for him, but leaped in with both feet when it came to blowing things up between them?

Fear. Baggage. Insecurity. Daddy issues.

Oh, shut up.

"Can you fix it?"

"I don't know." But Ashley's mind raced ahead, skimming over apologies, little gestures, big gestures, ways to show Ty that she loved him, was willing to wait for him, fight for him, whatever it took, as long as he was willing to meet her halfway. What if she— No, not that. Or— Nope, not that, either.

Then, in an aha moment of epic proportions, no doubt brought on by the punk rocker's manic glee and June Cleaver's down-the-nose sneer, she knew exactly what she had to do, and how she was going to pull it off.

Heart suddenly thudding against her ribs, she called, "Hen? Toss me the store phone, will you?"

"Are you calling Shelby?"

"I will, but I need to talk to Jenny first." Jenny, who had friends in television, and who could get the word out far and wide if she made it a big enough story. And who could maybe, just maybe, help make a big brother's dream come true.

Gilly rocked back on her heels. "I should go."

"No, stay. If you've got time, that is. I could use your help."

"Finishing the window?" she asked, eyes lighting.

"No, tearing it down and building it back up from scratch. I need a do-over."

Fingers crossed that it wouldn't be too little, too late.

24

Saturday, the day of the Midsummer Parade, dawned clear and warm, with a zero percent chance of rain and an eighty or so percent chance of Ashley melting down before the mayor's cavalcade reached the shop.

Not because she could smell the brownie bites, but because they didn't matter anymore.

"We're here!" Krista hustled around the corner of the storefront with Abby on her hip and Rose, Ed, Gran, and Big Skye behind her. "We're not too late, are we?"

"Nope." Ashley gestured to the next block down, where the mayor's banner-hung truck was parked in front of the bakery. "The judges seem to have stalled." She shot a look in Hen's direction. Standing with Jenny, Shelby, Danny, Gilly, Gilly's mom, and several other shop VIPs, she was chowing down. "And they're not the only ones."

Popping the last peanut butter brownie morsel into her mouth, Hen gave an unrepentant grin. "Just keeping tabs on the competition, boss."

Looking past the small crowd assembled out in front

of Another Fyne Thing, where a roped-off area would give the mayor a clear view of the window when it came time for the big reveal, Ashley said, "Where's Wyatt?" She didn't let herself ask about Ty. She had texted, asking him to come if he was back in town, but odds were that he was in Rapid City.

Heck, she might even be too late to help. She could live with that, though. At least she would have tried, and she would have given Ty something to think about.

Maybe. Hopefully. *Oh, God.*

"I'm here!" Her brother appeared from the other direction, coming through the sidewalk-jamming crowd that jostled beyond the competition area. "I had to park outside of town and hike in." He ducked under the rope and glanced at the two strangers standing just inside the roped-off area. "What's with the film crew?"

"They're friends of Jenny's. And it's a secret." Squelching her nervous butterflies, Ashley traded winks with Berry McNeil, the striking platinum blonde reporter who had, within her first five minutes in the shop, called dibs on two Designs by Della dresses and a fringed suede jacket. *Ca-ching!* Behind her, Mike the Camera Guy—that was how he had introduced himself—had everything up and running. They were ready to roll as soon as the mayor arrived.

Ashley had something to do first, though. Not letting herself think of anything beyond this very minute, she crossed to Wyatt, flung her arms around him, and said, "I just wanted to say I love you, big bro. You're the best. I know I don't say it enough, but I'm going to try to do better from now on."

He stiffened for a nanosecond, then went with it and hugged her back. "I thought I made you crazy."

"Well, yeah, but that doesn't mean I don't love you. You're the most functional piece of family I've got, and I know you'll always have my back. Thank you for that."

That got a chuckle, younger and freer-sounding than his usual where she was concerned. "What's gotten into you?"

"A reality check." She eased away, glimpsing Krista's pleased smile. "I've gotten a couple of reminders recently that family is forever, and I wanted you to know that I'm glad you're mine, exactly the way you are." She paused. "And speaking of checks, what are the chances you could write me another one?"

That got an eye roll, but it wasn't nearly so annoying as before. "You blew through the last one already?"

"I ripped it up." She had done it first thing yesterday morning in a fit of *I can do it myself.* "But since I'm throwing the contest, I'm going to need to borrow from you—emphasis on *borrow*—to make my next payment. I want paperwork, interest, the whole nine yards."

An honest-to-goodness grin curved his mouth. "Look at you, businessgirl."

"That's *businesswoman* to you, buster."

"I stand corrected. And ready to give you that loan, with or without the paperwork. After seeing what you've pulled off over the past six weeks"—his gesture encompassed the store, the crowd, the electricity in the air—"I trust you that I'll see the money back." But then he paused, frowned. "Hang on. What do you mean, you're throwing the contest?"

The cavalcade was on the move, heading toward Another Fyne Thing with the band thumping along and the mayor waving from the back of a bunting-draped pickup truck.

Ashley caught her breath. This was it. She was really doing this. "Change of plans," she told her brother. "I'll do the game show display next week. For today, I've got a whole new theory." Summoning a smile, she said, "If it goes the way I hope, it'll be the biggest surprise of the day."

Too bad it was aimed at a man who wasn't there to see it.

Wyatt wiggled an eyebrow. "I think you might be wrong about that."

"How so?"

"Just wait." As the truck approached with Mayor Tepitt waving and tossing mints into the crowd, he said, "This is your moment, kiddo."

The butterflies went vertical, launching into Ashley's chest and making it hard to breathe. *You can do this. You can.* "I'll make you proud."

"You already do, every day you live on your own terms and make your own way. And that's something I haven't said to you nearly enough, along with that I love you, too, sis." He nudged her forward. "Now go get 'em!"

It was time, she knew. The only thing missing was Ty. She had wanted him here, wanted to see his face when the curtains came down.

Too bad it turned out that her personal mantra was really *You don't always get what you want.* She was trying, though. She was working for it, even when the going got tough.

Aware that the camera was rolling, the crowd buzz was growing, and a whole lot of eyeballs were swiveled her way, Ashley took a deep breath, walked to the front of the roped-off area, lifted a hand, and called, "Howdy, Miz Mayor. Welcome to Another Fyne Thing, home of the best vintage wear in Three Ridges!"

Over the ripple of applause and the hoots of "Woohoo!" and "Way to go, Ashley!" Mayor Tepitt's amplified voice said, "Why, thank you, Ashley! I know you've got a real flair for window displays, and I've been looking forward to seeing your entry in this year's contest. But—" The mayor paused, drawing it out and preening a little for the TV crew.

Ashley stiffened. There was a *but*? No, there couldn't be a *but*. She had worked too hard for there to be a *but*.

Before she could do a *Wait, what?* the mayor continued. "First, I've got someone who wants to say something." She looked over to the other side of her truck. "Tyler?"

Ty!?

The butterflies hit warp speed and Ashley's vision tunneled for a second, as if she might faint right then and there. *Boom*, down on the sidewalk she would go, for all of Three Ridges—and the viewers of Channel Sixteen—to see. But then things cleared as hoofbeats sounded on Main Street and a mounted cowboy—*her* cowboy—came around the front of the mayor's truck, astride a familiar rangy chestnut, who had an arch in his neck and something hanging on either side of his haunches.

It was a realty sign, with HOUSE FOR SALE changed to HORSE FOR SALE and a diagonal SOLD slapped across it.

Pulse thudding, Ashley stared at Ty. "What . . . ? *Ty!* But you're supposed to be in Rapid City looking for Scilla!"

He reined up just on the other side of the rope and tipped the brim of his hat back so the sunlight reached his eyes. And instead of the wary, closed-off look she was expecting, she saw two of the most beautiful things she had ever seen.

Nerves and hope. Just like what was inside her all of a sudden.

"Nope," he said, loud and clear. "I'm right where I'm supposed to be, right where I need to be, though it took me a little while to figure out." He patted the gelding's neck. "You were right that I was marking time, keeping things loose, but it wasn't because of Scilla, not entirely. It was because having things meant I could lose them. And having things I love would make it even worse."

She couldn't breathe, but in the very best way possible. "You bought Brutus."

He nodded. "We can pick the dog together when it suits us, but this guy is nonnegotiable. Nobody else wants to put up with his grief, and I need someone who'll have my back against your devil cat." He paused, searching her eyes. "That is, if you'll give me a chance to set things right?"

The pause that followed was the longest of Ty's life, because her answer mattered the way breathing mattered to him, or music. But where breathing and music had always come naturally, this was new territory.

He could do this, though. She deserved it. She deserved to know that she was everything to him, and that he had enough inside him—he would *make* there be enough inside him—for her, even while he and Mac kept looking for Scilla, and dealt with whatever they found.

Just like Wyatt couldn't run his sister's life, Ty needed to make his own way. It was time to put down some roots, even if it scared the hell out of him.

Needing to move, he swung down, tossed the reins to Wyatt—the unexpected ally who had offered his truck and trailer to get him and his new horse to the parade when Krista clued him in on what was going down—and hopped over the rope. Aware they were being filmed by a TV crew from a station number he didn't recognize, he stopped an arm's length away from Ashley.

Pitching his voice to carry, he said, "This is me chasing you, or at least starting to. If you need more, you got it. I'll chase you, fight for you, bring you flowers and chocolate. Whatever you want, you got, because you're the best thing that's ever happened to me. And"—he took a deep breath—"because I love you." The last three words came out rough, rusty, and echoed in his chest in a way that said this was it for him. She was it. Whatever it took to win her back, he would do it. If only she gave him the chance. "Say something. Please."

Instead, she reached out, took his hand, and tugged

him closer to her, off to one side of the display window. Then, not looking at him, she called, "Mayor Tepitt? I hope you like my window. But it's okay if you don't, as long as Ty gets it."

Squeezing his hand, she shot a high sign to Hen, who was standing just inside the store. A quick yank, and the heavy purple curtains fell inside the store, revealing the huge display window.

Ty's. Heart. Stopped.

Instead of mannequins, butterflies, and vintage clothes turned trendy by Ashley's magical touch, there was Scilla.

Not in person, of course, but there she was. Her eyes. Her smile. Her photographs—the long-ago Polaroid, and a Photoshopped version of the mug shot, which cleaned her up and put trees behind her rather than a gray wall of lines and numbers.

And beside the photos, a plea for help. DO YOU KNOW PRISCILLA? PLEASE HELP US REUNITE HER WITH HER BIG BROTHER. HE'S BEEN LOOKING FOR HER SINCE THE DAY THEY WERE SEPARATED. Below that was a phone number and TV logo that matched the camera crew's. RAPID CITY'S TOP NEWS TEAM.

Ty moved toward the window, throat locking up as he tugged Ashley with him, tangling their fingers together and hanging on tight. She had done this. For him. Even after he had let her go, darn near pushed her away.

She was amazing.

"Ashley . . ." It was the most natural thing in the world to pull her into his arms. The crowd, the camera, even the mayor's amplified voice reading a brief, carefully worded statement about his search for his sister—none of it mattered compared to having Ashley in his arms again and knowing she had done this for him, even after he'd let her go. Pressing his forehead to hers, he rasped, "Thank you."

Looping her arms around his neck, she rose up and pressed her lips to his. "You're welcome."

The kiss was simple, chaste, and rocketed through him like lightning, tightening every fiber of his being with hope—that this meant what he thought it did. "Does this mean I get a second chance?"

"Only if I get one, too." Easing away, she looked up at him, all serious, and so adorable that his heart hurt. "I'm sorry I picked a fight about Rapid City. She's your sister. Of course you've got to do whatever it takes. There's plenty of time for the two of us to work things out after. Forgive me?"

He would have given her just about anything she asked for right then, but this one was easy. "Done. Do-over."

"How about we say we're moving forward from here?"

"Yeah." There wasn't even a twinge. It was right. *They* were right. "That'll work." He kissed her, deeper this time, and aware of a rising buzz from the crowd. But he was focused entirely on her when he eased the kiss to look down at her and say, "I love you, Ashley Webb. From now on, I promise to love you every day, and to fight for you when I have to, even if it means fighting myself."

Tears gathered in her eyes. "I love you, too, Ty. And there won't be any fighting." But then the corners of her mouth kicked up. "Well, maybe. I'm a work in progress."

"We both are." But for the first time in his life, he wanted to do that work. More, he wanted to do it together, as part of a team. Their team.

"So, Tyler . . ." A microphone appeared in his peripheral vision, held by a snazzy brunette with a definite *This story just got even better than I was hoping* twinkle in her eyes. "Does this mean you like what Ashley did for you?"

He would have rather ducked both of them out the back, or maybe upstairs—somewhere they could have privacy, where he could kiss her for real and revel in knowing that he didn't have to stop, that they hadn't lost their chance. But she had done this for him, and he wasn't going to waste the gift. This was his chance—*their* chance—to spread the word.

Maybe it would work; maybe it wouldn't. Maybe he would go to Rapid City for the winter and help Mac with the search. Maybe not. But if he did, he would be burning a whole lot of rubber between there and Mustang Ridge, and he'd be back in Three Ridges come spring, this time with the five-year contract Krista had offered him. Because Scilla might be his sister, but Ashley and the gang at Mustang Ridge were his family.

So, looping an arm around Ashley's waist and snugging her close to his side, he grinned at the reporter and added a little extra cowboy to his voice, the way he did with the greenhorns. "I'm so grateful to her that I'm about to bust. Here's hoping that someone who knows Scilla sees it, or maybe even Scilla herself." He looked into the camera. "I love you, little sis, and I've been looking for you for a long time now. Please call, or come find me." He snugged Ashley a little closer to his side. "And for the rest of you ladies out there, if you're looking for something a little different, come see Ashley here, at Another Fyne Thing!"

25

That evening, after everything wound down and the last of the steady flow of customers had waved on their way out the door, Ashley and Ty finally got some alone time.

"Well," she said, carrying their drinks around from the kitchen nook and making a beeline for the sofa. "That was quite a day."

"You can say that again. Here. Let me get those." He snagged his beer and her wine—she would've been channeling Shelby with a sedate white in a normal glass, if it hadn't been for the perky pink umbrella—and set them on the coffee table. "I still think your window should've won." He tugged her down, tumbling her onto his lap and drawing her in for a kiss.

"I agree, but still . . . Brownies." Because, really, chocolate was going to beat most anything nine times out of ten. Even a really good cause and prominent spots on the afternoon and evening newscasts.

"You sure you won't let me lend you the money?"

"Positive. Wyatt and I are going to draw up the paperwork this week. Collateral, interest, and everything."

"Collateral?"

"Bugsy." She grinned. "I'm going to be tempted to default, just to make my big, bad brother drive him out of town. The pictures would almost be worth it." She wouldn't, though. Snuggling into him, she added, "It's crazy. When I started this, I swore I would lose the shop before I asked him for money. Now it's no big deal."

"Actually, I'd say it's a very big deal." As Tunes jumped up on the coffee table to investigate, Ty reached forward, snagged his beer, and handed over her wine. "A toast. To making your second payment."

"Amen." They clinked, sipped, and kissed, and her heart turned over in her chest before settling back into the happy rhythm it had been bebopping ever since the parade. It was hard to believe how much things had changed in just a few hours. Then again, look at the past couple of months. The past two years.

A work in progress, maybe, but she sure liked the direction she was heading, and she loved the man who was going to be beside her for the next chunk of it, hopefully all the way to the end. It was early yet to think about things like *for as long as you both shall live*. But all of a sudden it didn't feel so far off, either.

She smiled into her wine as Tunes jumped up on the couch and pointy-footed his way over the two humans, giving suspicious sniffs at their drinks and wrinkling his whiskers in feline disgust. "And just look at you," she said to the cat. "You've come a long way." They all had.

"We should celebrate," Ty decided.

"A party for Tunes?"

He ruffled the cat's fur, got a sneer and a head butt in return. "He'd like that, wouldn't he? Actually, I was talking about when you hand over the check."

She wasn't sure which part of that warmed her right down to her toes—that he wasn't going to let her wallow in falling short of her goal when she had a workable backup plan, that he was thinking about her stuff as well as his own, or that he wanted to make a plan. All of it, really. Angling her face, she gave him a smacking kiss on the jaw. "Look at you, thinking ahead!"

His expression went wry. "Funny. You want to talk about the future? Fine, how about a vacation? I've always thought about heading south for a couple of weeks during the worst of the winter, but never did it. I think we should make a plan. Nashville, maybe, or New Orleans. Good music. Or Hawaii. Or is there someplace you've always wanted to go?"

"I . . . Hmm."

"Is that a *No, I don't want to go someplace warm and awesome in the dead of winter*? I know you'll be busy with the store over the holidays, so I was thinking maybe February."

More warm tingles. "Oh, definitely yes to the vacation part. It's just that nobody's ever asked me where I want to go on vacation before." Jack had taken her and her mom on a couple of cruises, and Kenny and the band had liked to party in San Fran, but that was about it. "I'll have to get back to you on that. Though Mardi Gras *is* on my bucket list . . ." She thought it would be like her brain—loud and chaotic, with lots of bright colors.

"No rush. But how about the party?"

"Definitely," she assured him. "I want to repaint the sign, do a big reveal, and christen the shop's new name with a champagne toast. I'm even going to invite Mom and Jack." Her mother would love Ty, God help her.

His eyebrows rose. "You're changing the shop's name?"

"I am." It was the first time she had said it out loud. Before, it had been all about the paperwork, legalities, and figuring out what script to use. Now, it was time for the shimmies of excitement. "Just a little—to *Ashley's Another Fyne Thing*."

Expression warming with approval, he said, "I think that sounds just about perfect to me."

"Good, because I was going to ask if you wanted to keep me company while I did the stealth painting Thursday night."

"Count me in," he said easily. "I'll take care of dinner."

And it really was that easy, she realized. It might not always be—probably wouldn't be—but for now, she would let herself enjoy being in love and being loved.

"Speaking of dinner," she began, then broke off when her cell phone rang its generic no-caller-ID melody. "Hang on. Hold that thought." She hit the button to connect. "Hello?"

There was a startled-feeling pause, and then a woman's voice said, "Um, hello. I don't know if I have the right— Is Tyler Reed there? This is . . . this is his sister."

Hot-cold-hot poured through Ashley and she was pretty sure her heart skipped a couple of beats.

"You're . . ." She couldn't get it out, was almost afraid to hope for him. Had her crazy plan actually worked?

"His sister. Um . . . I called the number on the TV, and the lady asked me a bunch of questions, then gave me this number." Her voice softened, took on new nerves. "Is he there?"

"Yes." Ashley got the word out, aware of Ty's sudden scrutiny, the tension in his big body that said whatever was upsetting her all of a sudden, he would deal with it.

Or, rather, they would deal with it together.

Hand shaking slightly, she held out the phone. "It's for you. It's Scilla."

His face blanked, then drained of blood, his skin going suddenly gray with shock. "You're kidding."

She put the phone in his hand. "The station gave her my number." Which meant she had answered the verification questions correctly. Which meant . . .

He lifted the handset, eyes stark on Ashley's. "Hel—" His voice broke on it. Clearing his throat, he said, louder, "Hello? This is Ty." Ashley didn't hear the reply, but his face blossomed suddenly with exquisite joy, as if he had been trapped alone with nothing but broccoli to eat and a bikini model suddenly showed up bearing chocolate. "Scilla." He blinked back moisture. "It's good to hear your voice."

Choking up, Ashley rose, figuring she would give him some privacy and give herself a good sniffle in the process. But as she moved past Ty, he shot out a hand, caught her arm, and tugged her back down beside him. He angled the phone so she could hear a soft sob, then Scilla saying, "I didn't think I was ever going to find you."

He tightened his arm around Ashley and breathed into her hair, and his voice was husky when he said, "It's all good now, darlin'. Because we finally found each other."

See how it all began at Mustang Ridge!
Turn the page for a preview of

SUMMER AT
MUSTANG RIDGE

Available now from Signet Eclipse.

"Okay, no pressure. We're just here to have fun. Ready?" Shelby paused with her hand on a pair of saloon-style swinging doors to grin down at Lizzie, hoping her daughter couldn't see the nerves. "Me neither, but let's do it anyway."

She pushed through into the dining hall of the ranch, which continued the Western theme from the log-style exterior, complete with rope accents, primitive furniture, and antler chandeliers. Thirty or so men and women wearing crunchy-new denim and unscuffed Western boots milled around long picnic tables with drinks in hand, creating a cocktail party's worth of noise, and a banner over the huge stone fireplace proclaimed HOWDY THERE, FILLIES AND STUDS. WELCOME TO SINGLES WEEK AT MUSTANG RIDGE!

The moment the doors banged shut behind Shelby, a dozen or so pairs of eyes zeroed in and gave her an up-and-down, making her very aware that her black pants, pin-striped jacket, and chunky boots probably said "straight from Boston" more than they did "we're stretchy and comfortable for a long car trip." Then the saloon doors swung again and her daughter came in behind her, and the eyes shifted away.

"Here!" A twentysomething blonde bounced up to them. She was wearing a green polo shirt embroidered with the Mustang Ridge logo on one side and her name—Tipper—on the other. She looked momentarily confused by Lizzie, but then shrugged and thrust two HOWDY, MY NAME IS _____! tags at them, along with a Sharpie. "You guys will want these!"

"But we're not—" Shelby began, but then broke off because Tipper was already bopping over to her next tagless victim, a curvy thirtysomething brunette with an elfin haircut. Shrugging, Shelby offered Lizzie the stickers. "You want to fill them out for us? No? Okay, I'll do it." She wrote *Lizzie's mom* on one and *Shelby's kid* on the other, and stuck them in place. "That should take care of it, but stay close to me." Which was a given.

"Hello, ladies," said a voice from behind them, making Shelby do a turn-and-tuck so she was in front of Lizzie.

The guy gained points by holding a soda rather than a beer, but lost them by having added another exclamation point to his name so the tag on his purple rodeo shirt read HOWDY, MY NAME IS BRAD!! Having gotten her attention, he leaned in too close to say, "I've got a confession to make—it's my first time. How about you?" An eyebrow wiggle lost him another point.

Not that Shelby was interested enough to add up the pluses and minuses, but keeping score was an occupational hazard, as was the propensity to turn everything into a slogan. *Tired of being single? Try our new and im-*

proved Brad!! He comes complete with a one-bedroom condo, convertible, and new caps. Ex-wife sold separately.

She gave him a half-watt smile. "I've never been to a dude ranch before, if that's what you're asking. And I'm not really—"

"Everyone?" an amplified voice broke in. "If I could have your attention?" A pretty, late-twenties blonde climbed up on a low stage beneath the banner. She was wearing figure-hugging jeans and worn boots, and holding a wireless microphone that fuzzed out her voice a little. When the hubbub died down, she caroled, "Welcome to Mustang Ridge! We've got an incredible week of riding, roping, and mingling planned for you. First, though, I'd like to start by telling you a little bit about the ranch and how we do things out here in the great state of Wyoming. So please have a seat, any place where there's a booklet, and we'll get started!"

Shelby waited until the others had filtered to their seats, jockeying for primo positions next to their first-choice singles. Then she nodded to an empty table. "Let's sit near the back." Lizzie hesitated and shot a long look out the door, making Shelby grin. "Sorry, kiddo, orientation first. But as soon as we're done in here, I'll take you out to the barn."

It was why they were there, after all.

"Why, hello, aren't you a big one?" a woman's voice purred through the barn. "Then again, I heard that everything's bigger up here in Wyoming."

Foster finished squirting antibiotics into Loco's cracked heel and looked up to find a blonde standing just inside the double doors, with generous curves stacked inside brand-new Wranglers and a snap-studded pink shirt that looked like the top fastener could go at any moment, and might take out an eye when it did. He stifled a sigh—*play nice with the guests; you're part of the local flavor*—and said, "No, ma'am. I believe that's Texas."

He wasn't all that big, either—maybe six feet, one ninety. Nowhere near as massive as his assistant wrangler, Ty, who always looked like something straight out of the pro rodeo tour in fringed chaps, flat-screen-size belt buckle, felt Stetson, and gleaming ostrich boots. Foster, on the other hand, wore his usual "it's my day off" clothes: a battered black felt Stetson, plain T-shirt, faded jeans, and scarred ropers. As local flavor went, he wasn't much. But Ty wasn't there. Foster was, and the blonde was looking to bag a cowboy in her first five minutes off the airport shuttle.

She sidled in, skirted a pile of manure like it was a diamondback, and sashayed over to lean against the wall beside him. Which just went to show that she had zero horse sense, because that put her right in the line of fire if Loco leaped sideways or swung a kick.

Granted, Loco was anything but loco. But still.

She leaned in too close, giving Foster a good look at the local topography—a pair of nicely rounded breasts inside pink lace that would itch like crazy once she was out riding, with all the sweat and dust, and the bouncing around that beginners were prone to. Not that she would take any of the advice she'd be given over the next couple of days about wearing comfortable, low-chafe underclothes as they geared up for longer trail rides. No, she would wear lace top and bottom, and then complain. He'd bet money on it.

"What are you doing?" she asked prettily. "Is he hurt?"

He let Loco's hoof down and shifted the gelding away from her. "It's more preventative maintenance."

"Like a lube job?"

Ohh-kay. "You're going to miss orientation."

"How about you give me a private tour?"

Not even with someone else's privates. "Sorry, ma'am. Ranch policy." Not really, but it was a handy excuse.

Her eyes picked up a gleam. "I wouldn't tell."

"Go on, now, and join the party."

She pouted, but then blew him a kiss and flounced away, ruining her exit—or improving it, depending— by stepping squarely in the manure. She skidded and squeaked, but kept up her sexy wiggle all the way out of the barn.

Moments later, Foster heard a muttered curse and some scuffing noises outside, as she scraped her boots.

Chuckling, he moved around to Loco's other side, ran a hand down the mustang's shoulder, and touched the back of his fetlock. "How's this shoe doing? Sounded to me like it might be coming loose."

And that wasn't the only thing, from the looks of it. Singles week. *Yeesh.*

After the herd in the dining hall had settled down to more or less pay attention, the blonde with the microphone announced: "My name is Krista Skye, and I'm one of the owners of Mustang Ridge."

Shelby stifled the urge to give her a resounding "Hi, Krista!" and opened the booklet in front of her.

The cover was emblazoned with the Mustang Ridge Dude Ranch logo, and the inner flap bore a glossy photo that she would've thought was Photoshopped if she hadn't seen the view on the drive in. The cloud-studded Wyoming sky was straight out of the *Simpsons* opening credits, the horizon was the poster child for "America the Beautiful"'s purple mountain majesty, sweeping fields ran along the ridgeline, and the ranch itself was nestled in a gentle valley beside a Crayola blue lake.

It was ridiculously gorgeous, assuming you liked the middle of nowhere.

"We're not going to go over everything in the book," Krista said, earning a few cheers from the hopped-up crowd. "Inside it you'll find daily schedules of our main events, along with alternatives if you need a day out of the saddle. The schedules and any updates will be posted here in the dining hall and out by the barn, so the main thing I'd like to go over right now is the rules of the ranch. We try not to go overboard, but you're in the Wild West, folks, and you're going to be dealing with livestock."

A big guy in the front row lifted a longneck in toast. "To fillies and studs!"

That got a sprinkle of laughter and a couple of eye rolls.

Krista grinned but stayed on task. "You've already read and signed the waivers, so you've got some idea of what I mean. We'll go over more safety precautions when we get to the actual riding part of things. For now, I'd appreciate it if you'd all look at page two and read along with me." Point by point, she went down a list of ten dos and don'ts that were mostly common sense, translated into dude-speak.

Don't kick dirt on the cook fire (pick up after yourself).

Don't take seconds until everyone's dished up their firsts (be courteous).

Leave every gate the way you found it (don't mess with the livestock).

Walk the first mile out and the last mile in (treat your horse well and he'll return the favor).

See to your horse before yourself (ditto).

When passing a cowboy, never turn and watch him ride away (trust your wranglers).

There's only one trail boss (follow orders).

When in doubt, tighten your cinch (always triple-check your equipment).

There's no such thing as a stupid question (never be afraid to ask a staff member).

And finally . . . cowboy up and have fun!

Giving Krista points for the presentation, Shelby tapped the page in front of her daughter and said in an undertone, "Read this. Know it. Love it. And I'm going to add number eleven: Don't go near the horses without a grown-up."

Ever since they had firmed up their plans to head west, Lizzie had been poring over her *Bridle Club* books until they were puffed up and practically disintegrating, and their Netflix account had given *My Friend Flicka* a good workout. But that didn't mean she knew what she was doing. Exactly the opposite, in fact, as she hadn't wanted to take lessons at a local riding school before coming out here.

"Basically," Krista continued, "we're asking you to follow the Cowboy Code by respecting your stock, your spread, your tack, and your fellow hands. In return, we'll feed you the best ranch grub you'll ever eat, bar none, and we'll teach you how to ride, rope, cut cattle, and square-dance. And because this is singles week, we'll also have a whole bunch of special getting-to-know-you events."

There was a shuffling in the crowd, and a stage whisper of "I'd like to get to know *you* better" from a woman in the front as she snuggled up next to Brad.

Shelby didn't get it but, hey, to each her own.

Krista continued. "Here in Wyoming, we're proud supporters of female empowerment. Since the eighteen fifties, Mustang Ridge Ranch has been bossed by Skye women four different times, seeing some of its most profitable decades and running thousands of cattle. These days the herds are smaller and our focus has shifted to giving you the best vacation of your lives, but the Skye ladies remain committed to this ranch and the people and animals on it."

She gestured to a nearby hallway, and an older version of her emerged from the shadows and came up to stand on the podium, shooting them a Mona Lisa smile. With fine white hair curled under at her shoulders, wearing jeans and a blue mock turtleneck, she looked to be in her sixties, maybe a bit older. At the sight of her, Shelby sat up a little straighter.

"This is Gran," Krista announced. "She and my grand-father Big Skye have been the heart of Mustang Ridge for more than half a century. She'll be cooking us some amazing stick-to-our-ribs ranch food this week, served family-style, the way it has been for generations. My parents are also integral to the ranch operations, but they're off-property right now. As a proud member of the third generation of the current Skyes, I'm in charge of guest services, and I help with the riding. I'll be hang-ing out with you guys and making sure you have a fab-ulous week. Tipper here"—Krista indicated the girl with the "Howdy" stickers—"and her brother, Topper, will be your servers. Mary is our head of housekeeping and Jo-seph is our head groundskeeper. But if you have any problems with your cabins or whatnot, please don't hes-itate to come find me, or leave me a message on the house phone." She paused, then grinned. "Okay, now for the good stuff . . . The riding is managed by our trail boss, Foster, along with his wranglers, Stace, Ty, and Ju-nior. They're some of the best cowboys in the territory, and they're going to put you through paces you didn't even know you had."

"Mmm," said a woman in the front, "cowboys! Love me some cowboys."

The crowd buzz edged up a notch, and Krista held up a hand. "We'll get to the horses tomorrow, bright and early after breakfast. For now, remember how I said we're going to have some extra time to get to know each other and see if we can make some love connec-tions? Well, in the spirit of Wyoming, we're going to have a few rounds of speed dating, ladies' choice. So, ladies, I'd like you to stand on this side of the room. Gentlemen, I'd like you to spread out, two or three to a table."

As the would-be speed daters started shuffling around under Krista's direction and with some nudges from Tipper and Gran, who were making sure nobody got left on the sidelines, Shelby whispered out of the corner of her mouth, "Lucky for us, we're not—" She broke off. "Lizzie?"

The bench beside her was empty.

Shelby's heart went *thudda-thudda* and adrenaline kicked through her in a mom's instinctive fight-not-flight response. But while she would've gone into berserker mode if she'd lost Lizzie back home, here she knew right where to look . . . and it was the most kid-like stunt her daughter had pulled in ages.

Grinning, she slipped out the back and headed for the barn.